ONE

IT IS a truth universally acknowledged that a woman is better at timekeeping and multitasking than a man. Whoever spread such nonsense was a tit in Ava's book.

This was the part of her working week that she had been dreading the most as she finally stopped her alarm on the twentieth snooze and reluctantly peeled the covers back from her face. Lemony light invaded the bedroom window as she glared at the sneering sun demanding she get up at the butt crack of dawn. Huffing, she faced the other way and groaned as two peachy bum cheeks grinned at her from the other side of the bed—a random man sprawled on his front and grunting in his sleep.

In hindsight, perhaps going out-out on a Sunday night wasn't the cleverest of ideas, but then again, these ideas were never her own. Her best friend, Samantha, was the type of lass who could be completely inebriated and then stroll into work the next day like a bouncing kitten on crack cocaine. Ava, however, would walk into work with a pair of large sunglasses obscuring half of her face, icily forbidding anyone from speaking to her, let alone even looking in her direction until late afternoon.

Today, she didn't have sunnies big enough for the shit-show that was work.

Now, don't get her wrong, she adored her job as a legal secretary and was often referred to as a freak of nature who bounced into the office with a genuinely sunny disposition. However, that was before her old man —and boss—suffered from a near-fatal stroke and had to take sick leave.

Tom Archer, a man well into his sixties and still working tooth and nail to keep his empire standing out from the rest, was the founding and managing partner at the prestigious law firm Archer and Brooks, a practice renowned for representing high-profile white-collar criminals and politicians. His corner office sat atop a skyscraper overlooking the River Thames with views of the London Eye and parliament—the location only adding to the esteemed reputation of his company.

The sudden decline in his health took everyone by surprise considering he lived an active lifestyle and enjoyed many country pursuits such as clay pigeon shooting, horse riding, and water polo. However, his favourite thing to do after a gruelling day at the office was spending time with his three beloved daughters: Suzannah, Heather, and Ava, his eldest.

Thanks to her father, it was safe to say that at the age of twenty-seven, Ava was doing well for herself. She had everything a woman could possibly ever desire: a "quaint" apartment down on Mayfair, a bustling social life, impeccable health nurtured through private care, and a job working for her old man that was easier than breathing. However, all of that was about to change now that

ILLICIT AFFAIRS

HOLLY DIXON

This book is dedicated to my mother.
From a young age, she always encouraged me to be creative
and channel that into writing.
Twenty-seven years later and I finally have something to
show for the creative streak she passed down to me.
This one's for you Mum :)

Nathaniel Brooks was standing in for her father for the next month.

Ava's morning started out like any other: sneaking out of her own bed with a note on her pillow for the lucky guy she hooked up with, a quick run to blow off the cobwebs, yoga to cleanse the soul, and her one-and-only hangover cure—a bowl of Coco Pops cereal. After that, she spent the best part of an hour getting ready since today was a big day, one where she had to stand out and make a lasting impression with her new so-called "boss". A man who had taken it upon himself to email her at one in the morning on a Saturday with a list of demands before he even had the decency to introduce himself!

"Well, personally I think you look bloody lush in red... even if that dress is a *little* revealing for work," Samantha said over a video call, still lying in bed with a cup of tea. Her short caramel locks stuck up in every direction as she rubbed her eyes and yawned. "But then again, you don't have spaniel ears for tits and can get away with that."

"But seriously, Sam, does it give the right first *impression?*" Ava sighed and ran her immaculate manicure down over the body-contouring pencil dress.

"Oh, you mean the 'back the fuck off, this is my daddy's office and I'm not taking orders from a loud-mouthed American' impression?" Sam trilled in thick Scottish and was clearly amused with herself as she hid her smirk behind her favourite llama-shaped novelty mug.

"That is the *very* look we're going for, my lass!"

"Aye, well, if yer whole ensemble doesnae say it"—Sam waved her hand in front of the camera—"yer big *gob* will!"

Ava lowered her brows at her friend before tucking a golden curl behind her ear and glancing down at her watch. "I best go, I'll see you in a couple of hours?"

"You sure will! I'll bring coffee...and sedatives," Sam quipped, causing Ava to giggle while she applied a scandalous shade of red to her lips. "Oh, and Ava?"

"Hm?"

"Try saving his little nut-roasting for when I'm in the office, will ya?"

AVA CHERISHED London city centre first thing in the morning and upon sunset. She loved her morning walk to the office where she'd awe at the autumn sun's smile tickling the wispy white clouds, its light glittering off of the monoliths of glass like candle flames licking up the sides of buildings and turning the sky into a Prosecco and gin candy floss cocktail.

She wasn't originally from London, an Oxford girl at heart, but she knew these streets like the veins upon the back of her hand, and on days where it rained, she would often be the one telling her chauffeur which shortcuts to take through her beloved city.

Ava's stilettos clicked against the concrete as she ran into the middle of a bustling road jam-packed with black cabs and transit vans. Horns tooted around her as she dipped between the gridlock traffic, peering up towards her glass palace. Seventy storeys high towered the Inchyra Business Hub, a building that upon the sixty-sixth to the seventieth floors homed Archer and Brooks.

"Good morning, Ms. Archer!" The cheerful security officer greeted Ava as she stepped through the metal detectors and into the ostentatious atrium.

"Good morning, Mike," Ava said, slightly bemused as she thanked him for darting to call the elevator for her.

"I do hope your father is keeping well?"

"His recovery is coming on nicely," Ava replied with a well-practiced smile, peering up at the elevator as it counted down from the twentieth floor.

"That's good to hear... So, Ava, I mean, Ms. Archer," Mike corrected himself, straightening his posture and clearing his throat, "I was wondering if you would like to go —" The chime from the elevator doors interrupted him as Ava stepped inside and looked back at Mike with her eyebrows raised expectantly. "To go...get your badge updated! That picture is several years old now." He pointed to the fob hanging from her coat, his cheeks matching the shade of her outfit.

"Perhaps later."

The elevator doors pinged closed, shutting down another of the security man's attempt at asking her out on a date. As she ascended, the elevator stopped at the fortieth floor to collect several people. Sighing, she scooted to the far corner of the metal box as white collars piled in, most of which were carrying their bitter-smelling caffeine fix. She stood there feeling like a ruby in a rough of coal cinders, her red coat standing out against the black suits.

"Ava!" A tall auburn-haired man with emeralds for eyes squeezed himself through the suited sardines and stood next to her. "Good weekend?"

"Hello, Peter." Ava's eyes smiled at his handsome face despite her lips remaining in a flat line. "As good as it could be, I suppose."

"Ah, I see...nervous to meet the new boss as well, Ms. Archer?" he teased as his elbow playfully jabbed at her side.

"I wouldn't say *nervous*," she scoffed and stood herself a half-inch taller by straightening her spine. "Slightly *peeved* at the whole inconvenience of it all but certainly not nervous."

"Yeah, a lot of the chaps in the office aren't looking forward to it. They heard this guy is a bit of a ball-buster," Peter explained as he ran a hand through his coppery mop.

"*Hah!*" Ava blurted and couldn't help but roll her eyes at him. "I'm sure the boys will be just fine. Everyone knows that the Yankees are all talk and no action." She smirked as the elevator finally stopped at their floor and the crowd vacated into the foyer of the busy department.

"I don't know about this one, Ava...chap's got a killer rep over in the States," he remarked with a sexy wink before leaning in to her, his breath tickling her ear as he whispered, "Best watch yourself, ol' girl."

Ava chuffed through her nose as Peter walked off in front, her ocean eyes dropping to his bottom adorned in grey tweed work slacks. She did enjoy his arse—especially when it was laid bare across her bedsheets every Friday night.

After greeting people good morning, she stood behind her tidy desk, shrugged out of her coat, and hung it up behind her before noticing the silhouette through the venetian blinds in the office next to her—her *father's* office, which was currently being invaded by America.

She pursed her lips together, already feeling irked at this man's presence as her long nails drummed on the table, deliberating on if she should introduce herself—after all, that would be the polite and adult thing to do. However, after this man decided to email her a list of demands for Monday morning and his "code of conduct" that he expected from all his personnel, she wasn't feeling like showing him any of her British hospitality. So instead of a warm welcome, she sat down at her desk and started up her computer. While she waited, she idly inspected the ends of her long curls just as an abrupt *bang* on her desk sent a shock wave through her body and she jolted upright in her seat.

"*Fuck me!*" Ava squealed, her skeleton trying to jump out of her skin as her eyes landed on two large veiny hands at the end of her desk, the knuckles of which were pressing down on the light wood to support their weight. With her heart in her throat, she dragged her eyes up the arm of a well-tailored, black pinstriped suit jacket and over the broadness of assertive shoulders before finally landing upon restless pools of chocolate and honey.

"Ms. Archer, I presume?"

TWO

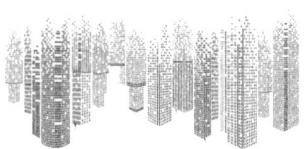

NATHANIEL BROOKS WAS jet-lagged when he woke up at the crack of dawn in his executive suite to disable the shrill noise of his alarm.

A gruff sigh left his lips as his fingers rubbed at the dark stubble of his beard, where thin wisps of hair peppered up the sides of his defined cheekbones into his hairline and cut along the sharp angles of his square jaw. His hands dragged down over his face with a tired sigh as he whipped back the hotel bed sheets and made his way to a hot shower.

Being in Europe was the last thing he wanted right now when things back in the States was going swimmingly; his slice of the company was booming and *damn* if he wasn't reaping the financial rewards of that. Having money meant he could *do* anything he wanted and *go* anywhere he wanted. From a young age, his life had been laid out for him, paving the way to his success, and at the age of thirty-five, he was settled with all the boxes ticked: wealth and good health, something that manifested itself in his appearance.

Nate knew himself to be every woman's darkest fantasy;

he was the epitome of tall, dark, and handsome, standing just above six foot and always dressed like a gentleman. A college football player, he still maintained his athletic build, something that did well to intimidate not only the women in his life but the fellas too.

Before reaching his thirties, he had already made a fortune in the legal profession. Smart, confident, and highly attractive? Yeah, he earned great respect before the judges and members of the bar alike.

However, life threw him a curveball when his business partner, Thomas Archer, took ill and Nate was summoned to London to manage Tom's firm.

It's just one month, he had told himself over a thousand times on the tiresome seven-hour flight from New York. *I just have to keep Tom's side above water, keep my side ticking over, and then I can head back home for Labour Day weekend—no biggie.*

The vibrations rumbling across the hotel desk in front of him tore his attention from his thoughts as he placed his phone to his ear. "Mr. Brooks, this is a courtesy call to let you know your driver is five minutes away." A polite-sounding woman spoke on speakerphone as Nate straightened his chrome-grey tie beneath his sharp white collar.

"Thank you," Nate replied, his baritone voice the type that demanded everyone's undivided attention. However, his tone was still rich and silken, like hot chocolate on a cold autumnal morning. He always spoke as though he had the entire world at his disposal, his experience and confidence seeping through every word.

He ended the call whether the woman had more to say or not, his attention upon his reflection as he shrugged his heavy shoulders into his black suit jacket and fastened the first couple of buttons. He looked as he did every day for work: refined and hard-edged, like that of his Bentley back home. The comb ran one last time through his thick dark hair, sweeping it up away from his forehead so it would sit neater into the faded shaven cut around his ears and down the back of his head.

A quick check of his wristwatch and he was off, suitcase in hand, with a hankering for a strong black coffee to subdue his jet lag.

He would have been on time this morning if one, the traffic hadn't been abysmal, and two, he had gotten off of the elevator on the correct *damn* floor. Now he was waiting for the elevator alongside several other men who were talking about some soccer match that was on the television the night before. He stood at the back watching them squabble like little boys, his thick brows knitting together and angling down into the bridge of his nose as he observed their inter-actions.

"So did ye hook up again with daddy's little princess at the weekend?" one Englishman had asked another as they stood next to Nate.

"Nah, mate. Ava's still milking the whole 'caring for her old man' thing." The redheaded man responded, causing Nate's hazel eyes to scroll down to his right.

The same Ava who was meant to be assisting me through this change of management?

"That's balls, innit? What are you going to do?"

"Nothing," Red boasted with a wink at his friend and a slimy smirk on his face that made Nate want to take his handkerchief and offer him it for his mouth. "She'll be back —if she knows what's good for her."

The elevator chimed and Nate's interest in the matter dissolved as the sea of suits moved forward and crowded into the silver death box from the fortieth floor. He fucking *hated* elevators but to hell with climbing a hundred flights of stairs. If there was one thing other than heights that Nate despised, it was confined spaces.

He was the last one into the elevator, standing rigid with men pressing against his suit from every direction and making him take a mental note to get his suit laundered.

"Ah, I see... nervous to meet the new boss as well, Ms. Archer?" Nate heard Red speak again, somewhere near the back, capturing his interest at potentially meeting his female subordinate here in the metal death trap.

"I wouldn't say *nervous*. Slightly *peeved* at the whole inconvenience of it all but certainly not nervous" came the sound of a young woman, a voice like vanilla pudding, sweet in the traditional sort of way, but the richness of her tone was utterly luxurious and warm. Nate had barely paid notice to what she had said, too absorbed by her sultry English accent.

"Yeah, a lot of the chaps in the office aren't looking forward to it. They heard this guy is a bit of a ball-buster," Red retorted, making the corner of Nate's mouth twitch to suppress a bemused smirk. Yes, it was true, he made all his personnel fall into line and preferred a more authoritarian approach in managing his fleet.

"*Hah!*" Ava, he presumed, laughed a cold sound that made his lips straighten into a thin line. "I'm sure the boys will be just fine. Everyone knows that the Yankees are all talk and no action."

Nate's ears pinned back at this, his already stoic expression turning frosty at the bigoted remark made by a woman who would need to be put in her place if she were to work under him.

The elevator chimed and the doors opened upon the seventieth floor, Nate being the first one out as he charged up the corridor and straight towards the office he would now take over.

His new office was situated at the far end of the department space, tucked away into the corner and encased in glass walls. After unlocking his door, the fluorescent lights flickered above the tiled ceiling before illuminating the spacious office. A large mahogany desk, with intricate carvings upon its front, sat at the front of the office, with several dark leather sofas at either side of the open space.

Nate was silent as he placed his suitcase behind the desk and began opening the blinds around his new working environment. When they were open, he raised his brows and let an impressed chuff through his nose at the panoramic views of London. However, the *real* impressive sight was when he opened his side blinds and saw the golden goddess sat at her desk—an impossibly beautiful face, the sunlight catching her hair through the window behind her and setting her locks alight.

Ava Archer.

She looked like a red exclamation mark against all the mundane black and grey suits in the office, sat there in that crimson dress that was almost *too* provocative for work—not that he was complaining.

With a crack of his knuckles, he decided it was time to show Ms. Archer some of that so-called action she believed he would be lacking.

Nate took long strides out of the office, approaching the desk of the young woman who was currently too busy playing with her hair to notice that her new boss was attempting to introduce himself.

Lack of attention—not ideal for an assistant.

The longer she continued absentmindedly inspecting her hair, the more Nate's patience thinned until eventually his nostrils flared and he slammed his palms down on the edge of her desk.

"*Fuck me!*" she squealed, her body jolting upright like that of a kitten getting spooked by a green vegetable and her reaction almost managing to bring a smirk to Nate's frosty face. *Such an odd way to greet her new boss*, he thought.

"Ms. Archer, I presume?" Nate raised his brows and watched as Ava scraped herself from the ceiling.

"Mr. Brooks, I presume?" she retorted sassily, causing Nate's expression to fall back into his signature stoic expression.

"Correct," he stated, pushing up from his knuckles and onto his fingertips, all ten digits pressed against her desk. "My office in ten." He pushed off her desk and began retreating to his office, but not before addressing her over his shoulder, "Oh, and bring coffee, Ms. Archer."

THREE

BRING COFFEE?!

Ava was furious with her new boss and they had uttered only a few words to each other. She had always gotten her father a coffee and it had never been a big deal, but there was just something about that condescending, smug, and misogynistic voice of her new boss, exaggerated by his accent, that made Ava want to pour the steaming cup of lava onto Mr. Brooks's crotch.

Preparing him a hot beverage from the coffee machine, she felt a hand upon the dip of her back that made her snap around to see a handsome smile beaming down at her.

"Told you so," Peter teased, leaning in to take the cup of coffee that Ava had just prepared for her boss before his touch lingered just that little bit lower, feeling across the band of her thong through her dress.

Ava didn't particularly care for Peter or his wandering hands, and frankly, he should know better than to flaunt their physical relationship while at work—such things were forbidden. She turned her head forward and gave him her icy shoulder as her finger jabbed the coffee machine again.

Directly outside of Nate's office, he could see Ms. Archer being a good little assistant, her heels punctuated by long strides as she stopped at the coffee machine while he sat scrolling through his emails. However, his attention paused on his assistant when Red placed his hand upon her lower back, cautiously close to her curvaceous derrière. They were far too cosy together for the workplace. Caring not to get involved with HR on his first day, Nate looked back down at his computer, his ever-expressionless face a constant state of winter.

"Coffee," Ava clipped, walking into the small office without knocking, much to Nate's annoyance. The woman strode towards his desk like she was modelling the crimson dress upon her back, her stilettos clicking against the floor as her feet seemed to fall expertly one in front of the other. His eyes fell upon the coffee mug placed *not* onto his coaster but to the *side* of it, making his jaw twitch.

"Ms. Archer, take a seat, please," Nate said, extending his hand to the chair in front of his new desk. When Ava had sat down, Nate stood with his shadow towering over Ava like a dark cloud as he walked around his desk and closed the office door. "I thought introductions were in order," he explained, the deep bass of his voice owning his newly acquired office space.

Ava glared at the name plaque replacing her father's, rolling her eyes behind her boss's back like a schoolgirl being reprimanded by the headmaster.

"It is my understanding that you are Mr. Archer's PA and have been for the past few years, yes?" Nate asked, his voice sneaking up on his assistant causing her shoulders to jump slightly.

"Legal secretary," she corrected, watching him circle

around her and the desk like a vulture. "But yes, I've worked alongside my father since I was twenty."

Her blue orbs watched as Mr. Brooks took his seat in front of her and crossed his arms with impeccably straight posture. She noted that he had the rosiest and fullest lips she had ever seen on a man before, his eyes so warm and yet his expression so cold like his face captured winter and summer into one season. He reminded her of a stormy day. A nice one. Even under the slight beard he had, she could tell he had a jawline for days, his face capturing the heart of Hollywood.

"No prior experience of administrative, legal, or assistant duties?" He asked it like he already knew the answer.

"No." *Has this twat actually read my résumé?!*

Her expression was glacial, however, her growing levels of annoyance with this man and his accusing tone was causing a small fire to burn in her belly. Sure, her father handed this job to her on a silver platter and his title and money fast-tracked her success, but she genuinely worked hard for her place here.

"Hmm..." Nate's eyebrows lifted; the corners of his lips turned down thoughtfully as he rubbed at his light beard. "It's interesting," he remarked, lowering his hand, "normally for a position such as your own, personally, I would hire someone with adequate exposure to the industry we work in."

He genuinely didn't mean to cause offence with his opinion; their job was to defend, more often than not, criminals with a lot of money. That was something that he'd seen a lot of people, himself included, lose sleep over. However, he could tell by the way Ms. Archer's eyes widened slightly that he had wounded her precious ego—*how cute.*

"I can assure you, Nathaniel, that I have been *exposed* plenty to this industry and that my skill set is more than competent for my role here," Ava stated, crossing her slender arms and long milky legs. "I find it peculiar also that a man of your age and background has managed to get to the top of the food chain so *early* in life. I mean, how old are you, *thirty?*" The corner of her lips pulled inwards and popped a dimple in her cheek that made her look coy and pixie-like.

There were many things about Ms. Archer's statement that irked Nate: the fact she didn't address her manager respectfully, the provocative way her ruby lips moved, and the teasing way she poked back at his own ego. He wasn't enjoying this little game with his lesser and didn't care to defend his Harvard degree in law.

"Thirty-five," he corrected. "And I think it would be more fitting if you were to address me as the rest of this department shall—Mr. Brooks or sir will be fine." He gave her a curt smile and reached forward for the cup of coffee. At first, he was impressed that she somehow knew to get him a black coffee, but as he sipped the cheap and foul-tasting beverage, he lowered his cup with his nose scrunched up distastefully.

"Yes, *sir.*"

Nate's eyes snapped up at the titillating tone which Ms. Archer used for that particular phrase. The sarcastic and sassy attitude on her face wasn't lost on him. His intense gaze trained on to her eyes, noticing the flames dance across her oceans, his stomach tensing slightly as an ache ran up his muscular thighs and the hand on his lap tightened into a fist. At that moment, Nate wanted nothing more than to bring this fiery woman to her knees, but the feeling was fleeting.

"There is one more thing I'd like to discuss with you before you attend to your duties," Nate said, watching as Ava casually relaxed back into her seat, raising her eyebrows to prompt him to continue. "I see on your contract that your start time is 8 a.m...."

Ava's shoulders lifted slightly, her head shaking as she said, "Yes, *and...?*"

"Well, considering you clocked in just before 9 a.m. this morning, I was wondering if there had been an error?"

"My father has always been flexible with my working hours," Ava disputed, showing a slight amount of annoyance as she uncrossed her arms and straightened defensively.

"Yes, well, I'm not your *daddy*, Ms. Archer, and I would prefer it if you were in the office promptly at 8 a.m. every morning," Nate stated, not a drip of amusement or emotion in his steel cold tone. He enjoyed the way Ms. Archer opened and closed her mouth as if her brain was struggling to load a comeback, and before she could whittle one up, he dismissed her. "That'll be all. If you would like to return to your duties, I will email over today's brief in due course." He rose from his chair and walked towards the door to show that this conversation was over.

For a moment, Ava couldn't move, gobsmacked, irate, and frustrated with what just went down. No one had ever spoken to her in such a dogmatic way before and she didn't like it one bit. However, she quickly composed herself, head held high as she walked towards her new boss without so much as making eye contact while exiting the office.

"Oh, one last thing," Nate called, causing Ava to halt and face him with her jaw clenched. "The best thing about being a Yankee is that you're a Yankee," he smirked, causing Ava's nose to scrunch in confusion before the penny dropped just like her stomach and her face became a picture of horror.

He had to admit, the cherry blossom upon her paling cheeks was a welcomed sight, but one he didn't have time for as he shut the door in her face.

"AYE, but you have to admit, he's easy on the eyes, isn't he?" Sam shrugged, her mouth latched on to a deli sub for lunch as she and Ava sat in their usual spot at the window inside their favourite café.

"I don't think there is anything *easy* about this guy," Ava scoffed, sipping on her tea. "You should see the mountain of work he dumped on me this morning. He's had me running around all day and there is no way I'm going to get it finished by home time."

"Awh, doll," Sam soothed, her warm palm rubbing the side of Ava's arm. "He's just flexing his muscle, you know, asserting himself on his first day in the office. Just be grateful he doesn't have a red room of pain just waiting to show you who's boss!"

"Yeah, well, he can piss off! We both know you're the only boss of me." She winked, glancing down at her wrist to check the time.

"You got a meeting after lunch?"

"What?"

"You've been checking that bloody watch constantly since we got here! It's like yer shitting yourself you'll be late for something," Sam said with a chuckle.

"Ugh, no. It's just that *sir*"—Ava sneered the new term like a child—"pointed out that he's tracking my time management and it's bloody well pissed me off. I'm *never* late."

"Uh..." Sam opened her mouth to speak but then shut it again.

"What?"

"Nothing." She scrunched up her nose and shook her head dismissively. "Anyway, work aside, how's Pops?"

"Oh, you know how he is; carrying on like he's in his forties, acting completely right as rain, complaining about the walking stick and his wonky face." Ava rolled her eyes but smiled. "Doctor says he's recovering well though."

"Give him my love next time you see him, will ya?" Sam asked, always seeing Mr. Archer as a father figure more than a boss.

"I will do; I'll be heading up to the estate on Friday to check in on him."

"Oh, will Trinny and Susannah be there?" Sam teased, an ongoing joke that both of Ava's younger sisters were like the famous fashion advisors.

"Most likely." Ava chuckled, looking forward to seeing her sisters. The three of them were very close ever since their mother divorced their father and moved off to some fancy villa in Spain with her toy boy partner. They rarely heard from their extravagant mother, but it was never a pleasant encounter when they did.

"Is Heather still pining after Peter?"

"Heather is pining over *any* man that has a heartbeat and cash in his back pocket, you know what she's like." Ava laughed.

"Mhh, speaking of," Sam prompted, swallowing her last mouthful of tea, "what is the script between you and the ginger ninja?"

Ava lowered her brows is an unamused manner, her

head shaking at Sam but her lips struggling to hide her amusement. "Nothing really...lovely bum and quite good in the sack, but we agreed we weren't looking for anything long term—it's just sex."

"You're nearly thirty, love. Are you not thinking about settling down yet?"

"*Thanks* for the reminder," Ava chided with a small laugh. "But no, you know I'm not fussed about kids, and that the whole marriage thing just isn't for me. Things are just simpler when there aren't any strings binding you to some-one, you know?"

If there was one thing Ava feared most it was the idea of her stood inside a kitchen with a dinner plate as the man lived his life, brought in the cash, and controlled how much independence she had. She had seen what it did to her mother and look how that turned out.

"So you're telling me Auntie Sam isn't getting any rug rats running about?"

"Well, I am thinking about getting a pet," Ava said, causing Sam to question what on earth Ava was talking about. "Yeah, maybe a nice rat or snake—could call him *Nathaniel.*"

FOUR

THE FOLLOWING days had tested Ava to a hellish extent. The workload Mr. Brooks was dumping on her was highly unreasonable. Twice she had to cancel on Sam to work through her lunch and once she had to stay back past finishing time to make her deadline on preparing the documentation for the Forbes negotiation. It wasn't that she couldn't handle the workload, it was the fact that her new boss was dropping it on her last minute while he still disappeared for his lunch every day at midday. Her father was always fair with her and they balanced the amount of work between them both. The American was all for making his life easier and Ava's hell.

She felt like she was being punished.

By the time Thursday blinked into existence, Ava was both mentally and physically drained, her nails chipped from how ferociously she had been typing up draft motions and subpoenas, her patience thin with the intercom machine at the *insane* number of times Mr. Brooks would call her into his office to ask her a question he could quite easily have instant messaged her on her computer.

However, one thing that came out of this hellish week was that Ava had noticed a pattern with Mr. Brooks. The man was completely unapproachable until he had his morning coffee in front of him. This would have worked well in her favour if her job didn't literally revolve around needing to assist him in every way she could other than wiping his own arse for him. Therefore, she found herself willingly going into work earlier and earlier, partly to cope with the increasing workload, and partly so she could make her life easier, starting with his morning cup of joe on his desk every morning for him.

However, this morning as Ava finished setting up her desk for the day, Mr. Brooks was already sat at his own. This put Ava in a foul mood before the day had even started, knowing that when she signed into her emails, there would be a list of demands from her boss jamming up her inbox.

Resiliently, she stuck to her routine and made her way to the coffee machine across from Mr. Brooks's office but stopped short before she reached it.

"What the—?" Ava faltered, the coffee machine no longer in its rightful spot. "Hey, Addy, did someone move the coffee machine?" she asked one of the data clerks.

"New boss got rid of it," Addy replied.

"He did *what*?!" Ava sputtered, looking at the blank spot where the perfectly good machine had sat for the several years she had worked here. "Why the hell would he get rid of our coffee machine?"

"Budget cuts?" Addy shrugged.

"Oh, this takes the bloody biscuit this does..." Ava grumbled under her breath before striding towards Mr. Brooks's open door. She blew into his office like a whirlwind, not caring to knock as she demanded, "Would you care to explain why the coffee machine is no longer in this department?"

Nate's head snapped up from behind his monitor, his eyes wide and his face a picture of surprise that Ava would have enjoyed if not for the fact her patience with this shitty week was already running on fumes.

It was rare that anyone caught Nate off guard but when they did it was rarely a good thing, and right now, it most certainly was *not* a good thing.

"Ms. Archer, now is not a good time," Nate affirmed, his hand motioning towards the door and dismissing her.

"That coffee machine has been there the entire time I have worked here. You show up for three days and get *rid* of it? People use that machine! My *father* uses that machine!" Ava protested, stood in front of his desk with her hands flapping about.

Nate hit a button on his keyboard, his eyes turning glacial as he peered back up from his screen at the stubborn, flustered woman in front of him who was failing to realise that *she* didn't call the shots in this department. He did.

"Ava," he ground out her name through his teeth and reiterated, "now is *not* a good time."

"Where else am I meant to get coffee? Do you honestly expect me to go out to do coffee runs? I have enough on my—"

"Ms. Archer, do you even *drink* coffee?" Nate interrupted.

"What? No, I don't usually dri—"

"Then it isn't a problem," he clipped out, his fingers drumming impatiently on his desk.

"Yes, it is! I'm not running around like a headless chicken to get you your caffeine fix every day!" Ava huffed, her hands on her hips before her eyes dropped to his desk, noticing too late the branded cup of coffee already sat there upon its coaster. "*Ohh.*"

"Nate, is everything okay?" came a woman's voice from his computer, making Ava's face pale when her boss slapped his keyboard with his finger again, unmuting himself.

"Yes, Mrs. Forbes, I apologise for the interruption," Nate said in his utmost professional manner as he glanced to the several square boxes on his screen whereby a video conference was taking place. "As you were." He smiled politely for the camera although his fisted hand thrust forward, his finger pointing towards the door.

Ava scuttled away to her desk and sat down. "*Oh, fuck,*" she said under her breath, her cold hand trying to tame the fiery blush across her cheeks. She couldn't believe she'd just embarrassed herself like that, over *coffee*, to an entire counsel, the client, and Mr. Brooks.

A small tap at her side caught her attention as she peered up and saw Mr. Brooks chapping on his window. When they made eye contact his finger curled back and summoned her and she made her way into his office.

"I didn't realise you were on a—"

"Ms. Archer, you may be my business partner's daughter, thus preventing me from disciplining you as I would see fit, but make no mistake that if you were my *own*, you would be out the door of *my* office for such a lack of respect and boundaries. Do I make myself clear?" Nate's voice boomed across the office space, his honey eyes like embers as he stood from his desk, his knuckles pressing to the wood as the veins upon his hands gave light of his obvious emotion. Never had he met someone so insubordinate, stubborn, and loud-mouthed as Ava. It awoke that side of him that demanded order, control, and above all else, *submission*.

Ava had been yelled at by only one man—her father—a

handful of times in all her twenty-seven years. As Mr. Brooks's voice roared at her like a whip of thunder cracking across the sky, she gulped down the lump in her throat and simply stood there, sheepishly looking at him. Despite him having no power over her job, she felt entirely intimidated by this man with his dominating stare and commanding presence.

"I said, do I make myself clea—"

"Yes, sir. It won't happen again," Ava interrupted with her eyes on the floor, an empty expression on her face.

"Good. Now send me across all reviewed documentation for the Forbes case," Nate said dismissively as he sat back down on his chair.

Ava's eyes widened at his garish request; she was only halfway through reviewing the mammoth number of files relating to Mrs. Forbes's trial.

"I haven't gotten together all reviewed documents yet," Ava said and nearly winced from the cold glare of his eyes slicing up into her as she quietly added, "sir."

Nate's expression softened ever so slightly upon Ms. Archer's attempt of a respectful address. It was a start, at least. His broad shoulders and chest rose as he took a deep inhale through his nose and said, "Have it on my desk tomorrow, 10 a.m."

As Ava walked out of his office, her chin lifted into the air defiantly, her expression like glass, avoiding the excited and amused faces of the department who had overheard the drama. She sat down at her desk with poise and the instant she did, a small pop-up appeared on her screen.

1 New Message, Samantha Eastley:

WTF?!

1 New Message, Ava Archer:

FML

1 New Message, Samantha Eastley:

Want a coffee?

1 New Message, Ava Archer:

Hah. Hah.

1 New Message, Samantha Eastley:

Wine??

1 New Message, Ava Archer:

Wine.

FIVE

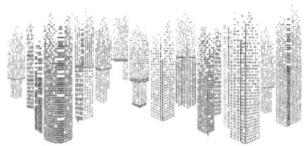

NATE WASN'T sure how long jet lag usually lasted but tonight he had a killer headache. His fingers pinched the bridge of his nose as he sighed, staring at his computer screen. He had spent the last three hours replying to emails and had barely put a dent in the mountain of unread messages sitting in his inbox.

This week had been killer.

Keeping two firms running was proving to be a challenge, especially when one of those firms was on the other side of the world. If not for the time difference, the fact that Nate wasn't there and couldn't be hands-on was starting to grind his gears. However, the branch back in Manhattan was ticking over relatively well, but here in London...that was a different story.

It was no wonder that Tom fell ill with the amount of work he took on at his age.

For the first time in hours, Nate finally looked up from his desk when he heard one of the cleaning staff roaming past his door with a vacuum. It was then that he realised the time as darkness sprawled in through the windows behind him, a red glow filling his office from the aircraft warning lights on the building opposite him.

He stood up and peered out at the London skyline, the city unapologetically urban. It spread across once luscious green lands like a vulgarly enlarged microchip. There wasn't much greenery or planted blooms, just monoliths of concrete and glass soaring out of the sidewalks in its uniform grid formation. At night, it was a glittering jungle with so many lights that as Nate looked to the sky, it was illuminated in a violet and blue haze that hid the twinkle of stars.

London was similar to his home, the monochrome buildings dominating the skyline, but the difference here was that a silver crack ran through the landscape—the River Thames.

After shutting down his computer for the evening, Nate loosened his crimson tie, hanging it over the corner of his desk, and popped the first couple of buttons on his shirt to allow him to rub at the back of his tense neck with a sigh.

As Nate switched off the lights to his office and locked it up for the evening, he turned around to the empty department and stopped short. Golden light lit up one corner of the office but it wasn't from a lamp, it was the transcendent glow from Ms. Archer's hair, the long, luscious waves of silk tumbling over each of her petite shoulders. The young woman was curled over at her desk, a highlighter in hand as she marked up several documents that were scattered across her workspace.

This woman clearly doesn't know the meaning of law and order, he thought to himself with a smirk on his face.

For a moment, Nate could only stand and observe her, his feet unwilling to move as he held his suitcase at his side. Ms. Archer was undoubtedly beautiful sat there in a burgundy formal dress that clung to every sumptuous dip and curve of her sinful body. He had a feeling that the young woman was more than aware of her sexual prowess for no woman could carry themselves in such a refined and assertive manner as she without using their looks to their advantage.

However, Nate was starting to see that there was more than what met the eye with Ms. Archer. It was closing in past eight at night and here was his assistant meticulously reviewing the documents that he had asked for with such unreasonably tight timelines. Truthfully, he didn't need the documentation until Monday, but he thought it best to set an example after her atrocious behaviour in front of his department. Her outburst hadn't gone unnoticed by his personnel or his clients. And all over *coffee*.

At this, a small smirk twitched at his lips as he recalled the way Ms. Archer ran her wild mouth and huffed like a bratty adolescent. If she were behaving this way out of work he could think of several salacious ways to make this untamed woman fall back in line, but no, such tempting and disreputable thoughts had no place at work, nor did he have room in his settled life. Those days were long behind him.

Making his way over to her desk, he stood in front of her and had to bite back his smile as she continued to stare down at her files, highlighting down the page as though doing a word search. Her lack of awareness never failed to amaze him.

"Late night, Ms. Archer?" he asked politely but furrowed his brows when the blonde didn't respond or even react to him. "Ava?"

When the small tinny noise tickled his ears, Nate soon noticed the white cable running down the front of her body, his eyes lingering upon her supple cleavage before looking at the cell phone her headphones were plugged into. He carefully set his suitcase on the desk in front of her.

"*Fuck me!*" Ava screamed out, jumping upright into her seat as though an electrical charge had bolted through her body. With her hand against her jackhammering heart, she gawked up at Mr. Brooks, sweeping a curl of hair that had flown across her long lashes. "*Nath*—Mr. Brooks," she corrected herself, much to Nate's delight. "You're still here."

Nate had to muster up all his self-control to not chuckle or even smile at the flustered expression on the young Ava's face—she looked like a bunny caught in headlights.

"I'm here," Nate confirmed, raising his eyebrow at the confused look on Ava's face. Where else did she expect to see her boss if not at work? "I was working the Forbes case," he explained, unsure why he felt the need to, but when he saw Ava's shoulders slump, he wondered if his punishment had been too much for her, even if he was somewhat impressed by her staying back and seeing out her sentence.

"Me too." Ava sighed, sitting back in her chair, tossing her hair over one shoulder as she rubbed her tense neck. "I'm almost done with the files for the Forbes negotiation. I've nearly finished drafting the subpoenas, however, there is just one problem..."

"And that is?" Nate frowned, peering down at the pages Ava was flicking through.

"I think there's perhaps a mistake with the filing of evidence; these signatures don't match, see?" Ava explained, holding up two pieces of paper.

Nate sighed, having thought that the young and cunning Mrs. Forbes would pull such a thing as one of the executors to her late husband's estate and trust. He walked around the desk, standing behind Ava, and peered over her shoulder down at the mismatched signatures of Holden

Forbes. Ms. Archer's innocence on the matter was admirable but an inexperienced error in judgement. Nate could sniff a gold digger a mile off but he didn't fight for justice, he fought to win the case and bring in revenue to his firm.

The proximity of Mr. Brooks disrupting her personal space made Ava's spine straighten, the blood wakening her brain and tickling her senses as she became as still as mouse right before a cat pounced on its prey. Besides the heat radiating from his mass, it was the top notes of his cologne—mint, lavender, and cinnamon—that coiled around her emotions, slowing her heartbeat to the kind of rhythm usually reserved for the deepest of dreams. However, the spicier notes of his scent hit the back of her throat, the cedar, amber, and sandalwood making her heart flutter like the wings of a hummingbird. His scent was equal parts freshness and softness as it was strength and sensuality.

"I might have known she'd try to pull a stunt like this," Nate grumbled, his warm breath brushing past Ava's shoulder and painting goosebumps down her arms.

"What do you want me to do?" she answered, her voice barely above a whisper. No need to raise voices in an empty office where her boss was leaning over her shoulder and reaching for the documents, flicking the pages casually as though he were unaware of how his closeness affected Ava.

"Remove them from the case; we fight her corner clean. If she wants to retain ownership of the estate from his kids, she's gonna do it my way," Nate answered simply, pulling back and pausing for a brief second in the intimate space so close to the nape of Ms. Archer's neck that had taken his senses prisoner.

It would be fitting that she would smell as enticing as every natural bloom, as alluring as a red rose, as free as springtime blossom rain, with just a hint of debauchery. She was an aromatic song, her essence the floral orchestra of the soul, and it was something that Nate knew he would forever crave.

Ava was somewhat impressed at Mr. Brooks's moral compass as she timidly turned her chin over her shoulder, her bluebells peering up at him from beneath the canopy of her luscious dark lashes. Her oceans met the expanse of his rich forests, his eyes like the soft moss that clothed hazel trees, and in that moment she saw that familiar look of desire in his dilating pupils.

It had been years since Nate had felt the familiar feeling stirring deep within his core—the flames, the itching at his fingertips, the tingling upon his tongue...the ache. Attraction was a fickle thing to Nate, as the concept of love was to a cynic. A semi-euphoric, temporary chemical reaction that fades over time—that was something that Nate had first-hand experience with.

"Was that all...Ava?" he asked, saying the young woman's name as though testing its softness upon his palate.

The way he said her name brought chills down the nape of her neck, and if it hadn't been for the past few days with this imperious man, she'd have maybe stuck around and played with fire.

Perhaps a part of Nate had hoped their business was not finished here as his glance fell upon her two delicate petals that parted ever so slowly, but he could tell it was over when the young woman let go of a small breath and faced forward in a composed manner.

"Yes, sir."

SIX

NATE AWOKE in the early hours, long before the sun kissed the horizon as stars tickled the sky behind the curtain of city light. Sweat glistened upon his bare chest like the rain upon the windows of his hotel room, hands fisting white cotton sheets as his heart burned and pumped steam throughout his veins.

He could still feel it.

Her touch was haunting him. Not the physical touch of her fingertips ghosting across his flesh but the touch of her fingers running down his soul and teasing his subconscious. The type of touch reserved for the most vivid of dreams. The more he sought refuge from his darkest of fantasies, the more the memory of her scent taunted and tempted him to sink back down into his bedsheets, back to the bottom of her oceans.

His body ached, certain parts more than others, his hormones in a state of turbulence much like the storm rumbling outside on the sodden streets of London.

Knowing he wouldn't be able to go back to sleep, Nate dragged his heavy body out of bed and into the bathroom embellished in gleaming chestnut-coloured tiles. It was an opulent space lit in a warm glow, with a black-and-white rolling-top bathtub sitting up against a wall-length window and an oversized shower against the opposing wall.

White noise and steam filled the bathroom as a monsoon of water fell from the square showerhead and drizzled down Nate's chiselled body. The more he tried to wash away the images of her lips upon his neck, the more he awoke his arousal and the more the coarseness of his loofa scrubbed harder at his flesh.

But it was useless; he couldn't rid her from his mind.

Her rose-scented silk plagued his mind like an addict craving another hit. One unwarranted and sensual dream had the white-collar executive losing his control as his hand slid down his sculpted stomach towards the pulsing hot ache demanding his attention. His dark hair turned virtually black now saturated and soapy as it clung to his face. He locked his fingers around himself as though he were grasping that irresistibly smelling neck of hers, a breath hissing in-between his teeth as he closed his eyes, dropping the loofa and with it, his self-control.

Flashes burned in his mind of her face: the high rise of her cheekbones, those thick lashes, those baby doll eyes, and that beautiful accent that purred, *Show me where you want to be touched?* His imagination ran rampant, his hands in her wet hair as he watched those delectable lips wrap around his...

"*Fuck*," he gritted out between his teeth, his palm slapping against the cold tiles, hanging his head in sin as his hand worked to draw the illicit lust from his body. Steam seeped from his pores, salt mixing with the water dripping down him as his mind worked hard to create scenes of her body against his in that shower, to conjure the idea of her high-pitched whines tickling his eardrums, the sound of his name screaming from her hot lips in that mouth-watering accent of hers.

His orgasm blindsided him as his silken fluids bathed the tiles, his hand in a fist against the wall as his body quaked from the pleasure rippling up his thighs and ricocheting around his core with explosive sensation. As he came down from his high, the image of her naked, glistening body in front of him slowly dissipated along with the steam.

Nate's muscles corded tightly together as the veins bulged down his arms—the only evidence left behind of his desire as he washed the sin from his body and watched it swirl down the drain.

Nate had known Ms. Archer for only a few days but there was one absolute thing—her tempting beauty had sunk its claws into him and he would not allow something as basic as a primal instinct ruin everything he had worked hard to secure.

FRIDAY MORNING— *THANK fuck.*

Ava was overjoyed when she awoke that morning believing it was midweek only to realise it was the day that every worker looked forward to.

This morning she was the first one into the office, determined to have her workload completed so she could enjoy a stress-free weekend back at her family estate in Oxfordshire.

Arms loaded with boxes of paper, she made her way to fill the photocopier when a black shiny object suddenly caught the corner of her eye as her heels scuffed to a halt. There filling the empty spot on the counter sat a coffee machine, but not just any coffee machine, a *new* and improved machine.

"What in the—" Ava blinked, staring at the new model, perplexed as her brain worked to piece together the puzzle.

Did he get rid of the old one to replace it with a better one?

This revelation made colour rise to her cheeks, but not from flattery, from guilt. "I'm such a tit," Ava whined to herself in the empty department as she mentally facepalmed herself and continued with her duties.

At the time, Mr. Brooks's small kindness had been misinterpreted as an act of assertion as he assumed his new position of power. A gracious and welcoming gift to their department was the last thing she would have expected from her new boss. Ava was starting to realise that she had perhaps been overly cold and chauvinistic to this man, domineering and arrogant as he may be.

As a way of offering a small olive branch, Ava prepared a coffee for him, timidly unlocking his door and entering his vacant office space. The lights flickered on as she approached his desk and placed the hot beverage down upon his coaster, taking extra care as she turned the mug until the handle pointed in the right direction.

"There," she uttered to herself, her good deed done for the day. She turned to leave but stopped as she saw the red tie hung over the corner of his desk. That moment, late last night, was still fresh in her mind: his scent, the warmth of his body close to her own, and that inviting look in his eyes.

It was no secret that Mr. Brooks was an attractive man, but then again, it was no secret that he was a giant pain in most people's arses either. Ava was not succumbing to the domineering charm of her boss, and instead, would remain professional despite that gaze of his being so intense that it nearly set fire to her bloody dress.

However, as she stared down at the red silk draped over his desk, something deep, dark, and rooted within Ava caved and she reached to pick up his tie. Her eyes glanced behind her at the empty department before she took the hit she had been needing since last night. She inhaled deeply, basking in the strong aromas clinging to the threads of silk, her mind walking through fields of lavender, fingers touching the green spines of cedar as her mouth salivated from the peppery essence capturing her senses. She couldn't remember a time where a man's scent alone had this power over her.

In the distance, the chime of the elevator doors opening alerted her as she jumped with a squeak and neatly placed the tie back where she found it, turning to make a quick getaway. However, as she did, her ample hip caught the pencil holder on the side of Mr. Brooks's desk and sent it clattering to the floor, scattering pens and pencils everywhere.

"*Oh*, fuck me," she hissed in frustration as she dropped to her hands and knees, scrambling to pick the stationery back up.

It would just be my luck that I try to do one decent act of goodwill and then this would hap—

"Good morning, Ms. Archer."

SEVEN

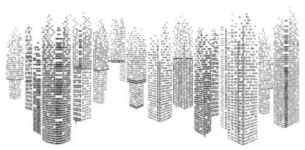

THE LAST THING Nate needed or expected to see was his personal assistant upon her hands and knees, presenting a rather sumptuous and plump derrière to him first thing in the morning—especially after the night he'd had. But alas, as he walked through the empty department, hesitating as he saw his office lights on, he turned the corner into his workspace and dropped his jaw as his wide eyes fell upon Ms. Archer.

Her skintight dress stretched over her peach, the silver zip running from her nape to tail appearing to be at breaking point as it held the material intact around her tight little body. She was quite literally a piece of liquorice just waiting to be unwrapped.

The young woman looked to be tidying something up beneath his desk in a rush, but he wasn't in a hurry at all, not when he had a view of two black lines running up the back of her creamy thighs, her suspenders holding up her sheer black stockings.

Damn, if I wouldn't sell my left nut to see her crawl

towards me without that dress on right now—shit, no! Head in the game, Brooks!

"Good morning, Ms. Archer," Nate announced, not wanting to devour the sight of her in that state for too long since his recently satiated member was stirring beneath his grey work slacks, and for fear of labelling himself a pervert. However, he couldn't blame himself for stealing a look—he was a hot-blooded man after all.

A high-pitched squawk left Ava's lips. She shot upright, startled from the presence behind her, the top of her head banging against the corner of the desk.

Nate hissed in empathy for her, watching the young blonde rub at her crown and curse under her breath. Normally, he detested such profanities, but when she did it in that fruity accent, it was endearing.

"A hand?" Nate asked, extending his hand for her to take, his lips in a bemused smirk as he peered down at glaring eyes.

God, this kitty has claws.

"Thank you," Ava chided, her tone cold and full of pride as she carefully put her hand in his and slowly rose to her feet. Warmth engulfed her small hand as his large paw wrapped around her. Her eyes landed upon his, which were surprisingly soft for once, two pools of honey for her to swim in.

"Are you alright?" he asked, his tone laced with genuine concern as his thick brows knitted together and his eyes traced her face for signs of distress.

"I'm perfectly fine, thank you very much," she replied, reluctantly pulling her hand away from his as she brushed down the creases in her dress and placed the pencil holder back in its rightful place.

"If you don't mind my asking, why exactly are you in

my office?" Nate asked, his level of bemusement at Ava's flustered face evident in his tone.

With a dent in her pride, Ava was becoming increasingly ticked off by the cocky smile upon her boss's mouth, even if it was sexy in an arrogant kind of way. She noted that he wasn't in a hurry to take a step away from her, their bodies standing a little too close for comfort.

"I was getting you a coffee."

"Ah, so you saw the latest addition to the office, hm?"

"Yes," Ava hissed, slowly crossing her arms, refusing to be the person to take the first step back. Her eyes dipped to his crisp linen shirt, the first couple of buttons undone and exposing his angular collarbones, noticing a small freckle on the right side of his clavicle as though a drop of chocolate had landed there for her to lick.

"Do you like it?" Nate asked teasingly.

Ava's eyes snapped up as though she had been caught with her hand in the cookie jar, and stealing a glance at his sun-kissed skin, she wondered if his flesh tasted as nice as it smelt before she squawked, "Do I like *what*?"

"The coffee machine!" He laughed, a deep, rumbling noise that resembled rolling thunder through dark clouds.

"Yes, I guess it's *one* good addition to this department," Ava sneered, still not keen on her new boss's arrival, nor did she particularly enjoy his teasing attitude this morning.

Before he could test her patience any further, she turned on her heel and made for a quick exit, a small smile twitching at her lips the second her back was to him.

Nate couldn't help the grin flashing onto his face when his assistant left him stood there, chuckling at her smart mouth and shaking his head. Ava Archer was a definite firecracker.

THE DAY HAD DRAGGED on as Nate attended meeting after meeting, his eyes wandering to an unsuspecting assistant of his. He couldn't pin what it was about her that got under his skin; was it her bratty mouth that needed to be tamed, her obvious beauty, the fact she was off-limits, or was it as simple as her being the only woman not giving him the eyes in this department that drove him wild? There was just something about Ms. Archer that irked him and kept his mind drifting back to his erotic dreamscape that morning.

It had been years since he found himself so infatuated with a girl—no, a *woman*. Years since he had felt the bite of desire, years since he found himself wanting someone to take a chunk clean out of his soul. Such thoughts were detrimental to everything he had amassed.

Ava thought Fridays were meant to be the easiest day of the week but with Mr. Brooks leading the department, it would appear that Friday was just another day to grind down the workload. By the time late afternoon came around, Ava was gladly logging out of her computer, about to slip one arm into her coat when the beep of the intercom sounded on her desk, her eyes turning glacial as she stared at the red dot on the machine.

"Ms. Archer, my office, now," his commanding voice summoned, making her sigh as she shrugged out of her coat and strutted into his office.

"Yes?" she said with a feigned positive smile, her eyebrows raised as she popped her head around the door frame, hinting that she was in a hurry to leave.

"Come in and close the door," Nate ordered, sat at his desk and not peering up from his computer, his face as frosty and composed as ever.

Ava's brows creased together as she hesitantly shut the office door behind her and took a seat in front of Mr. Brooks. As always, her boss was his usual dark and mysterious self, oozing authority as he rose from his chair and prowled around the large mahogany desk and stood in front of her, leaning back with his hands on his desk.

"Ms. Archer, as you know, the Forbes negotiation is fast approaching and is taking up a lot of man-hours in this department. The problem is, however, that I alone am running two firms at once *and* trying to lead this high-profile case, which just isn't practical." Nate sighed, a part of him wishing he had someone to offload his busy and crappy week to. Every day he had skipped lunch just to hold a call with his Manhattan branch; there just weren't enough hours in the day. "I appreciate your father did the bulk of the work here and that you acted as more of a cler-ical assistant to him, however, I require you to be on the front line with me for this case." Truthfully, he did need her help but it was more than that. He felt a level of guilt for punishing her so harshly on their first day together, especially when she worked so hard to support his every need. She deserved a medal for what he had put her through.

Ava's eyebrows shot up in surprise. Even as her father's legal secretary, her old man had never once given her a front-row seat to the nitty-gritty of the war zone. Coming to think of it, he barely ever gave Ava the responsibility to handle any of the trials that passed through here. She never had a chance to shine. Everything she did was in the back-ground, running the show to a degree.

"Of course, what do you need from me?" Ava asked, trying her best to hide the glee inside her belly, but she had a feeling that her excitement was showing when Mr. Brooks gave her a small admiring smile, one that made her belly do a flip-flop.

"Well, first things first, Ms. Archer, if you are to be working this case behind closed doors with me, I need you to sign this," Nate answered, reaching behind him and holding up a document.

"And what exactly am I signing here?" Ava squinted up at the file, watching the smirk climb up the corner of Mr. Brooks's handsome yet nefarious face, feeling as though she were about to make a deal with the devil himself.

"This, Ava, is a non-disclosure agreement."

EIGHT

"I MEAN, it's pretty impressive when you think about it, one million steps in one month and it's for a good cause." Peter's voice droned on somewhere in the distance over the noise of the busy cocktail bar, but Ava's mind was elsewhere as she thought about the terms of the NDA she had just signed.

The contract was straightforward: do not speak to anyone other than the client, her attorney, or Mr. Brooks about the Forbes case. However, it wasn't the legal bindings of the agreement that was playing on Ava's mind. Mr. Brooks had been very clear that every day she would be required to work after hours with him. The contract detailed that a private meeting would be held daily, in his office, to discuss the details of the case, that their calendars should be booked out during this time, statuses set to do not disturb, and for the office door to be locked. Something about that last condition put Ava on edge, sparking her excitement at the thought of being alone with him, but she couldn't quite understand why he had that effect on her. It was one thing to be attracted to a man, but it was something else completely when you lusted after one to the point of it becoming an obsession.

"Ava?" Peter asked, waving his hand in front of Ava's vacant stare fixed on the street outside the bar window, the glass a series of bokeh lights from the raindrops trickling down the glass.

"Hm?" she asked in a daze, turning her attention towards him again.

"Hey!" He laughed and took a sip from his pint of lager. "You were a million miles away, ol' girl."

"Sorry, my brain is still in work mode." She sighed with a smile, sweeping her long hair back from her face and resting her head on her hand. "What were you saying?"

"I was just talking about the charity ball coming up. I presume you'll be my arm candy for the evening?"

"Very presumptuous of you, Mr. Taylor. What makes you think I don't have a date already?" Ava teased, her long legs slowly crossing underneath the high bar table as she hid her smirk behind her glass of wine and enjoyed Peter's staggered expression.

"You do? Who?" Peter inquired, a hint of envy laced through his tone that brought the green out in his eyes.

"Why does it matter?" Ava shrugged, her coy smile evident as she lowered her glass.

"Just so I can size up the bloke."

"*What?*"

"You know, so I can cut him down to size and politely tell the gent that he is punching way above his weight with a lady such as yourself," Peter explained confidently as he rolled up the light-blue sleeves of his shirt exposing the ink running up his forearms.

Ava threw her head back and laughed. "You absolute *knob*!"

Peter's face lit up watching her laugh like that, his hand slowly snaking around her knee and making Ava's expression turn sober when she saw that familiar look on his face.

"Let's get out of here, yeah?" Peter asked, his bottom lip caught under his teeth.

THE FRONT DOOR banged open as it did most Friday nights and the pair tumbled into Ava's apartment like a hurricane, a frenzy of copper and gold as jackets were tossed and shoes were kicked. Books thumped against the floor as Ava pushed Peter up against the bookshelf in her hallway, her mouth latching on to the side of his neck and tasting the bitter spice of his cheap cologne. Hearing him hiss from between his teeth only spurred her on as she tugged at his shirt, roughly untucking it from his work slacks and jerking apart the lapels until his buttons popped open and his chest was exposed for her hungry mouth to lap up.

"*Jesus Christ*, Ava," Peter huffed hotly, his fingers digging into her ample hips, bringing her closer. "The hell has gotten into you? Not that I'm complaining," he scoffed before groaning as Ava's teeth grazed against his left nipple, his eyes closing as he leaned his head against the shelf behind him.

Truthfully, Ava didn't know what had gotten into her, so amped up after a stressful few weeks with her father taking ill and working the week from hell with her enigmatic new boss. Something had her desperate for a release, needing to vent all that pent-up energy and take it out on her plaything.

"*Shut up*," she snarled erotically, looking up at Peter with a burning demand in her eyes, a dark grin sprawling across her face that Peter mimicked before he yanked her body forward and crashed his eager mouth against her own. Her tongue chased after his, fingers tangled around auburn strands as feet stumbled through her apartment leaving a trail of clothes in their path.

"Bloody hell," Peter laughed incredulously as his back bounced against Ava's mattress, the blonde woman standing at the end of the bed smirking down at him like a cougar about to pounce on its dinner.

"I *said*..." Ava warned, reaching behind her to slowly pull the silver zip down her dress. The material eventually sprung apart before the shoulders slid down her arms and sensually revealed her underwear as she sneered, "Shut...up."

She couldn't help but revel in Peter's reaction, his mouth snapping shut before his jaw slowly descended upon seeing the French lingerie adorning her voluptuous body. She had an affinity for all things luxurious and her lingerie certainly fell into that category.

"Yes, madam." He gulped, nodding his head and propping himself up on his elbows to get a better view of this woman that he couldn't get enough of, even after the several times they fucked. That black lace teddy with red roses embellishing her smooth tummy was enough to bring any man to their hands and knees.

This was Ava's game; one she had mastered after many one-night stands. The fiery little vixen crawled provocatively onto her mattress between the redhead's legs before eventually straddling his lap and peering down at the many tattoos covering his bare chest.

"Good boy," she cooed down at Peter, guiding his hands onto her petite waist, and slowly sliding them up to her chest, noticing his growing arousal pressing up against her thigh. Her hands moved his southwards towards her sweet centre but at the last minute she snapped and pinned his hands above his head, her eyes daring him to try to resist her. With one quick, assertive movement, she had taken his belt and bound his wrists with it.

Temptation was something Ava knew well, and it was something she always impulsively acted on. She knew that the only way to get rid of that lustful urge was to yield to it.

All week she had felt the unwarranted itch of desire and now she was using Peter to scratch it for her.

MORNING BROKE through Ava's curtains, her lashes fluttering into consciousness as she watched the specks of dust floating in the sunbeams.

"Good morning, gorgeous!" Peter's voice reverberated off all four walls in her bedroom making her brain ache as she hid beneath the sheets. "Coffee," he chuckled, placing a mug down onto her nightstand.

"I don't drink coffee," she grumbled, peeking only a pair of sapphires out of the sheets as she squinted up at Peter's messy mop. "What time is it?"

"Back of nine."

"Back of *what*?!" Ava squeaked, shooting upright and not caring that the upper half of her body was exposed and igniting a greedy gleam in Peter's eyes.

"It's alright, love. It's the weekend." Peter laughed, sipping at his cuppa, his presence starting to irk Ava as she got out of bed and resisted his attempts of pulling her body close to his. "What's the hurry?"

"I've got things to do, places to be!" Ava sighed impatiently while peeling his arm away from her waist and padding into her en suite with Peter in tow.

"Oh," he said, a little disappointed. "I thought we could maybe have breakfast together?"

Her feet skidded to a stop against her bathroom tiles. *Not this again.*

"Peter..." Ava's tone was a warning as she slowly turned around to face his wandering eyes dragging down her model body.

"I know, I know"—his hand motioned at her to slow down—"*just sex* and all that, but we can still have breakfast together for Pete's sake!" He laughed, putting down his coffee and stepping closer to her until his hands landed upon her upper arms. "C'mon, it'll be nice, I'll make you a hangover smoothie."

"I can't," Ava stated sternly, taking his hands and placing them back at his sides. "Sorry, I'm just very busy today," she added a little more softly before coaxing him out of her bathroom, "I'm visiting my father at his estate this weekend and I promised I'd be on time for brunch which I'm now going to be late for."

"So? I'm sure he'll understand—breakfast is the most important meal of the day!"

"Perhaps next weekend. Just...see yourself out, alright?" Ava called through the bathroom door that she now shut in his face as politely as she could manage.

That was the trouble with her arrangement with Peter; it was no longer just a one-night stand. The sex was above par and he was certainly a very attentive lover, but there was more than just the problem of things getting too familiar with them both now...

Peter hadn't managed to scratch her itch.

NINE

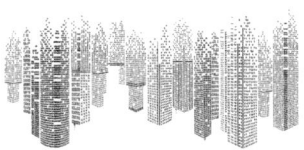

THE BRITISH COUNTRYSIDE was always a welcome sight for Ava when she was constantly surrounded by stone and glass. It wasn't that she didn't adore her concrete jungle, it was just that there was something very freeing about driving through the rolling green hills that were patched with vibrant yellow fields of growing rapeseed flowers.

Ava's chauffeur pulled through a set of grand gates fit for a castle as they drove up an avenue of majestic oak trees, the road lined with sunny daffodils and snowdrop flowers.

The Crestwell estate soon came into view, the ivy-covered manor showing off the ego of Mr. Archer, laid out in sandstone brick that sprung out from the well-manicured lawn as if it were insulted by the soil it sat on. The house was overly large and ostentatious to the point it was almost intimidating, but to Ava, this had been her home all along. The large rectangular windows were oversized, every room bathed in daylight from the first kiss of dawn to the twilight hours. The driveway was grandiose, sweeping into a wide circle in front of the stately home with an ornate fountain in its centre.

"Thank you, David," Ava said to her driver as he carried her suitcase up the stone staircase that led to the front of her childhood home. Before her stood the large oak doors that were sheltered under a wide porch supported by stone pillars. One of the tall doors burst open as a man walked out into the late morning sun.

The gentleman wore a green tweed blazer over a button-down shirt and a pair of well-pressed sandy-coloured trousers. Despite his summery attire, his hair was turning to winter, greys fading into silver as time creased his handsome, yet slightly lopsided face. His right leg stepped forward while his left dragged behind, the walking stick he leant on tapping against the concrete tiles.

"Hello, little bug!" Mr. Archer beamed, stick pointing to the side as his arms extended wide.

Ava's face burst into life as she ran like a child towards her beloved father and wrapped her arms around him. It may seem odd to some that this was their style of greeting after last seeing each other only just over a week ago, but Ava saw her dad every day and enjoyed his company so even a short period of time without seeing him had felt longer than she'd care to admit. Also, being the eldest daughter, she felt a certain level of responsibility to keep an eye on her father and make sure he was well.

"Oh, I missed you, old man!" Ava cooed, squeezing her arms tightly around him before easing off when she felt the tap of his cane against her leg.

"Steady on you with the 'old man'," he chuckled, his voice personifying the British summertime. "I might be going grey, but I've still got youth in me yet!"

Ava wasn't sure if it was the time spent apart or the fact that her father was still healing from his trauma, but something about him felt older and more fragile since last they met.

"Yes, boss!" Ava laughed, saluting her dad in their usual bantering way. "How are you feeling? How's the leg?"

"I'm perfectly fine, bored out of my mind in this big bloody house with your two squabbling sisters driving me barmy!" he jested, placing his hand onto Ava's shoulder and guiding her through the grand doors of the house that creaked and echoed into the main atrium of the building. "Speaking of which, *don't* mention Suzy's hair..." her dad warned with a grimacing shake of his head.

"Why? What's wrong with Suzy's hai—"

Suddenly a set of doors burst open from her right and a tall woman with a sharp black bob greeted her. "Ava! You're bloody late, brunch is going cold!" Heather huffed, a polka-dotted apron wrapped around her thin frame. "Get your arse through here!" she barked, disappearing back through the doors but not before poking her head through them again and adding, "Oh, and for the love of God, do *not* mention Suzannah's hair!"

AFTER SPENDING the afternoon with her father, reassuring him that everything was all rainbows and sunshine at his firm, Ava was now sprawled across her youngest sister's bed ranting about her new boss and the week from hell she had had. She lay staring up at the high ceiling with her legs dangling over the side of the four-poster bed.

"He sounds like Christian Grey," Suzannah giggled, making Ava's eyebrows lower into an unamused expression as she propped herself up on her elbows and glared at her youngest sibling who was still at college studying fashion.

"Why do people keep referencing that bloody movie?!" Ava chided, shaking her head and crossing her arms. "I *wish* he was Jamie Dornan; I'd climb that man like a tree."

"*Ava!*" Both of her sisters gawked at her.

"What? I bloody would!" she scoffed as the three of them burst out into laughter that slowly faded. "Not to point out the elephant in the room but speaking of fifty shades of *grey...*" Ava winced as she pointed at Suzannah's hair.

"It was meant to be *ash*-blonde, not grey!" Suzannah whined, slapping at Ava's knees before throwing herself face down onto her bed and squealing into the quilted sheets.

"I'm teasing, poppet. I'm sure the salon will sort it out on Monday, but *hey*, blonde suits you!" Ava soothed, patting Suzy's back.

"Not everyone can possess the golden child gene, isn't that right, Ava?" Heather teased as she swung upon a hanging loveseat in the corner of the room. It was an ongoing tease between her sisters that Ava was the only blonde in the family, but apart from that, Suzannah and Heather enjoyed winding her up about being Daddy's favourite.

"Envy isn't a good look on you, dear sister," Ava retorted with a smirk.

"Neither is that outfit," Heather bit back, causing Ava to drop her jaw in offence.

"What's wrong with my outfit?"

"You look like a thirty-year-old single mother who drives her ex-husband's Range Rover."

"I do not!"

"You kinda do," Suzy chipped in, her voice muffled with her face still planted.

Outraged at this, Ava got up and peered at herself in the mirror. She couldn't understand how her peach blazer, white loose-fitting shirt, and high-waisted jeans made her look like a divorced mother, especially with her lips painted red.

"I think it looks chic," Ava said defensively, shrugging.

"No, darling sister, *this* is chic," Heather sighed, coming up behind Ava to remove her blazer, tuck her shirt into the waistband of her skinny jeans, and then roll Ava's sleeves up to her elbows.

"You need a belt for that waist," Suzannah added as she stepped in to loop a brown leather belt around Ava's slim centre.

"Honestly, you pair," Ava sighed but had to admit that her sisters were right. The ensemble *did* look better with their fashionably skilled touch. Ava didn't have bad taste in dress sense at all, but compared to both her fashionista sisters, she had no chance.

Once the sisterly antics had died down, dinner was being served which smelled like a delicious Sunday roast despite it being Saturday. Fatty, smoked, and succulent aromas filled the hallways of the large house as the trio made their way downstairs.

"So, tell me, have you split up with my future husband yet?" Heather teased.

"For the last time, Peter and I are *not* an item." Ava rolled her eyes, her hand grasping the dark wood of the bannister at the bottom of the stairs as she swung around it out of old habit.

"Suzy said you guys *shagged* last night—becoming quite the regular occurrence, don't you think?"

"Keep it down!" Ava hissed, not wanting her father to know of the raunchy misconduct happening behind his back in his office. "It'll be the last time it happens; he offered to make breakfast *again*..." She bared her teeth at Heather, who was only a year younger than Ava and less naive as Suzannah, who still didn't agree with Ava's a-romantic outlook on life.

"*Again?*" Heather mirrored Ava's expression, walking through the large hallways as the aroma of dinner grew stronger. "Well, if you're pulling the plug with Peter, I call dibs. You can go on the prowl for Jamie Dornan," she jested as Ava peered back at Heather from over her shoulder.

"Or I could just fuck my current boss!" Ava joked, her shoulders shrugging up with a whimsical expression on her face before she turned around and stopped dead as she smacked hard up against a muscular roadblock. A squeak left her lips as she timidly peered up and stared into restless pools of honey that sent heat flaring to the surface of her face.

TEN

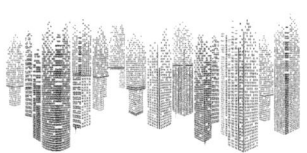

NATE'S HANDS grasped handfuls of Ms. Archer's hips, his fingers itching to reach back to her plump behind and pull her forward. He hadn't been expecting to find her here this weekend but was highly pleased when Tom had mentioned all *three* of his daughters were visiting. As per usual, Ava's colourful mouth never failed to impress or amuse him, nor did her beautiful flustered face. She looked different outside of work—less sharp and filtered, her curves softer and more delicate, a type of carefree demeanour to her that he enjoyed.

"*Mr. Brooks?!*" Ava piped, her voice breaking from the high pitch she addressed him with. It didn't help matters that Heather was snorting back her laughter behind them both.

Why is this fucker always around at the worst possible times?

"Ms. Archer," Nate didn't attempt to hide his amusement as his lips lifted into a perfect smile that dimpled his cheeks and reached the corners of his eyes. "I was just catching up with your father," he explained as a common courtesy, his eyes dipping down to the pleasant placement of her warm palms against each of his pectorals.

Ava couldn't help but stare up at him, her feet frozen in place, and her fingertips unwilling to move from the solid muscle beneath his fitted lilac shirt which was rolled up at the sleeves and only emphasised the power beneath the stretched and rumpled fabric.

When he eventually made a move to step back from her, she noticed the way his fingertips applied a slight amount of pressure into her sides, his thumbs pressing into her hipbones and causing a surprised gasp to leave her lips as their magnetic gaze remained on each other.

"Ah, Ava, I see you bumped into Nate!" Mr. Archer exclaimed, stepping out of his study and into the hallway where Ava sprung apart from her boss as she tried to remember the use of her tongue.

"Quite literally," Heather quipped, passing by Ava with an impish smile on her face and receiving daggers from her elder sister.

"Nate, we were just getting dinner, why don't you join us?" Mr. Archer beckoned generously as he staggered up to Nate and placed a hand down upon his broad shoulder.

Nate didn't need to look at his assistant to know her expression would be horrified at the prospect of him joining their dinner party, a small amused chuff escaping his nose at the thought.

"Oh no, I couldn't possibly impose, Tom," Nate replied, deciding to let Ms. Archer off the hook and save her any further embarrassment. However, he did intend on quizzing her as to why she would "fuck her current boss".

"Pish-posh, you wouldn't be imposing at all, we'll set you a place at the table now."

Ava felt her stomach rocket into her throat as she

quickly made her way into the dining room and sat down at her usual spot at the table. This was a nightmare.

Home is meant to be a sanctuary and here the bloody devil is!

"Well, that wasn't painful to watch," Heather whispered next to Ava, her thin lips rolled inwards to suppress her laughter.

"*Shut your mouth!*" Ava hissed, elbowing her sister and uttering, "You don't think he heard, do yo—"

"High maintenance, expensive to upkeep, and desperate to see the Italian coast," Nate chuckled, suddenly appearing in the room alongside Mr. Archer and causing Ava's mouth to snap shut.

"Ah yes! As are most," Mr. Archer laughed as he took his seat at the top of the table. "But a fine beauty she is! We sailed the coast of Sicily many years ago—why Ava, you must have only been a little sprout!"

Ava sat upright, giving her father a meek smile as she downed her glass of water to quench her suddenly dry mouth. It was a pleasant but odd experience seeing Mr. Brooks dressed down and wearing dark navy jeans that clung to his strong thighs and emphasised the tightness of his bottom—he certainly had a bum that rivalled even Beckham's. It also wasn't lost on her, or her sisters for that matter, that Mr. Brooks's tan leather belt matched perfectly with his brogues and designer wristwatch. Of course, a man of his stature would be effortlessly stylish as he were handsome, making it near impossible for Ava to keep her eyes off him as he took his seat directly across from her at the large table.

AVA WAS glad that during the meal, the conversation was steered mostly towards Suzannah and her college work. However, Ava did find out snippets of information about the mysterious Nathaniel Brooks and how he studied law at Harvard, was an only child, and grew up just outside of the big city in a town called Southampton, confirming that her boss was from new money just like her.

"Yeah, well, Cynthia was telling me about the internship she got, you know, for work experience, so it's something I think I should look into as well. What do you think, Daddy?" Suzannah asked, her fork moving around the peas on her plate, an annoying habit that Ava thought her little sister would grow out of after twenty-odd years.

"Absolutely, pet. Exposure to the working world is critical in any industry," their father agreed and suddenly Ava's head popped up as though a light bulb switched on above her.

"What about an internship at the firm? We're always hiring data clerks!" Ava insisted, knowing their father would show his own daughter the same kindness he did to her best friend. However, as her father and Mr. Brooks exchanged a disconcerting look, Ava furrowed her brow and asked, "What?"

"That's partly why Nate came over, bug. During the annual financial review, you'll know we look at ways to save the business money, and as it turns out, data entry isn't required anymore," Mr. Archer sighed, removing his glasses with a heavy look on his face.

"What are you say—"

"What your father is trying to say, Ava," Nate interrupted, wiping his smug mouth with a napkin, "is that it is the twenty-first century and with robotics in place these days, there is no use for a data clerk—we're practically tossing cash down the drain."

"*Wait*, you're not telling me you're getting *rid* of the data department, are you?" Ava's attention snapped between Nate's composed face and her father, who was now rubbing at the bridge of his nose. She felt the prickle of anger up the back of her neck like a flame held against her reddening skin.

"I was going to tell you after dinner, bug."

"You cannot get rid of that department; *Sam* is in that department!" Ava scolded, her hands bundled into tight fists upon the table's edge as her father stuttered and stumbled for words.

"It's smart business, Ava," Nate cut in.

"This was *your* doing, wasn't it?" Ava angrily accused across the table towards her boss as her sisters sat back in their seats sending each other worried glances that Britain and America were about to start a world war.

"*Hey*, I'm just doing my job"—Nate raised his palms defensively—"if you've got a conflict of interest in this matter, we can discuss it in the office on Monday."

"*Are you fucking kidding me right now*?!" Ava exploded at her new boss, the legs of her chair scraping loudly against the wooden floors as she suddenly stood with her fists banging down on the dinner table, rattling the china, and causing her family to jump whilst Nate remained as glacial as ever.

"Ava, calm down!" Heather gasped.

"No, I will *not* calm down!" Ava raged, turning her attention to her paling old man. "This is *Samantha* we're talking about; she is like a daughter to you! She is not fucking *expendable*!" Her eyes snapped back onto Nate as he calmly got to his feet.

"Ava, you should listen to your sister, this is not a conversation for the dinner—"

"*Oh, fuck off, you knob!*" Ava barked, interrupting Nate as she tossed her napkin on the table and stormed out of the room before she had a chance to see the gobsmacked expression on her boss's face.

ELEVEN

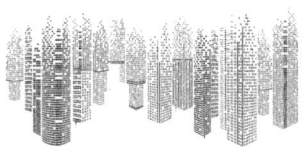

NEVER HAD Ava felt so utterly powerless.

Her feet thudded against the loose stone chipping pathing the way to their family's stables. This was her happy place, the one place growing up that she would come to whenever her parents were having screaming matches and tossing expensive china at each other.

It was a small shelter for their remaining two horses, a hut made from weathered oak planks with a sloping corrugated iron roof that made even the briefest of summer showers sound like a hail of bullets. Straw covered the floor, golden hues rivalling Ava's hair as half-empty hay nets hung limply along the walls alongside buckets of water for the horses.

Ava ran into the wooden hut, slamming the creaking door behind her, the rusted iron hook on the door clattering loudly against the hut and spooking the horses.

"Shit," Ava sighed, looking up at a large black horse that huffed disapprovingly down at her from behind his gate. "Sorry, old boy, I didn't mean to scare you," she soothed, running her palm down the silken snout of her father's horse, smiling at the tickling of silver whiskers across his warm nose as she carefully pressed her forehead against his and closed her eyes.

Just a few brief moments and already her heart rate was calming down, put at ease as the sun dipped across the hills and burnt-orange light crept between the slits of wood holding up the stables. However, all that burst from her as the black beauty huffed and pulled away from her as the stable's doors were ripped open, the sunset flooding in and blinding her.

"Suzy?" Ava asked with her hand shielding her eyes. It was always her youngest sibling who would find her here.

"Guess again."

Ugh, not this wanker.

"What the hell do you want, Nate?" Ava sneered as her boss entered the stables, the amber glow cutting around his powerful silhouette.

Nate felt a shiver of pleasure run through his body as he heard his name against her scarlet lips. Of all the hues of autumn, her hair was the most divine as the sunset caught it and sent molten gold carelessly flowing down her shoulders. A golden goddess in her purest of forms.

"Oh, we're on a first-name basis now, are we?" He smirked, stepping towards her bratty demeanour as she crossed her arms and exaggerated her cleavage through the unbuttoned V-neck of her shirt.

"Well, for starters, we're not at work so I'll address you however the hell I want, and besides that, you're the one who started calling me Ava instead of 'Ms. Archer'," she mocked his American accent and quoted the title with her fingers, much to Nate's amusement.

"Are you always such a *brat*?" Nate laughed, a hearty sound that caught Ava off guard as she peered up at his handsome face and felt something defrost inside her—but then she remembered this was the *arsehole* who was laying off her best friend.

"Are you always such an egotistical *knob*?" she fired back, taking an assertive step towards him but shrunk in his bold shadow as he challenged her by taking a step towards her also, the pair coming to a standoff in the middle of the stables.

Nate steadily trained his gaze down on her, impressed by her backbone, if not amused at how adorable she was when she was feisty. Surely, she knew he could flip her tiny body on its ass with one lift of his finger? She likely did know that, which just made him admire her more.

"You should really watch that mouth of yours, Ms. Archer."

"Oh, yeah?" she challenged with a defiant rise of her chin, meeting his death stare head-on.

"Yes. It'll get you in trouble one day," Nate replied, taking a step towards her, and forcing her to take a half step back.

"Well, it's a good thing I like trouble then, isn't it?" Ava sassed, dropping her arms by her sides and straightening her spine as she took a step forward, insisting that he took a step back, but he remained firm in place.

"Has anyone ever told you that you have a serious attitude problem, Ava?" he ridiculed, growing tired of her smart mouth as he began pressing forward, making her retreat backwards despite her provoking expression.

"Has anyone ever told you what they say about a woman with an attitude, *Nate*?" she challenged with a coy smile, taking small steps back as her boss closed in on her like a lion closing in on its prey, but she refused to back down, a lioness asserting its position in the pride.

"Enlighten me," Nate prompted, stopping when Ava's back pressed up against a wooden support beam holding up the small hut. If she felt intimidated by his presence, she certainly did not show it.

"A fierce man can handle a fierce woman. A fragile man will say she has an *attitude*," Ava stated, her hands tucked behind her back casually as she leaned her head against the beam and stared up at Nate from beneath the canopy of her dark lashes.

Nate watched her carefully, his eyebrows raised in surprise at her statement. This woman wasn't like the rest, he could feel it in his bones as he stared down into her passionate eyes, the sun behind them both now setting on the horizon of her oceans.

"Is that what you want, Ava?" he teased despite his serious expression as he pressed his knuckles to the wooden structure above her head, his arms outstretched above him. "A fierce man?"

Ava's heart began fluttering again just like it did that night in the office when he leant over her. She was starting to suspect that it was his proximity to her that had that type of effect on her cardiovascular system, that and his heady aroma that did a number on her hormones.

"What I *want*..." she began, peeling her back away from the wooden beam and closing the distance between their bodies while Nate remained grounded in his position. Her eyes stayed focused on his whisky-coloured orbs, feeling the heat of his stare tingle down the back of her neck, her breath turning shallow as she edged forward until her thighs pressed against his. It was like her body was betraying her despite her mind being set. Yielding slightly, she took a step back before continuing, "Is for you to not lay off my best friend."

Nate was lost in her presence, the woman blonde from root to tip, born to bring more golden sunshine into this world, and it showed too, it showed in those soulful blue eyes as bright as any orchid, clear as any glacier yet so very warm too. Under the ambient lighting, her hair wasn't so creamy up close as it was far away. It was streaked with warm tones of honey and butterscotch, the warmth complementing her pale skin rather than washing her out. Ava was the essence of summer, a rare beauty with lips like the most exotic of roses.

"Consider it done," Nate settled affirmatively, causing Ava to scrunch her nose up in confusion before he explained, "If I knew Ms. Eastley was your friend, I would have arranged another position for her sooner."

"Why didn't you say that earlier?!" Ava gasped, humbled by Nate's sudden generosity.

"In case you haven't noticed, it's a bit hard to get a word in edgeways with yourself." He chuckled, a deep sound that reverberated in his chest, as his hand lowered from above her head and gently pinched at her chin, his thumb hovering over her lower lip. "The trouble this mouth stirs..."

Ava felt her blood simmer in her veins from his touch, her tongue wanting nothing more than to taste the salt upon his fingertips. It was clear to her, in that moment, that lust was coiling around her bones, making her feel weak and melting her self-control down into a puddle of hormones.

"You should do something about that then," Ava breathed hotly, her lips moving and skimming past his pad, watching as Nate's eyes flicked back up to meet her own and squinted at her in surprised contemplation.

"Should I?" he asked in a low tone, asking more himself than Ava despite her nodding her head slowly and staring directly at his mouth. Flames licked up Nate's thighs at her daring and provocative conduct, his heart driving the blood in his veins away from his brain and clouding his judgement in a haze of lust. He wanted her. Nate Brooks wanted her like nothing else in this world, his desire making him feel starved for connection.

With his head in the gutter and his primal urges dominating his actions, his delicate grip on her chin lowered, fingertips brushing down the side of her sweet-scented neck, his thumb gliding down her throat before squeezing just enough to register her excitement from the pulse kicking against his palm.

"Yes..." Her answer was delayed, her brain feeling starved as the blood swirled below her naval and made her ache, that steady pulse growing stronger and stronger. She had never felt such until feeling his grip on her throat, but she wasn't rolling over like a submissive kitty for him. Her hands slowly found their way to Nate's hips, her fingertips feeling along the rim of his belt before climbing up the buttons on his shirt with shallow humid breaths filling the small space between their bodies.

The pair came to an impasse as Ava's hand wrapped around Nate's thick neck, showing she wasn't a kitten to be played with as she pushed against his hand and purred close to his mouth, "...*sir.*"

Nate's hand fisted tightly against the wooden strut above Ava's head as she tested his dominance and control. He'd fuck her in this hut right here, right now, just to make a point. He didn't give a shit if someone walked in. He couldn't care less about the repercussions of his immoral impulses.

"Say that again," Nate dared, the bump in his throat feeling crushed against Ava's hand as he pushed forward, his head tilting as he dipped down to her eye level.

"Make me, *sir*."

Fuck, Nate thought as his hips twitched like a car riding its clutch. Her voice was so low it practically snarled at him, making his nails bite into the heel of his palm.

She was a firecracker and he just lit her damn fuse.

Their lips were practically on each other's, exchanging sultry breath, and yet neither made the first move, in a dead-lock for power as they stared into each other's bruised and battered souls.

"Hello...?" Suzy's voice suddenly came from outside the stables making the pair of them jolt away from each other. Ava's petite sister walked into the stables, too naive to sense the electrically charged atmosphere as she beamed, saying, "Oh, good I found you! Mr. Brooks, your driver is here."

"Thank you," Nate said in a composed manner to Little Archer, despite his body pulsing as though he were running a marathon. "And please, call me Nate." His eyes slid down to Ava at his side. "I'll see you on Monday, Ava." He didn't give Ava a chance to respond as he nodded at Suzy and walked out of the stables, eager to leave before his prominent arousal was spotted bulging through his tight denims.

The sexiest thing a woman could do to a man was crawl, and here was Ava Archer who had now crawled inside his imagination and made it run wild.

TWELVE

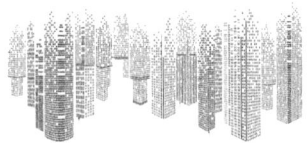

THE REST of the weekend was one big messy blur for Ava. She kept replaying what happened in the stables until the memory was forever burned into her mind. The taste of Nate's breath was still on her lips, the feeling of his soft grip on her throat, the way his hazel forests gazed down at her, spreading heat throughout her body like wildfire—he haunted her.

Ava had been over it a million times in her head and every time she concluded that it was highly inappropriate to have those types of relations with her boss. Peter Taylor was different; he was just a lawyer like the rest of the white collars filling the department. He was expendable. Nathaniel Brooks was her father's business partner, and for some reason, it felt like she was betraying her old man by having these illicit thoughts. However, she couldn't shake the itch that was Mr. Brooks; the way he stood above her and didn't silence her demons, choosing instead to play with them—was *that* what she wanted? Was that what she *needed*?

Monday was on her doorstep before she had time to

think of an appropriate way to approach her boss and explain to him that whatever *nearly* happened in the stables would *never* happen. It was a near moment that could be devastating to both of their careers. However, it was coming up midmorning and Ava hadn't seen Nate all day despite him appearing online. He even stood her up when he was meant to be briefing her on the Forbes case. His evasiveness put her on edge, especially when his calendar was free, and being his assistant, she had no idea where he was. It didn't help matters that the initial Forbes negotiation was today— the first time Ava would have sat in one—and she had utterly no idea what the finer details of this case were. She felt completely unprepared.

Brushing down her white blouse, she tucked her shirt into her tailored grey work slacks, and perfected her high ponytail, letting the waves fall to the middle of her back. She knew Mr. Brooks would have to be at the Forbes negoti-ation so decided to go early to the board room and hopefully catch him before the meeting.

Ava's heels echoed down the long hallway, her laptop in her arms as she swung around a corner and stopped dead, her jaw dropping at the scene unfolding in the board room. There inside, stood Nate with his back to her, dressed in his usual sharp work attire as he leaned his hips against the back of a chair, his knuckles white from how tight he gripped on to the table behind him. But it wasn't seeing him stood there that made Ava feel like her stomach was about to fall out of her arse. It was the brunette woman in front of Nate, on her knees and gripping his thighs.

NATE HAD TAKEN FAR TOO many cold showers that weekend. That vexing little blonde was all he could think about, his body in a constant state of ache and yearning that he alone could not relieve—no matter how many times he tried.

By the time Monday came around, he was glad that his morning was jam-packed, giving him some respite from his newfound and lethal obsession. First things first, the promotion of Ms. Samantha Eastley. With Mr. Archer's permission, Nate opened up a brand-new position for the young woman, appointing her as data analyst and systems manager for their sector, and giving her a handsome bump in pay too.

"You're bloody kidding me right now?!" Sam trilled in her thick Celtic accent, squealing the meeting room down and practically bouncing in her seat like an excited toddler over the incredible news. "Eh, aye! I absolutely accept!" She beamed, tucking the ombre caramel waves of her shoulder-length bob behind her ears.

Nate could see why this woman was best friends with Ms. Archer; they both shared that vibrant zest for life and were both hyperactive in their own ways.

"Good, then your new position will commence in three months' time, but I would ask for your utmost discretion on this matter, Ms. Eastley." Nate spoke professionally even though he was breaking every HR rule in the book right now.

"*Abso-fucking-lutely*, mouth shut, got it," Sam promised, nodding her head as she zipped her lips and tossed away the key.

Nate was struggling to hide his amusement as he escorted her out of the meeting room but called after her, "Oh, and Ms. Eastley?" He waited until Sam turned around to face him. "That discretion does not extend to Ms.

Archer." He winked, a small smile slipping his lips as Sam beamed him a cheery grin and all but danced her way up the hallways. Chuckling to himself, Nate began making his way back towards his department when the elevator doors pinged open and a flash of emerald green caught his eye.

"Nathaniel!"

Nate halted and turned to see the eccentric and widowed Charlotte Forbes approaching him. Charlotte was the definition of wealth, practically dipped in gold from her late husband's pockets. The middle-aged woman was dressed in a designer green jumpsuit that showed off the body that her personal trainer likely handcrafted for her. She reminded Nate of a viper, a very lethal viper. "I'm glad to have caught you," she cooed in prim and proper British that was pretentious as it was tasteless. "Can we discuss somewhere private prior to the negotiation, darling?" Charlotte asked, removing her unnecessarily large sunglasses and sitting them atop her sleek brunette hair that was so flawlessly long and straight, Nate doubted it was her own.

"Certainly, Mrs. Forbes," Nate answered and respectfully ushered her into the meeting room he had just vacated.

"Honestly, Nate, for the umpteenth time, please just call me Charlotte." She laughed, her hand resting on his elbow and making him feel as uneasy as a jaguar entering an anaconda's territory.

Nate had dealt with these types of clients before, women that desired nothing more than money, a succubus that would corrupt any man to get what they wanted.

"What would you like to discuss, Mrs. Forbes?" Nate asked, standing at the top of the long conference table and watching as Charlotte made her way to the refreshment table and poured herself a glass of water. A woman of her stature had a way of acting like she was at home anywhere she went.

"Well, it's nothing pressing, of course, I very much wanted to thank you for your help in setting up my case." She prowled closer to Nate, making his guard climb higher as he casually dismissed her gratitude for him just doing his job. "Oh, *but no*, your firm really has been highly supportive during this stressful and *lonely* time in my life." Charlotte sniffed, a practiced melancholic smile on her face as she idly sipped at her water. "I am just very appreciative is all. I'm having a hard enough time grieving my beloved Holden without my stepchildren trying to ostracise me from the family like this"—she scoffed a sardonic laugh—"not that it isn't something they've tried to do since I joined the family!"

Nate remained guarded, his face revealing nothing despite him wanting to ask if Charlotte could blame Holden's kids for having a strong distaste for her; not only was she ages with his offspring and marrying their seventy-year-old affluent father but now she was clearly trying to hijack their inheritance.

"Again, Mrs. Forbes, this firm is here at your disposal," Nate announced, hoping to shut down the conversation, but Mrs. Forbes had other ideas as she stood before him, waving her hand about expressively, the contents of the tumbler she held worryingly sloshing up the sides of the glass.

"And a fine firm it is—*oh my!*" Charlotte gasped, her hand waving to motion at the room and inadvertently spilling water down Nate's crotch and thigh.

Nate recoiled as the ice water saturated the dark fabric of his slacks and stung at his skin. He cursed under his breath swiping his hand down over his lap before stopping short when he found Mrs. Forbes down upon her knees in front of him, his eyes blown out wide.

"I'm so very sorry!" Charlotte fretted, dabbing his thigh with paper napkins. "I'm so jittery these days!"

"That's quite fine, honestly, I got it!" Nate hissed, trying to take a step back from this erratic woman but finding he was blocked in between her and the table behind him. His hands gripped the wood behind him, his jaw clenched frustratedly, wanting to bark at this nutjob to get off of his damn leg and kick her away like a petulant dog—even if it meant losing money and a client.

He was just about to snap when a loud thud behind him alerted both him and Mrs. Forbes. Snapping around, he saw his saviour set their laptop down onto the table, their hands on their hips with glaciers shooting icicles at him.

"Ava." Nate's face lit up, his stomach somersaulting and causing him to worry at the effect his assistant had on him. He felt like a pining schoolboy around her!

"Mr. Brooks," Ava clipped out, her eyebrows raised expectantly as her glaciers dropped to the woman who was currently clung on to the sides of his thighs. "Am I interrupting?"

Two and two were put together, Nate's attention snapping between Ava and Mrs. Forbes before he quickly realised what this scene looked like from Ms. Archer's perspective.

Agh, shit.

THIRTEEN

THE NEGOTIATION MEETING WAS LONG, tiring, and unresolvable. Without a prior brief, Ava had gone into the meeting blind but quickly learned that Charlotte Forbes was the wife to the late Holden Forbes, a seventy-year-old man who owned several well-known whisky distilleries across the isle and had died suddenly from a fatal heart attack. His three children—Jenson, Oliver and Freya Forbes —were in disputes with Charlotte, accusing their step-mother of trying to steal their inheritance. Whereas Charlotte decreed that the estate was very much a part of her entitlement as much as it was Holden's children.

"Yes, darling, but you can't settle those types of demands yourself for you are not the *only* trustee on the will, now are you, Oliver?" Charlotte's lips lifted into a mocking and provoking smile at her stepson, a man who couldn't have been that much younger than her with shock-ingly blonde hair that was tied into a bun at the back his head.

Ava noticed then that all the Forbes children were blonde, with pale blue eyes, looking like they were made in a test tube. The only one not dressed as though they were attending a gala was Freya, a young woman who couldn't have been much older than Ava's youngest sister. The girl sat wearing a simple black dress, her thin lips dry and cracked as she gnawed upon them nervously.

Oliver's face turned a perfect shade of cherry as he rose from his chair and pointed an accusing finger across the table at Charlotte. "You wretched woman! If my father were still here and saw your true colours—"

"We are in agreement that we have reached an impasse on the settlement, yes?" Nate's voice boomed across Oliver as everyone's attention snapped to him.

Ava couldn't help but stare too. Her boss was in his element in this environment, the entire room at his disposal as he sat composed as ever at the top of the table and demanded control and order.

Oliver scoffed at Nate, "Well like hell she's getting the bloody business! She's already got her claws into my father's—"

"Good, we are in agreement that this will be settled in court then," Nate interrupted him casually, not caring for his tantrum, shut his laptop, and glanced at his watch. "We are three minutes over and I have another meeting to attend. Peter, wrap this up and we'll reconvene in three days' time." He rose from his chair, carrying the same aura that a magistrate would as he left the room without so much as a look in anyone's direction.

As the tense meeting dispersed, Oliver cursed Charlotte's name to his sister as Peter, acting as Charlotte's attorney, and the lawyer serving the Forbes children tried and failed to defuse the bickering across the table.

"Freya dear, do try and remember the auction this weekend," sighed Charlotte.

"We're still going ahead with that?" Freya squeaked like a mouse.

"You cannot be serious?! It isn't enough to try and steal what our father wanted for us, now you're trying to sell his possessions too?" Oliver growled.

"Holden stated it clearly in his will that he wanted to donate his possessions to charity, dear." Charlotte tilted her chin up before rising to her feet and peering down at them. "You shall all attend and keep face."

"Father would have wanted it..." Jenson finally broke breath, looking at his brother.

"Fine," Oliver said as he stood up and glared at his stepmother. "But be sure that I will be accounting for *every* penny that goes to charity. Come on, Freya." He motioned at the young girl before dramatically making his exit.

Ava sat there with her teeth clamped on the inside of her lip, staring at Peter's emeralds, and trying hard not to show her amusement at the Forbes family drama. If she had known this was what usually went down in these types of meetings, she would have brought some popcorn.

"CONGRATS AGAIN." Ava beamed, her arms wrapped tightly around Sam as the pair returned to the office after a cheerful lunch. "We'll need to celebrate!"

"Thanks, my lovely— *Oh!*" Sam pulled back, her face lit up in excitement as she sang, "I almost forgot what is happening in a few weeks..." When Ava didn't jump on her cue, Sam pushed her away to meet her gaze. "Your birthday, silly!"

"No."

"Don't you 'no' me! We are getting blitzed whether you like it or not, Mrs!"

"Nuh-uh." Ava clenched her jaw and shook her head like a petulant child. "I do not wish to celebrate another nail in the coffin."

"You're bleeding twenty-eight, not sixty-eight!" Sam scoffed, rolling her eyes and crossing her arms before settling it once and for all. "It's happening either way because we need to celebrate *my* happy news anyway, so like it or not, you're coming out and getting blitzed on bubbles with me."

"Are all Scottish people alcoholics?" Ava teased.

"Eh, lass, I'll have ye ken I drank whisky before I drank my maw's ti—" Sam began to rant but Ava quickly clamped her hand over her friend's mouth before any more Scottish atrocities came out in the middle of the busy department.

"I have spent *way* too much time with you; I understood everything that just came out of your mouth just then," Ava laughed and lowered her hand. "Okay look, I have to get back to work, but yes, I'll go out with you and get 'blitzed', *happy*?"

"Yup, *elated*!" Sam beamed, mocking Ava's English accent and slowly walking backwards away from her. "Just remember and wear your red coat"—she winked, causing Ava to ask her what the hell she was talking about—"so that I can warn everyone that 'the red coats are coming' and yell 'freedom', of course!" Sam disappeared around the corner dramatically waving her hand like the Queen, leaving Ava stood there shaking her head in laughter.

It reminded Ava of the day she met Samantha at St Mary's Boarding School for young ladies. Ava had been stood outside the head mistress's office pinning flyers to the noticeboard when she saw a young girl, who struggled to follow the strict uniform guidelines, flip off the headmistress as she rounded the corner and bumped straight into an amused Ava. If not for the large sum of inheritance money that Sam's parents left behind, she doubted that St Mary's would have put up with years' worth of Eastley mischief. It was from that moment on that Sam became part of the Archer family, always around at Ava's family home for Saturday brunch and Sunday roast dinner.

From then on, the duo were inseparable.

Sam was perhaps the craziest and most unhinged person she had ever met, but Ava would be lost without her bringing light and colour into her life. They had the type of friendship where they would look at each other and burst out laughing at absolutely nothing, the type of laughter that made your ribs ache and filled your soul with love.

Samantha Eastley wasn't just a friend to Ava; she was her soul sister.

IT WAS WELL past finishing time as Ava slumped into her seat and stared at her screen. After her lunch with Sam, she had worked flat out all afternoon and was still no closer to clearing the mammoth pile of work needing to be done. However, she couldn't blame the increased workload on Nate anymore as she had seen him hunched over his desk all day in the same manner she had been. It was starting to dawn on Ava that her old man had perhaps been holding back a tsunami of stress from her. She didn't know what bothered her more: the fact that her father had done this in the first place or the fact that if he hadn't, Ava could have potentially stopped his stroke from happening if she had just taken on more work. The thought made her feel accountable and sick to her stomach.

Looking through the blinds into Nate's office she saw him sat there looking utterly spent and exhausted as he dragged his hands down over his face. She hadn't seen such a vulnerable side to him before and knew if he saw her looking, he'd likely act as though he were in control and coping.

Everyone has two hands: one to help yourself and one to help others, her grandmother had always told her. For some reason, looking at Nate just then, she couldn't shake the thought from her head.

With a small sigh, she made her way to his office and leaned her hip against his door frame, a sympathetic smile on her lips when he hadn't noticed her presence and continued yawning and rubbing his eyes.

"Need a hand with anything...*boss*?" Ava asked with a delicate smile, pushing the last word of that sentence out of her mouth and reminding herself to play nice.

"Ava." Nate's heavy eyes sprung up from his desk for the first time in over an hour. "You're still here?" He knew it was past finishing time but as he glanced down at his clock and saw just how far past home time it was, he couldn't help but feel bad that the young woman had stayed back as well. "You should head home and get something to eat, Ms. Archer."

"My name is *Ava*," she corrected with a pixie-like smile teasing her features as she pushed off of his door and padded towards the front of his desk, "and *you* need something to eat also."

Nate chuffed through his nose, a small appreciative smile on his lips as he sat back in his chair scratching his beard contemplatively and asked, "Do you like Thai?"

FOURTEEN

"WHAT HAVE you done to my office?" Nate gaped, walking back inside his office carrying the Thai takeout he had gone out for. One section of the floor was covered entirely in pieces of paper, Ava sprawled out across the files on her stomach, heels off as she swung her legs in the air behind her, a highlighter pen in hand.

"I'm finding and securing all of Mr. Forbes's assets," Ava chirped, pulling her earphone out with a proud grin on her face that made Nate struggle not to smile in response.

"It's a mess..."

"Yes, but an *organised* one," Ava challenged, pointing her pen up at Nate and shattering his icy demeanour as a small chuckle escaped him.

"Just come and get something to eat." He shook his head with a simper, sitting down on the two-seater and unloading the takeout cartons onto the table in front of him.

Ava jumped to her bare feet and made her way to Nate's computer to save her progress when she noticed his screensaver of an impressive white yacht named... "*Natalia*," she said aloud causing Nate's head to snap up in surprise until he saw the image on his monitor. "Nice boat." She shrugged, not fazed by expensive things as she switched the screen off.

The red haze from the aircraft warning lights sitting atop other skyscrapers oozed into the office in a series of red stripes through the slits in the blinds.

"Do you like dumplings?" Nate asked as he loosened his tie and undid the first two buttons of his shirt.

"I love *all* Thai food." Ava beamed, joining Nate on the leather sofa and tucking her legs underneath her as she admired the spread of food on the coffee table. "The only thing missing here is a bottle of vino," she sighed softly and balanced her noodles on her lap.

"You mean *this* bottle?" Nate smirked, producing the bottle of wine as if by magic and causing Ava's eyes to widen.

"Where did you get *that*?" Ava gawked with a mouthful of dumpling, her eyebrows raised as she pointed a chopstick at the bottle of red. "Are we even allowed to drink that in the office?"

Nate's expression darkened into one of mischief, a cocky smile on his lips as he pointed at his face and bragged, "*Boss.*" He watched Ava's head tip back as melodic laughter bubbled from her rosy lips. "As long as you don't go telling your pops, my ass ain't gonna get handed to me for this, and I can do whatever I damn well want."

"Are *all* Americans this overly cocky?" Ava teased with her lips pursed playfully and her eyebrow raised.

"Only the good ones, *ma'am.*" He winked, making Ava's breath hitch in her throat as her thighs tensed slightly. It was perhaps the first time that his New Yorker drawl had enticed her in such a way.

The night continued with banter and laughter, the

bottle of wine nearly finished as half-eaten takeout cartons scattered across the coffee table.

Ava removed her hair from its high ponytail, her roots sighing in relief as she ran her nails through her golden tresses and allowed the unruly and voluptuous waves to tumble down her shoulders.

Nate stared at her as she did, envious of the mug she placed to her lips and in awe of how someone could be so beautiful and not have been snatched by a proud, adoring man. He knew it had to be *her* doing, that the bold Ms. Archer surely had men lining up at her door, but she refused to be tied down to any of them. Some birds weren't meant to be caged. She wanted her freedom, and for that, he admired Ava, even if he was envious that he didn't have the same flexibility in life as her. She was a red moon during a starry night sky.

"Thank you for this," Nate professed, his plastic coffee mug of wine sitting on the arm of the sofa as he rested his feet on the coffee table.

"*For...?*" Ava frowned, sweeping her long hair over one side of her head as spirals of silk curtained one half of her face.

"Well, for one, staying back and helping me out, but mainly for *this*." His finger waved between the both of them sat comfortably on the leather chesterfield. "It was nice to not think about work for five minutes." He chuckled, leaning his elbow on the back of the sofa and dragging his nails through his hair, making it softer and less refined.

"Don't mention it." Ava smiled sweetly, her back against the arm of the sofa as her long legs filled the space between them. "I guess being the boss has its disadvantages, hm?"

"Yeah, you could say that...but stress is just part and parcel of the job."

"You should hire Mrs. Forbes to sort that stress out for you then," Ava uttered, inspecting the ends of her hair, internally berating her bitchy mouth and the wine's influence on it.

"And what exactly is that supposed to mean?"

"Oh, come on, let's not pretend that I didn't see what you were both doing in that empty meeting room today," Ava scoffed with an eye roll as she teasingly prodded the side of Nate's thigh with her toe.

"You shouldn't jump to conclusions," he stated with eyes down on her foot.

"Shouldn't I? *Oh, please*, the woman was on her knees in front of you, grasping your thighs! I might be blonde, but I was certainly not born yesterday, Nate."

"She intentionally spilt water down me," Nate countered with a dismissive shrug of his shoulders. "Why she was using seduction as a tactic, and for what reason, I'll never know."

"Maybe there was no reason or tact involved," Ava snipped as she crossed her arms, lifting her shoulders up to her ears as she theorised. "Maybe she was just seducing you for the sake of it."

Nate couldn't help but notice the change in Ava's body language, the coldness of her tone and the lack of eye contact as he teased, "Why, Ms. Archer...are you jealous?"

"*Jealous?*" Ava scoffed with a sassy eye roll. "And *why* exactly would I be *jealous*, Mr. Brooks?"

"You tell me."

Ava met his testing gaze but yielded first, her icy manner shattering as she giggled. She kicked at his thigh again, this time with a little more force, but yelped as Nate suddenly grabbed her foot and pulled it onto his lap.

Gasping, she tugged her foot and began to ask, "What are you—"

"Your feet must ache wearing those heels every day," Nate wondered aloud but didn't require an answer as he trailed his thumb down the delicate curve of her instep. His grip tightened around the sides of her bare foot, his thumbs pressing deeply into the fleshy pads beneath her toes and eliciting a hiss from between her teeth as he massaged her worn out sole. When she resisted and attempted to remove her foot from his lap, he tugged harder and kept her in place as his thumbs pressed deeper and deeper into her tired tissue until she slowly surrendered and sank back into the sofa.

His intentions had been innocent, even if the wine was clouding his judgement, but as Ava began pressing her thighs together and soft whines left her wine-stained lips, those intentions steadily became more and more sinful. He found his hands moving of their own accord as he squeezed at her heels, his fingertips running up her calf beneath her work slacks and eliciting more of those delicious noises from her lips that were causing his skin to prickle with heat.

Ava's lashes fluttered closed and she found herself submitting to his touch. Nate's fingers expertly knew just where to apply pressure, his assertive grip listening to her body as her mind told her to retreat and her body begged her to stay. However, Ava knew this was like sipping fine red wine—one taste of that high and you wanted more and more. She felt like she was melting from the way his fingers brushed against her flesh, edging higher up her trouser leg. A steady pulse found its way between her legs, demanding attention that the pressing of her thighs could not tame this time.

"*Fuck,*" she moaned, biting down on her lower lip before suddenly remembering just *who* was giving her this intense foot massage, her leg abruptly recoiling with her knee bent up. "I don't think this is a good idea," Ava cautioned, glad that there was some sobriety left in her brain despite her erratic heart pumping the alcohol around her body. "I think I best go," she announced, swinging her legs over the sofa and standing.

"No, wait—" Nate panicked, jolting upright as his hand reached forward and gently took her wrist. "I won't stop you, it's just that...I don't want you to go...yet." The amount of neediness in his tone made him feel uneasy, but he couldn't deny the level of comfort Ava had brought him tonight, a type of solace that he hadn't found in another for so long. However, as he looked up and saw the troubled expression on the young woman's face, his stomach sank as he let her go and sheepishly looked down at his shoes. "I'm sorry, that was very rude of me," he uttered, shaking his head, and trying to come up with an excuse for his dishonourable conduct, "The wine, it's—"

"A lovely bottle," Ava interrupted, causing Nate to look up at her with dazed eyes. She was like a bee to the honey in those eyes and couldn't stand to see him upset, especially when she knew that his actions were not unwarranted. Ava could have any man she wanted with just a bat of her lashes, but with Nate, he was off-limits out of principle and that drove her insane. She had everything but she couldn't have him.

To ease his feelings of guilt and to reassure him, she settled back down on the sofa next to him, her legs safely tucked beneath her as she diverted away from the awkward train wreck and asked, "You mentioned earlier that your family have a vineyard back home?" Nate was like a deer caught in headlights, staring at her as though she may well disappear into thin air. "Why don't you tell me more about it?"

FIFTEEN

WAVES CRASHED upon a shore in the distance, pulling Nate back towards the familiar sound of home. His eyes fluttered open as he rubbed the sleep from them and peered down to the warm weight pressing up against his side, sat on the chesterfield sofa in his office.

Ava.

He quickly realised the sound was her soft breathing, every heavy exhale like that of frothy white waves as she slept peacefully, curled up next to him like a resting kitten with his large suit jacket draped around her petite body. She was serene in this state, like seeing the sea calm down after a turbulent storm.

Nate couldn't resist, let alone miss his opportunity, as his fingers ghosted down over her nose, tracing the little button tip turned up at the end, before tenderly brushing across her petals and sighing quietly—her lips were as soft as he imagined. However, his touch disturbed her slumber as her eyes creased, lips pouted, and the bridge of her nose wrinkled in the most adorable frown he had ever seen. Staring down at her in curious fascination as her eyes blinked into consciousness, he knew then that he could watch a billion sunrises and would never find one quite as beautiful as her eyes opening in the morning.

White light flooded Ava's retinas, her mind foggy and body heavy as she stared up into the hazel forests that she had walked through in her dreams. A sleepy sigh left the slight curve of her lips as she closed her eyes, pulling a blanket around her and draping her arm over the warm pillow next to her. However, when that so-called warm pillow began jiggling beneath her and the husky noise of Nate's quiet laughter came from above, her hand felt across her pillow, over the hard ridges of Nate's chest until her eyes snapped open in alarm as she realised she wasn't dreaming and wasn't in her own bed. Gingerly, her eyes peered up at Nate to see his lazy smile.

"Good morning, Ms. Archer."

I fell asleep in the office with my boss. Shit, shit, shit!!

Ava squeaked in a panic and recoiled away from Nate, rolling backwards off the couch and landing between it and the coffee table with a large *thump*.

"*Shit!* Are you alright?" Nate gawked, peering over the edge of the sofa and down at the tangled body of his assistant, laughing when she flapped and struggled under his suit jacket like a wild animal caught in a net.

"I'm fine!" she squawked in exasperation, tossing the suit jacket from her and blowing the stray strands of hair from her eyes. Ava turned to look at the takeout cartons, the empty bottles of wine, and the plastic coffee mugs before glancing at her watch. "Fuck, *the time!*"

"It's fine, I don't mind if you are late today." Nate rolled his eyes, bemused by how flustered she was over, yes, a little unorthodox situation, but a harmless and innocent one at that.

"Perhaps *you* don't mind but I don't want people thinking that I slept with my boss!" she berated, jumping to her feet and picking up her heels before running to her desk outside.

Nate's eyebrows jumped at this.

Did she mean sleep as in sleep or sleep as in...?

Either way, she had a fair point; considering their dishevelled appearance, the fact they were in yesterday's clothing, and the odd scene in the office, one's imagination could easily come up with an explanation for what went down.

"*Where the fuck is my phone?!*" Nate heard Ava hiss, saw her cell on the floor amongst the paperwork, and took it out to her. "Thank you."

"Don't mention it." He smirked, perching on the corner of her desk and watching her hurry about, looking as though she were trying to escape a burning building.

Ava hopped as she quickly pulled on her heels and turned to look at Nate to say goodbye but froze on the spot when she saw him leant against her desk.

Sweet heavens above, she thought.

He looked irresistible with no tie, his shirt untucked and unbuttoned just enough for her to see the dark wisps covering his chest, and his hair unruly and sexy in an undone and natural way.

Oh, to sit on that man's fa—no, shit!

She shook the thoughts from her head and rushed towards the elevators before those thoughts could manifest into physicality, tossing over her shoulder a brief, "See you in a bit!"

"Ava! Wait up!" Nate called after her, chuckling as he caught up to the frantic blonde, his hand slipping around her waist and coaxing her to turn and face him. Her dazed eyes found his and Nate would be lying if he said he didn't adore the way her stare dipped to his lips expectantly, that once confident fire in her gaze now diminished to a flickering flame and giving light of her desires. "The Forbeses have invited me to a charity auction at their estate this weekend. Do you wanna tag along?"

Is he asking me on a date?

"Sure, just forward me the invite," Ava replied.

Nate grinned down at her, catching her by surprise as he grabbed a hold of her wrist when she abruptly went to turn away again. "Wait! One more thing..." he said in a lower register, raising his hand as his knuckles delicately brushed over the sweet blush upon her cheek and tucked a single spiral of gold behind her ear.

Ava didn't dare move, her heart in a state of frenzy as her breathing was heard through her lips. His touch was magnetic and had a way of jamming all her thoughts. Her lashes fluttered upon feeling his caress across the burn in her cheek before Nate pulled something from her hair and waved a rogue piece of paper from a fortune cookie in front of her face.

"You forgot this," he teased, chuckling as she snatched it from his fingers with a squeak, crumpling it into her jacket pocket and dashing into the elevator.

Ava stared at her reflection in the elevator mirror as her mind drifted to the previous evening. After the awkward encounter, Nate and she had talked long into the early hours, trading secrets and embarrassing tales, showing each other their biggest scars, reminiscing about their childhood memories, and laughing at times gone by. Ava couldn't remember a time where she had spoken to a near stranger without running out of things to say, but Nate was as full of stories as he was an exceptional listener. She never tired of his company.

A smile toyed at her lips as she remembered his mannerisms, the way he spoke with his hands when he was passionate about a subject, the way he'd pinch his nose when he laughed, his attempt at a British accent that had her ribs aching from laughter.

Seeing that side of Nate, that part of him that no one else she knew had access to, felt like having backstage tickets to a gig. It made her feel high on life, a feeling she couldn't get enough of. However, as the dopamine slowly faded and her attention focused back on her starstruck reflection, she became gravely aware of the dangers associated with what she was feeling. Ava had felt a similar sensation throughout her active sex life, and yet last night felt more intimate than any one-night stand she had ever had. Nathaniel Brooks touched her in ways that hands couldn't.

SIXTEEN

AUTUMN DAYS FADED towards the inevitable colder weather ahead, each nightfall coming sooner than the one before. However, on this autumnal Saturday, the foliage awaiting Ava's gaze out of her bay window was like that of an infinite dream of scarlet and gold with branches taking root into a cloudless azure sky.

The shrill buzz came from the phone mounted to the wall as she cursed under her breath and took one last look at herself in the mirror. She wasn't sure what to wear to a charity auction so ebbed on the side of caution and went with a long, pleated, tan skirt with a tucked-in black sweater and a pair of heels to add some class.

"Bloody heck, Brooks! I'm coming," she growled, the buzzer going off repeatedly as she finished tidying the stray curls of gold tied up into a braided bun.

Stepping out into the crisp air, she breathed in the gold and felt it extend throughout every part of her before peering down at the silver executive car and climbing in.

"You don't bloody have to take your time, old girl!"

"Peter?" Ava's nose scrunched up as she slid into the rear seats next to him. "Where is Mr. Brooks?"

"Must be meeting us there." Peter shrugged, idly picking lint off his green peacoat.

"Oh." *Definitely not a date then.*

"Everything alright?"

"Yes, splendid," Ava said with a tight smile.

"Rightio, time to go!" Peter grinned, giving her knee a quick pat before chapping on the chauffeur's window.

Fortunately, Ava didn't have to listen to Peter's obnoxious droning for too long as the car pulled into the Forbes estate. They drove up a long avenue of trees that decorated the rolling green hills on either side and made Ava feel as though she had stepped inside a Jane Austen novel.

"It's quite impressive really... I've been sat here for twenty minutes and my resting heart rate is 25 bpm, see!" Peter thrust his arm across Ava's vision, obscuring the picturesque countryside and catching her by surprise. "Oh look, 24!" He beamed down at his fitness watch as Ava gave him a quick yet pained smile. "You should really consider coming out running with me; it'd do you the world of good, old—"

"This is as far as I can take you," interrupted the driver from beyond the small partition.

Ava peered through the small window up front and saw a sea of people gathering within the long driveway that was lined on either side with vintage cars.

"That's fine!" Ava blurted as she abruptly opened her door before the car had managed to crawl to a stop. She had made her way into the small crowd by the time Peter caught up with her and casually linked his arm through hers. "Mr. Forbes certainly had a lot of cars," she mused as they sauntered up the aisle of collectable vehicles going up for auction.

"Old fellow is barmy selling all of these if you ask me! I wouldn't be letting any of these beauties go... I mean, these aren't just cars, Ava, they're—*no bloody way!*" Peter slid to a stop and gawked at a particular black and white car that looked like something Cruella de Vil would drive. "He surely can't be getting rid of *this*?" He turned and looked at Ava's blank expression. "Ava, this is a Rolls-Royce Phantom!"

"And...? *Gah*—!" Ava squawked as her hand was pulled forward to stand in front of the antique lump of metal.

"You don't just get rid of gems like these!"

"Well, it's not like he's going to need it anymore..." Ava blurted and received offended looks from the people peering into the windows of the vehicle. "Swell... I'll just be heading on inside now and grabbing some of that lovely free champagne." She excused herself with an awkward smile before scuttling up the long driveway.

The Forbes manor was deceivingly large as it hid behind majestic oak trees. It was a red brick building wrapped snugly in green ivy, the perfect backdrop to an Agatha Christie mystery.

Ava stepped inside the opulent foyer that was littered with London's upper-class socialites as a caterer handed her a glass of champagne. She meandered her way through the many rooms showcasing various pieces of Holden Forbes's life that were up for grabs. His wealth was shown in the randomness of some of his possessions—an obsession with vintage arcade games such as pinball and penny machines, a creepy wooden fortune teller, and a retro pro-boxer machine.

She sipped idly at her flute before stopping short inside

an empty room and peering up. Hanging shamelessly upon the wall was a grossly large oil painting.

"Oh, dear God," Ava scoffed, rolling her lips inwards to suppress her laughter at the gauche family portrait. Dressed in white, the Forbes family posed classically with expressionless faces, apart from Charlotte Forbes, who held the slightest of smirks—the type that held a secret.

"How long do you think they had to stay still like that for?"

"*Fuck me!*" Ava's squeal reverberated off the high ceiling, her shoulders jumping as her attention snapped back to the imbecile who snuck up on her.

"Ms. Archer," Nate greeted her with a smirk teasing his lips, his honey gems staring up at the artwork rather than her.

Ava huffed and faced forward again, ignoring his proximity to her back as she shook her head up at the painting. "What I find most impressive is how one could hold their poker face for that length of time," she quipped.

"Meh." Nate shrugged behind her before whispering coyly into her ear, "I think the Botox helps with that." His mouth lifted into an accomplished grin as bubbly giggles left her lips, his eyes down upon her as she slowly turned around and peered up at him from beneath those long lashes. He felt as though someone had reached inside his chest and squeezed the air from his lungs.

"What, is there something in my hair?"

"No! It's nothing...you just look"—he paused, deliberating over the correct word as his eyes drank in her effortless beauty—"casually remarkable."

"You're not so bad yourself, love," Ava joked, hoping her snide tone would cover the blush upon her cheeks. It baffled her how a man could make dressing in suits look as though it were his staple outfit. The stone-coloured suit jacket hung easily from Nate's broad shoulders, his crisp white shirt unbuttoned to show delicate tufts of dark hair, a belt securing his dark tight jeans that drew the eye to his well-framed package.

"Love?" Nate challenged with a raise of his brow, his heart secretly flip-flopping with the term of endearment from his subordinate—even if it was said in a cheeky tone.

"Shall we?" Ava swerved with a grin, holding her elbow out and causing Nate to shake his head and chuckle as he escorted her towards the civilised garden party out back.

The air was perfumed by fresh petunias, the well-groomed lawn stretching out as far as the barley hills in the distance. Upon the opaque green sat a large white gazebo housing the main auction event.

"Ah! There you both are," Peter cut in as he made his way over to them and casually took Ava's other arm, much to Nate's distaste.

The trio sauntered across the formal garden, a string quartet growing louder the closer they got to the tent. Despite being from money herself, Ava felt incredibly inse-cure around these money-thirsty snobs who drooled over a dead man's possessions.

"Oh, good, you made it!" Charlotte Forbes cooed, excusing herself from a group of ladies and dragging her stepdaughter with her as she joined them. "You all look absolutely *darling*! Don't they look *darling*, Freya?" She motioned to the quiet girl on her arm who nodded her head and sipped upon her orange juice from a champagne flute.

Ava couldn't help but cringe at this woman who was straight out of an *Absolutely Fabulous* sketch and feel sorry for Freya who seemed like the only normal one in this family.

"Sorry to interrupt," Oliver cut in, his hand delicately upon Charlotte's shoulder as he advised with a polite smile, "The bachelorette auction is about to begin, Charlotte."

"Thank you, my dearest," Charlotte replied, turning to press a small kiss on Oliver's cheek, which caused Ava, Nate, and Peter to exchange confused looks as the Forbeses played nice together as though they weren't at war in a financial lawsuit. "Oh, Ms. Archer! You should put your name forward for the auction! I'm sure some dashing young fellow would sweep you off your feet!"

"Uhm...no...I'm quite fine for that, thank you." *I'd rather shag a cactus.*

"Come on, old girl. It's for charity!" Peter egged her on.

"Let's go take our seats, yeah?" Nate veered, saving her from any further awkwardness as he led her to the front row.

"I'll be back in a mo!" Peter grinned, disappearing with Charlotte.

"Where are those two off to?" Ava asked Nate, who gave her a meek shrug.

"So...not your idea of fun, hm?" he asked, nodding his head towards the bachelorettes lining up at the side of the stage and checking their makeup in their compact mirrors.

"Being objectified and sold to the highest bidding man? No, I think I'll pass."

"Considering it's for charity, I doubt folks will see it so chauvinistically." He chuckled.

"Then why don't you put *your* name forward, Mr. Brooks?"

"Because it's a women-only auction."

"*Exaaaactly*..." Ava sang, batting her lashes at him and grinning at the way he pinched the bridge of his nose and shook his head with suppressed amusement.

"Fair enough," he said with a smirk, his tongue wetting his bottom lip as he stared at her. Although he would never admit it, he admired the fire inside this bold vixen. She was perhaps the only person in this room, maybe even his life, who could call him out for his shit, and he loved it.

"What's up with you?" Ava squinted up at Peter as he rejoined them with a menacing smile on his face.

"You'll see." Peter grinned, cracking his knuckles and reclining in his seat.

"Thank you, everyone, for coming to today's auction," Oliver announced on stage with a mic held to his mouth. "As some of you may know, our beloved father was taken from us due to his ill heart. He was a generous man and very passionate when it came to giving to charity. That is why all proceeds from today's event will be going to the British Heart Trust."

The audience filling the gazebo applauded as Charlotte joined him on stage, however, Ava's attention was on Jenson, who placed his hand on top of Freya's, their expressions sombre over their father's death.

"Thank you, son," Charlotte said over the sound system before pressing a quick kiss to Oliver's cheek. "Holden would have adored seeing you all here today. We are all so grateful for your contributions so far but would like to give special thanks to Archer and Brooks for their generous donation of ten thousand pounds!" She encouraged the crowd to applaud as Nate gave a simple but courteous nod in her direction. "Well, let's not keep the ladies waiting any longer, fellas, as we commence our bachelorette auction!"

Nate chuckled, knocking his knee against Ava's as she tutted in disapproval. A table was rolled onto the stage housing a red glittery box that Charlotte dipped her arm into.

"The first lucky lady you have the chance to win a date with will be..." She pulled out a red envelope and peered inside with an excited giggle. "Why...is it the beautiful Ms. Ava Archer!"

Ava choked looking up at Mrs. Forbes, the blood plummeting in her body as she felt her stomach nearly falling out of her arse.

"Go on then!" Peter laughed, nudging at Ava to stand up.

"Did you do this?" Ava snarled at Peter, slapping at his grip on her arm before he all but threw her up onto her feet.

"*Gerrup* there!" He howled with laughter, his fingers in his mouth as he whistled and applauded with the crowd.

Gulping down the bile in her throat, Ava dragged herself onto the stage, standing beside Charlotte and grimacing down at the horny men who were straightening themselves in their chairs to angle a better view at their soon-to-be prize.

"Don't be nervous, darling! I'm sure they won't bite...*much*!" Charlotte jested, eliciting laughter from the crowd that made Ava feel as though she were stood naked inside her own living nightmare. "Give us a twirl!"

"I'd rather not..." Ava said through a plastered grin, her uncomfortable response causing the crowd to laugh harder at her obvious dismay.

"Gentlemen, I'm sure you will all agree that a date with this fine beauty"—Charlotte motioned her hand over Ava as though showing off a piece of art—"is simply priceless, therefore, shall we start the bidding at say...five hundred pounds?"

"Here!" one man shouted instantly at the back making Ava's eyes widen.

"Five-fifty!" another shouted.

"One thousand!"

"My, my, Ms. Archer. You are very popular with this crowd!" Charlotte nudged Ava, who felt like at any second she was going to lose her stomach contents or scream bloody murder. She knew these men were wealthy, but would they honestly stoop so low as to spend hundreds, if not thousands, of their money on a goddamn date?!

"Five *thousand* pounds!" A new bidder stole gasps from the crowd as everyone turned to see the mysterious man at the back: a red-faced, round man dressed in tweed and nearing retirement age.

Ava's eyes widened in horror as she looked down at Nate and Peter, pleading with them to do something, but Peter simply shrugged his shoulders and laughed at her misfortune.

Something twisted inside Nate's gut. This auction had suddenly taken a perverse turn now that it was Ms. Archer's dignity that was at stake. He knew she was no damsel, a woman who was far too fierce ever to be saved from distress, but here she was pleading with the halfwit redhead next to him who was letting her dangle by a noose.

"Seven thousand five hundred." Nate rolled his eyes at Red and raised his hand in the air.

"Eight thousand five hundred," the tweedy man boasted from the back of the tent.

"Ten thousand," Nate countered with cool composure.

"*Twenty* thousand!" the man boomed across the drama-thirsty crowd.

Ava's palms were going to be scarred for life with the indents from her nails, anger and anxiety tearing through her veins from the humiliation of it all. Never before had she felt so tiny and minuscule, a second-class citizen being fought over by two men without her say in the matter. It was so degrading.

Nate turned his head over his shoulder to peer at the imbecile at the back. Clearly, this stubborn ass of a guy used his pay packet to measure his dick. He was going to call it quits in the bidding war, turning around to give Ava the bad news when he saw her blue eyes on her feet. She looked so small on that stage, so submissive and caged like a lion at the circus. It made him feel sick to his stomach to see the fire in her diminished to just a flickering flame.

Ah—fuck it!

"Fifty thousand pounds." Nate's offer caused a crescendo of gasps from the audience before a tense silence dropped upon the auction. He watched as Ava's eyes met his, but the surprise on her face didn't show any relief.

"Do I hear fifty-five?" Charlotte asked the man at the back, who was rubbing his face before growling and throwing his hat to the ground. "Going once...twice...*sold* to Mr. Brooks! Come get your prize!"

Humiliation, anger, and a touch of relief filled Ava as Nate came up onto the stage, his fingers linking through hers as he gave a quick nod to the wolf-whistling crowd and abruptly escorted her off stage and out of the tent. The second they were clear of the crowd Ava suddenly hitched up her skirt and bolted towards the house.

"Ava!" Nate shouted, receiving concerned glances from people, darting after her as she stormed inside the house.

"That was so fucking *humiliating*!" Ava snarled, stomping inside the room that showcased arcade games from the 1930s and causing people to turn around with their jaws dropped.

"Ah, c'mon, it coulda been worse...look who ya coulda

ended up with." Nate tried to lighten the situation but was half expecting her loud reaction.

"*Could have been worse?!* Oh, easy for you to say when you're flaunting your bloody wallet and testosterone around!"

"*Hey*! A thank-you wouldn't hurt considering I'm gonna have to sell one of my goddamn cars for that!"

Ava's scornful gaze snapped up to the people drawn towards the commotion. "In here," she hissed at Nate, yanking the lapel of his jacket and pulling him inside a retro photo booth.

"The hell are you do—"

"I've had quite enough of people ogling me like some spectacle!" she snarled, yanking the velvet curtain closed behind him. "Now, where was I?"

However, her brain stalled at the lack of personal space inside the cramped box and made for a dizzying reaction with her hormones as her nose twitched against the alluring scent of Nate's cologne.

"I believe you were acting like an ungrateful brat after I saved your ass back there." Nate's arms crossed as he scowled down at her.

Ava opened her mouth to unleash hell, but something stopped her. Perhaps it was the restless pools of honey she was swimming in, perhaps it was the heat radiating from his body, or maybe it was just her conscience. "You're right," she began, choosing to ignore the way his eyebrows jumped in surprise. "Thank you for what you did."

"*Wow.*" He stared down at her as his arms slowly uncrossed. "Who are you and what have you done with the real Ava?"

"Don't make me regret it, Brooks. Now move, the dust is bothering my nose."

"*Annnnd* there she is." Nate chuckled, adoring the nickname she gave him as he retreated out of the photo booth. However, as he did, his elbow knocked a lever and a flash blinded them. "Might as well?" he asked with a raised brow and nodded at the camera.

"Only if you pull a funny face." Ava smirked.

"Not a chance," he replied, deadpan.

"Are you always so serious?"

"No."

"Do you always say no to everything?" She raised her brow.

"No."

Nate watched her face flatten dubiously and couldn't help but to laugh as he poked his tongue out at her just in time for the flash to go off again. Her eyes lit up brighter than any camera flash as she tossed her head back and laughed the type of hearty laugh that came from the soul. He couldn't help but marvel at this side of her.

"These are brilliant," Ava chirped, handing him the monochrome photos. "Here, you keep them. Let it be a souvenir of your time here in London."

"How thoughtful," he joked, peering down at the photographs. "I'll keep it in my wallet until the next time I have to save a damsel." Nate laughed at her reaction as she shoved at his chest, his feet stumbling forward and tripping upon his shoelace as he fell up against her but luckily caught himself on the wall of the booth before he could crush her.

"I think you're the one needing to be saved," she jested in breathy laughter that fell quiet as she watched his intense gaze fall upon her lips.

Her back slowly peeled from the wall, encroaching on unknown territory as she stared up into not the eyes of her boss, but the eyes of a man that she desired. If he didn't want this then he certainly did not make that fact evident as he remained firmly in place, his breathing growing louder as though he were struggling to remain composed. She was playing a dangerous game, contently caged in by his arms as her fingertips curiously stepped up the buttons on his shirt, closer towards his exposed clavicle before suddenly a loud bang snapped the moment in two.

"You're a bloody disgrace, brother!" Oliver roared from outside in the hallway.

"What the hell?" Ava gasped as she and Nate stepped out of the booth in time for Oliver to throw Jenson across the room. The pair crash-landed upon a foosball table that clattered, snapped, and banged into broken pieces on the floor which they wrestled upon.

Nate jumped into action, gripping at Oliver and yanking him off of Jenson, whose nose sat at an alarming angle, blood staining his pink shirt.

"Father would turn in his grave if he knew! You disgust me!" Oliver spat at his brother before roaring at Nate to get off him.

"Do everyone a favour and walk it off, buddy," Nate ordered, easily dominating the situation as he pushed Oliver out of the room and into the now crowded hallway. "You that way." He thrust his finger down the hall at Jenson, sending the squabbling pair in opposite directions before returning to Ava and huffing in exasperation.

"What the bloody hell was that all about?" Ava gaped up at Nate. "They were all acting fine two minutes ago!"

Nate sighed, rubbing the back of his neck as he leaned against the door frame and said, "You wanna see who people *really* are? Just add money to the equation and that'll unmask them."

SEVENTEEN

"WHY DO I always miss out on this shit!" Sam whined as the elevator climbed towards another tiring day at the office.

"It was bloody horrific. You should have seen the twat that was bidding for me." Ava shook her head trying to rid the images.

"I bet he was sexy."

"Samantha. He smoked a pipe, used a cane, and wore a bonnet!"

"Oh, you lucky bitch!" Sam laughed, elbowing Ava in the ribs and causing her friend to chuff slightly at her own disarray. "Speaking of booze—"

"What? We weren't speaking of booze?" Ava screwed up her face.

"Aye, we were," Sam said, deadpan, before her face lit up in mischief. "This weekend, you, me, and Mr. Malbec?" Her brows wiggled enticingly.

"You really are something else." Ava laughed as the elevator doors pinged opened on their floor. They both stared out onto a department that was in a state of pandemonium. Phones were ringing from every corner, people were yelling orders over the table at one another or dashing back and forth.

"Well, fuck that for a game of soldiers. I'm off to hide in the kitchen and pour vodka into my cuppa," Sam remarked as she raised her handbag to her face and stealthily dashed towards the kitchen.

Rolling her eyes at Sam, Ava stepped out of the elevator as she hesitatingly walked through the chaos and finally saw Peter, who looked at her as though she were his saviour.

"Thank God you're in today!" Peter sighed, wiping his brow as Ava set her things down on her desk.

"What the hell is going on?" Ava peered up at Nate's office and worrying that the blinds were shut. They were never shut.

"Haven't you heard the news?"

"What news?"

"Oliver Forbes was found dead in his apartment at the weekend," Peter explained, causing Ava's eyes to bulge. "They're saying it's suicide."

"Suicide?" Ava gasped.

"*Taylor!*" Nate's voice boomed from his office, and Ava and Peter simultaneously jumped.

Peter gave Ava a nervous look and advised, "Do yourself a favour, ol' girl, and stay out of the boss's way today."

Staying out of Nate's way was surprisingly easy considering he never once came out of his office and Ava didn't dare chap on his door when the blinds remained shut, the door closed, and his status set to do not disturb. Whatever he was caught up in would no doubt be testing his patience and making him work for his salary.

Ava remained busy also, put on edge that her intercom was no longer being used as Nate pinged his orders at her. She wasn't upset at it, oddly feeling sympathetic towards him as she worked fast to assist him in whatever way he needed.

Ava had blinked and it was suddenly finishing time, perhaps the fastest working day she had ever done, but she wasn't ready to leave just yet. As per their contract together, Nate and she had a meeting scheduled to discuss the details of the Forbes case which Ava no longer knew for certain was going ahead since the scandalous news this morning.

"Ms. Archer, I need you in my office," Nate's voice beckoned over the intercom and for once, Ava jumped at the chance to see him.

"Yes, sir?" she asked with a small smile, hoping her politeness would save her from his bark. However, as she took in his appearance, her lower lip descended, and her brows lowered in concern.

The executive desk was covered in a mess of white papers strewn about as if a window had shattered and the wind had placed the sheets where it saw fit. Nevertheless, in that chaos, Nate saw order. He leaned onto the dark wood with his knuckles pressed upon its surface as he diligently studied the papers. His black suit jacket hung around the back of his chair, his white shirt unbuttoned at the top, and his red silk tie wrapped around his clenched hand—a sign that he was as deep in thought as he was frustrated.

In light of the news this morning, the Forbes civil case had blown into a full-on criminal investigation, the press breathing down his client's neck and therefore his own too.

"Come in," Nate said, pleased that she had come so quickly, "and close the door."

Ava did as instructed, noticing that the scene from last night had been erased from existence, more squeaky clean than that of a murder scene. "What do you need?" she asked as she approached the front of his chaotic desk that coincided with his appearance and likely his emotional state.

"I had it this morning," he explained, slowly tapping his fingertip against the hard surface of the desk. The cuffs of his shirt were rolled up, exposing his muscular forearms, which could only mean one thing—he was all business now. "I saw it. I saw it, but now I can't seem to damn find it," he grumbled, the ragged furrows of his forehead capturing his frustration as his eyes scanned the scene. Nate was searching for a particular paper among many, that had lost its rightful place in the file and was crucial at this moment in time. That sort of thing drove him wild, and not in a good way. "I'm looking for a certificate that has a gold foil seal on its front, can you help me find it?"

"Of course." Ava nodded, her fingers pressing against his desk as she leaned forward slightly, her eyes trying to catch his attention as concern etched into her features. "But will you please just sit down and take a breather?"

Nate's eyes flicked up from the papers, landing on snowy globes bursting from his assistant's skintight dress as she leaned slightly over his desk. However, his eyes rose quickly and sheepishly to hers, hoping she didn't catch him stealing a look. As their eyes met, for just a moment his celestial being floated in her oceans, a sudden sense of serenity overcoming him as his brow relaxed. She had a deleterious effect on his concentration for whatever reason and it made him pin his plump lower lip between his teeth as he gazed into her eyes with a carnal desire. Nate wanted to take her, right there, but today his self-control would prevail.

With perfect posture he straightened his back and brought his fist to his side, the tie still wrapped around his hand, the edges of which dangled loosely, epitomising his predicament.

"I'm fine."

"No," Ava insisted, walking around the large desk, pressing his shoulders down and coaxing him into his seat. "You're *spent* and need to take a breather, Mr. Brooks."

For some reason, Nate flinched at her addressing him in the way he had originally requested; it felt impersonal and cold. However, that coldness suddenly evaporated from him as dainty hands found his broad shoulders. Ava stood in front of his chair between him and the desk as her hands squeezed at him, eliciting a hiss from his teeth as the tension egressed through her feminine touch.

Maybe a five-minute break wouldn't hurt?

"Better. Now, let me have a look for this certificate." Ava smiled sweetly down at him for doing what he was told. She turned around at the mess across his desk, meticulously flicking through the many documents and hummed, "Gold foil seal..."

Nate sighed heavily, the sensation of her fingertips lingering happily, sending tingles down his arms and through his core. However, his attention flicked up as Ava reached over the far end of his desk, her heart-shaped derriere pushing back towards him as though the sight was for his enjoyment alone. His hands gripped the arms of his chair, the blood rushing towards his centre as the black dress pulled higher on her legs, revealing the black lace of suspenders securing her sheer stockings.

It took every ounce of restraint he could muster to not grab her hips at that moment.

Now he had a *real* problem, the concern for the lost document paling in comparison. Under the neatly pressed

Italian fabric of his work slacks, a monster awoke and took form, pushing against the pleated pants.

"Hm, how odd... I could have sworn I saw it earlier..." Ava pondered as she set three piles of paperwork across his desk. "You're sure you've checked everywhere?"

"Every inch..." Nate answered, stammering, his sudden loss of vernacular the direct result of observing more and more of Ms. Archer's underwear, unable to discern a panty line.

"Ah, wait! Is that..." Ava saw the sheen of gold from beneath his desk and got down onto all fours, crawling beneath the desk as she pulls the crumpled certificate from between the mass of loose computer cables.

Nate's eyes nearly sprung from their sockets as she lowered in front of him, her dress bunching so high up on her thighs that the under curve of her peach was as clear as day. At any rate, he was glad her attention was turned away, the misdirection giving him a chance to stave off the growing crisis in his pants, but his member had grown involuntarily at an alarming rate just seeing her bent over his desk. The more his pressing palms sought to conceal the bulge, the more the pressure and friction, the more the problem grew.

"Gotcha!" Ava beamed, crawling back out of the tight space and rising to her feet, but as she did, her head caught the lip of the table eliciting a squawk from her mouth as she stumbled backwards, her heel catching on a cable under the desk and tripping her. "Agh!" she squealed out, her balance thrown as she took two clumsy steps backwards and tumbled down onto her boss's lap, the certificate in hand.

Nate was an alpha male and whenever he was aroused, his instincts turned animalistic so as his assistant stumbled backwards on the cord, he saw it happen almost as if in slow motion, reacting quickly as he caught her in his assertive grip. His strong hands wound around her waist, fingers pressing against her hipbones as he secured her in place, the red tie draped against the bare skin of her inner thigh as he released his clenched fist.

Perhaps it was the rosebud notes diffusing from the golden silk now covering his face or maybe it was the sudden warmth he felt over his lap, but either way, it made him twitch in pleasure.

Nate knew he should let her go right now but for some reason, his grip tightened around Ava's hips and pulled her back down into him. This woman was his ultimate temptation.

Ava shivered feeling the crimson silk running down a place where only her lovers had touched. It aroused her to no degree that something of Mr. Brooks was now touching between her milky thighs, the very thought bringing a noticeable pulse between her legs.

A curl of hair had found its way across her pixie-like face in her dishevelled state, but she didn't care to move it just yet, her arms and legs unable to move. Her mind and body were transfixed upon the strong hands gripping her slender hips that jutted through the skintight material of her dress, her sumptuous peach pressing down against her boss's crotch.

Ava sucked in a hiss through her teeth as Nate pulled her down against his lap, the stiff outline of something pressing up against her fleshy globes making the whites of her eyes pop. His warmth seeped through the expanse of his solid front and oozed into her back making her teeth clamp down upon her lip.

Nate was no longer in control of his actions, his face

dipping into the gold silk as he inhaled the scent clinging to the side of her neck until he was drunk on it.

A part of Ava wanted nothing more than to reach her hands behind her and grip the top of Nate's luscious dark hair, her back against his chest as she would slowly roll her stomach in a type of sensual dance, her hips circling, grinding her rear down into whatever teasing object was prodding into her bottom. She could imagine it now, his hot breath on the side of her throat, and could only dream of the deep groans he'd pour into her ear, the feeling of his hands tightening around her hips and maybe even one around her throa—

"Shit, sorry!" Ava yelped, snapping out of her corrupted thoughts as she jumped off of her boss and dusted down her dress. Her pale cheeks now blooming like a cherry blossom tree as she glanced at the closed blinds, grateful that no one saw. She knew she had to get out of there before she seriously jeopardised both of their careers and quickly made her way to the door.

"Lock the door." The authoritarian dimension of Nate's baritone voice filled the hollow of the room and subdued the silence. Three little words were all it took to cross that line. His assistant peered timidly over her shoulder and their eyes met in an unwavering expression of carnal lust; she knew, and he knew of the base things that were about to happen in this office.

EIGHTEEN

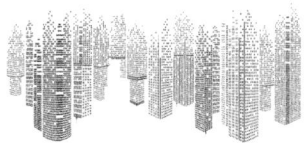

BANDS OF AMBER sunlight flooded through the blinds hiding the garish fluorescent light and contaminating the rest of the office space. Nate's heart pounded out of his chest as he stood from his chair, his legs feeling weak from the blood that was engulfing his centre. Winding the red silk tie tightly around his clenched hand, he fixated on the woman he would soon ravage as he struggled against letting the out-of-place lock of hair that sat across Ava's eyes make a mess of him.

Ava didn't utter a word as she faced the door again and twisted the lock in place, her eyes down on her feet as curls hung and curtained her face.

Nate stood like an uncut bull behind his desk; this was his domain and Ms. Archer knew it. His burning gems tracked her delicious silhouette as she did as instructed, her submission intoxicating. He took a step, and then another, pacing towards the gorgeous Aphrodite, a polished leather toe leading each deliberate movement. His stride was slow but confident as the taps of his soles against the tiles echoed their heartbeats and matched in cadence. The sweet scent of her flesh filled his flaring nostrils once more as he breathed her in, her luscious blonde hair now touching his chiselled face. Only his earthy cologne and the mint upon his breath was her way of knowing just how close he was, an air of caution between them both as the lion closed in on its prey.

"If we do this..." Ava warned, her voice a pitiful volume as though scared to confess her lust. She wanted to fight this impulse in her but already her brain was rationalising that sleeping with your boss or your father's business associate wasn't as bad as people made it out to be. It was only her reputation and morals that were on the line, that and her self-respect.

"If we do *what*?" Nate quizzed, standing perpendicular to her as he dragged his fingertip lightly down the centre of her back, following the silver zip from the nape of her neck, down to her panty line, his other finger delicately moving one section of her hair down her back so to expose the side of her thin neck. "On-the-job compliance training?" he teased with a smirk.

Shivers ran down Ava's arm, her spine straightening from his touch as she took a step back until her bottom pressed up against him, his embrace oddly familiar yet exhilarating at the same time. Nate's lack of concern over what they were about to do irked it, spurring her on to push his buttons.

"I think you know *what*," she challenged, lifting her arms into the air and looping them behind Nate's neck. Her entire body was at his disposal, stomach flattening as she stretched upwards, her sinful curves flowing down her sides like a piece of sculpted art as her supple breasts sat higher up on her chest plate. Leaning the back of her head against his shoulder, she turned her face up and into the base of his throat, feeling woozy on his spicy aroma as she whispered against his flesh, "It's the thing you've desired since that moment in the stables, the thing that pisses you off more than disorder, the thing that fuels your thoughts right before bed..."

Nate's eyes widened before closing over, his jaw clenched as he listened to the sultry words come from her delectable lips, trying not to lose his damn mind as she idly skimmed her nose up over the slight peppering of stubble on his neck.

Her suggestive words bound his wrists tighter than any rope, his knees wanting to kiss the floor and yield to this golden deity.

"Guilty as charged," he confessed, his hands cupping her tiny waist. "I know what I want," he whispered into her ear before wrapping her small frame in his strong protective arms, holding his prize securely in place as he breathed, "You."

The white shirt he wore contrasted sharply with her black dress, his dark hair with her blonde, the entangled pair resembling a human yin yang.

The smooth baritone of Nate's voice reverberated through Ava's bones as he slid his strong arms around her and claimed her body as his. He confessed his sins, the low rumble of his voice comforting as it wrapped around her and carried her off to a place where sound had the power to change everything wrong in the world.

Nate's curious fingers explored her outstretched body like a teenaged boy touching a girl for the first time. Yes, he was an experienced lover, but something was different about Ava. He had never been with anyone like her—driven, intelligent, feisty, fearless, yet soft and submissive at times. Imperfectly perfect.

Taking his time, he traced the jutting bones of her hips, crossing the soft expanse of her tummy, exploring every valley and curve, and playfully lingering on the barely noticeable elastic band of her panties, his fingertips sliding slightly further south. Nate was meticulous and thorough; with enough practice, he would know her body like he did his files. She was like an uncharted map, his hands explored every city, town, and village, mapping her body as his lips chased her soul. He kissed her forehead first before turning his head to the sensitive part of her inner arm and planting kisses.

Admittedly, he was getting drunk on her pheromones, his temperature reaching a fever from the small whines he elicited from her lips, his heart rate accelerating with excitement raging through his veins.

From her left shoulder, he plotted a path to her neck, taking his sweet time with each kiss to cover every inch of her, and then moving from her clavicle to her ear.

Craving Ava had been the most delicious ache he had ever felt, worth the torment and worth any repercussions that were now pushed to the back of his mind. The only thing that confused him was how this didn't feel wrong; the sin he was committing felt heavenly.

Ava felt as though her blood was replaced with steam, her legs barely keeping her upright. She had been with many lovers but none as attentive as Nathaniel Brooks. His touch was intensely intimate from the delicate strokes on her stomach to the touches down her sides as though his fingers were paintbrushes upon a blank canvas, her legs like that of an easel. A small hiss pulled through her teeth as his touch ghosted just south of her panty line, her lashes fluttering closed as she became lost in a haze of sensation that was growing a fiery wet mess between her milky thighs. He made her blush in all the right places.

Nate's fingers sensually ascended her sides, all the way up her raised arms until he gently turned her around to face him, dropping her hands when he saw those sapphires and looking at her in a way he had never looked at a woman before.

Her hands landed like two butterflies upon his shoulders as he reached to cradle the back of her head. He knew this was the worst thing he'd ever do, knew he was about to throw caution to the wind, but just the thought of her body and the whisper of his imagination left a fully grown man completely incapacitated. With Ms. Archer, there were no thoughts, no concentration, only desire and the ache of waiting for something that should never happen.

His head tilted slightly, eyes closed as he advanced, but he stopped just before his mouth pressed to hers, deliberating on if he should go through with this. That single remaining thread of morality was stretched so tight that one breath from Ms. Archer's tempting lips snapped it and blew it away.

NINETEEN

FIRST KISSES WERE NORMALLY the making of some-thing, but this kiss was like taking a wrecking ball to any previous relationship they had made for themselves.

Ava pressed forward until all of Nate's hard edges melted into her smooth contours.

A soft wet click was heard as Nate kissed her top lip, just once, pulling back slightly and peering down at her to confirm that this wild fantasy was quickly becoming reality. She answered him by way of her mouth turning up into a devilish smirk that popped the dimple in her cheek, an expression that Nate mirrored as she clasped her hands behind his neck.

With brute strength, his muscular arms cinched her body close to his, but his lips drew hers in by a different less visible force, an unearthly sort of magnetism. Nate kissed her passionately, destroying any semblance of the employ-ment relationship. In that moment she was not his assistant, nor his business partner's daughter, she was simply a woman, a marvellous, beautiful woman who he had craved the taste of for what felt like an eternity. He couldn't get enough of her cinnamon dolce crème as he tenderly sucked upon her lower lip, their timid tongues finding each other like old lovers reuniting, tangling like two people sampling sweet passion after a long fast and dancing to the melody of their erotic song.

Ava needed little to no reassurance as she abruptly took a step back, her hands gripping dark tendrils as she pulled Nate with her until her back thudded up against the office door and her greedy mouth demanded every last drop.

While his fleshy explorer rhythmically darted in and out of her mouth, his lower half emoted pent-up longings as his hips pinned and gyrated against her body, not caring to hide the bulge in his pants. Breathlessly, he took a step back and took her hands in his, lifting her arms above her head and pinning them high against the heavy door with his left hand as his crimson tie hung down from her wrists and arms. He needed her to stay still, to stand there and let him devour every piece of her just like in his dreams.

He involuntarily growled like a savage bear, his tongue flicking at the soft lobe of her ear, then he surveyed her front with his dominant hand, digits caressing the softness of her lower jaw, down the side of her neck, pausing briefly to wrap lightly around her throat and squeezing the sides playfully as if to say *you are mine*.

Ava moaned softly, her tongue leaving a glisten of moisture on her upper lip as she smirked at him as if daring him to take a chunk clean out of her throat like the piece of forbidden fruit she was. She wasn't afraid of him; she wanted to see what darkness hid in his shadows. She wanted him to play with her black soul.

After the detour, Nate's eyes followed his fingers as they continued to her breasts, tracing the dip of her neckline, and then down over the fabric, registering the black lace beneath and the two hardened buds of her nipples protruding through the dress. He bit his lip with delight, a quirky smile coming to his lips as he wondered what may be happening between her legs.

Being pinned to that door by Nate felt like swimming in the sea with thunderclouds looming overhead, a type of electrical current pulsing through Ava's body and tingling static across her gooseflesh. His primal growls and intimate touches were richer than the concentrated chocolate of a truffle, his noises that sent waves of fire down between her loins now pooling with heat and making her fear that the flimsy covering of her thong would do little to hold back her arousal.

Frustrated by the fabric blockading his assault, Nate slipped his right hand behind her back and his fingers found the zipper head of her dress.

"Shh," he hushed, referencing the muffled voices heard on the other side of the door. It was getting close to quitting time for the remaining staff and as the sun set and warm horizontal rays ascended the walls of the office, Nate realised that the silhouette of the lovers may well be visible. He eyed the leather ottoman nearby before looking back to Ava and slowly pulled down her zip, unwrapping his present. As her dress parted at the back and cool air kissed her snowy flesh, he observed the goosebumps rising down her spine while the fabric dangled from her shoulders. Nate ran his hand up the back of her exposed thigh and grabbed a handful of her soft, doughy derriere, exhaling heavily as he did. He nearly crumbled from the beautiful sensual whine that she made for him but leant in hushing her again, his smirking lips at the shell of her ear.

Ava bit back a giggle, relishing in the adrenaline, her knee bending as she skimmed the inside of her warm thigh up the outside of his pant leg until she hooked the back of her defined calf muscle around him and tugged.

"Be quiet," he growled by her ear, secretly enjoying her disobedience as his hand found its way to her inner thigh, his mouth taking her entire lobe into his wet, hot mouth for a gentle suck, nibbling lightly on her cartilage. "Or I'll make you." The disciplinarian emerged, the tip of his tongue drawing a jagged line from her lower jaw to the auricle of her ear before pulling back to see her reaction.

Ava didn't like being told what to do and was always up for a challenge. To make this point clear, she playfully snapped her teeth at him like a feral kitten, her leg tightening its grip until his crotch pressed up against her own and in one swift movement she leaned forward and flicked her tongue up his chin.

"Then *make me*," she dared with a small giggle. After all, what was the point in playing with fire if you didn't expect to get a little burnt?

Nate's eyebrows rose in surprise at her confidence before his eyes squinted at her.

Rules were rules.

He lifted his right knee between her legs, grinding his upper thigh against her heated crotch, just enough to dissolve her giggles into a hot moan before withdrawing it teasingly. He didn't care for her protesting whine as he returned his attention to her clavicle, kissing the smooth ridge from its terminus at her shoulder to her mid-neck.

Something about this moment, the sweet smell of her flesh, the little noises escaping her voluminous lips, the way she tempted him, whatever it was, it summoned inspiration from deep within his loins and unleashed a powerful new sexual energy. Ava Archer would be the first to experience him in this hyper-aroused state.

With strategic placement of his lips, his mouth sucked on her neck before biting down hard and sucking even harder, slurping on her deliciousness, and claiming her as he saw fit. She may not bow down to him but at least the red-purple evidence left behind on her pale skin was his stamp, like the gold seal on the certificate of title.

Every breath Ava took was humid and laboured against the assault of his kiss delivered to her neck. She swore she could feel the sensation being mimicked right at the burning throb between her thighs. Her arms pressed to the cold wood of the door began to twitch under his grasp, her nails biting into her palms as his teeth marked her neck and made her mouth salivate with pure ecstasy. Despite her self-restraint crumbling, she whimpered, "That the best you got, Brooks?"

When she tempted him, the dam of pent-up sexual energy inside of Nate broke. Done with the chitchat getting in his way, he could take no more teasing with these little games as he released her dainty wrists, allowing her arms to fall to her sides and for her dress to fall to the floor. His whisky eyes revealed a hunger now not seen before as he took in the sight of her three-piece lingerie and his lips formed a coy smile at the thought of the nasty things he would do to her.

Nate aggressively twirled her near-naked body to face away, pressing her up against the door and smirking as she gasped in shock, her palms slapping against the wood.

"If we do this, there will be rules. Do you think you can play by the rules, Ms. Archer?" he asked with a smirk, not requiring an answer as he expertly slipped the red tie between her lips and made a neat knot behind her head.

Ava gawked as she felt the makeshift gag go between her lips, no man ever having done such a kinky thing to her, and it made her both aroused as it did on edge—normally it was she who delivered the kink. She didn't protest as he then escorted her away from the door, his dominant hand softly caressing the lower boundary of her jutting shoulder blade as he guided her forward.

Nate stopped in front of his desk and turned them, biting his lip as he stared down at her body, his own feeling oxygen deprived as her sight stole his breath. Yet breathless, he maintained his military stance. In his mind, he had disrobed this young woman countlessly since he arrived, but no reverie could do justice to the delectable beauty now standing before him.

He took a half step back, almost stumbling as he perched on his desk, fully appreciating her attire or the lack of. The French lingerie fit her body perfectly as if designed exclusively for her feminine curves. The ends of the red tie fell from her golden locks, framed by the black straps of her balcony bra, pointing to the contrasting black lace thong dividing her alabaster cheeks. The suspender straps provided dimension to accentuate the gorgeous length of her toned legs, leading the eye to the Louboutin heels which matched his silk accent.

Nate could not have imagined at sunrise that she would be wearing his tie by sundown.

TWENTY

HERE AT THE FIRM, it was strictly forbidden to fraternise with the staff, especially for Nate in his position of power. She knew it, he knew it, everyone knew it. Indeed, if their illicit engagement was discovered, not only would it limit her employment prospects with leading firms, but it could destroy Nate's legal career and his status in the professional community. Not to mention, it would invite a sexual harassment lawsuit against the firm. However, the undaunted Icarus defied the rules of gravity in his seduction of the sun.

Nate took another step towards her, watching her chest heave up and down erotically in the bra that he'd soon remove. His fingers swept around her middle just above her suspender belt as he leaned in to inhale more of that intoxicating perfume, his heavy breath hot against her neck like a bull about to breed. The warmth of her tender flesh was cruelly tantalising on the pads of his fingers which grazed the peak of her hip before he abruptly removed his touch and smiled at her whine and furrowing brow.

"Can you be discreet?" he asked in all seriousness, removing the tie from her mouth and letting it drape around her neck. "There's more at stake here than you think. Can I trust you?"

"Yes," she answered automatically, the question seeming absurd since their predicament also affected her. "This won't get out." Ava couldn't deny her desires, but she couldn't stand the thought of her father disowning her for giving in to them either.

"Good girl," he sighed softly, the term of endearment making Ava laugh and making Nate raise his eyebrow.

"I am *anything* but a good girl, Nate."

"Fine, how about...kitten?" he teased, pulling her close until she was stood between his legs with her palms resting against his chest.

"Don't call me kitten unless you expect to get a little *scratched*," she purred like a feline, kissing his grinning mouth as her fingernails ran up the front of his throat before flicking down his lower lip. A gasp left her as Nate ensnared her finger into his hot, wet mouth, closing his eyelids in a moment of escape as he sucked the bitter taste from her digit and then released her.

He couldn't help but smile down at her, his two forefingers sneaking under her bra straps and simultaneously cajoling the luxurious material from her smooth shoulders, his fingers then returning to outline the margins of where the straps had rested. However, his delicate touch abruptly shifted as he aggressively yanked the cups of her bra down and exposed her two fleshy mounds which his large hands engulfed.

Ava gasped against his burning hands but was silenced as his mouth came crashing down against her own. It was in the heat of a kiss, such as this, that passion transcended the words of the greatest poets and writers alike. Her fingers were clumsy as they unbuttoned his shirt, nails eagerly grazing down over the stepping stones of abdominal muscle before grasping the buckle on his belt and tugging him forward, pulling his ass off the ledge.

Nate was frenzied, done with the foreplay antics as he gave in to his lust and kissed this woman back like she deserved. His hands slapped against her peach as he grabbed it, kneaded it, and then picked her up, spinning in a one-eighty to sit her on his desk, his mouth never leaving hers while her persistent fingers removed his belt.

He moved as quick as her, breaking the kiss once to toss off his shirt as she whipped his belt through his pants loops and lassoed it around his neck to draw him close and latch on to his lips once again.

Ava wrestled with his zipper until she yanked it open. Her hand eagerly cupped his package and she revelled not only in the way he pulled back from her lips to groan but his impressive girth twitching against her palm also.

With her legs wrapped around his waist, she reclined as Nate coaxed her to lie back, her hot flesh sizzling against the cold wood of the desk as she sprawled out over it and the paperwork.

Nate stood over her, peering down at the black and red lines shadowing across the front of her perfect body as a crimson glow seeped in through the blinds in flashes of light from the adjacent skyscrapers.

She was the personification of a rose, beautiful in every sense of the word, velvety skin, fragile like petals but sharp as thorns, delicate in scent and floral in taste.

Her mouth hung open as she moaned upon Nate's lips worshipping her chest, her fingers clenching around his dark tendrils and eliciting grunts from his mouth. She hadn't felt anything like it, the power of attraction, the intensity of raw desire, her thighs quaking just from the way his teeth abused her rosebuds.

Nate was losing his damn mind, drowning in the sensual noises coming from the lips that he'd never get enough of. His tongue rolled her sensitive little teat this way and that before trailing a path of wet kisses down her stomach, his nails biting into her plump cheeks as his teeth nipped at her cashmere flesh.

It had been months since Nate had last had sex, hell, it had been months since he so much as *kissed* another. Being with Ava was like having been in prison and put on a staple diet only to find his freedom at an all-you-can-eat buffet.

She peered down at the dark mass of hair between her legs, her heart nearly flatlining at the seductive and somewhat dangerous look in Nate's eyes as his teeth pulled upon the dainty waistband of her panties, his eyebrow raised before his teeth released it, snapping them back in place and sending a jolt of energy straight to her core.

Ava squirmed on the desk with her back arching, his mouth like nothing she had experienced before, so curious and adamant that it was kissing every inch of her. She couldn't tear her eyes away as the roughness of his stubble made her thighs sing, wanting nothing more than him to paint her inner thigh with purple kisses. His hand moved in the opposite direction as he carefully peeled the flimsy black lace down over her hips and shimmied them up her legs and off.

Any woman that Nate had undressed usually blushed and hid away but Ava was different, she seemed to flourish like a flower coming in bloom. He wanted to take his time with her, he really did, but seeing her sprawled out like that and smelling her sweet musk made him lose his sanity. His nostrils flared like an angry bull, his eyes eating her up before he tugged her hips to him and feasted upon the dewdrops quivering upon her wet petals.

Ava had to slap her palm over her mouth to stop her from screaming out as his hot mouth latched over her sex and smothered the flames. He had her eyes rolling back in her head, back arching high as his tongue wrecked her.

Nate was like stone in his pants, her sweet glaze making a mess of him as he slurped against her, his hot flesh grinding down against her bundle of nerves as his fingers spread her apart craving more. He never knew that sin could taste so sweet, but then again, that was before he had met Ava.

Suddenly, the phone on his desk began ringing causing Ava to jump upright in panic. Nate lifted his head for a brief second as their eyes connected.

"No," he growled, his strong arms wrapping around the top of her thighs and tugging her back down to his face again, forcing her to submit as he sucked roughly on her intimate lips.

Fuck work, fuck social politics, fuck morals, was all Nate could think as his tongue whipped through her silken lips.

She was drowning in a sea of euphoria, her back flopping on the desk again as she fisted sheets of paper next to her and sang a symphony of praises for Nate's ears. Her nails clawed at his shoulders before managing to pry his attention off her dripping mess long enough to plead how much she needed him.

"You want me, sweetheart?" He smirked, wiping his glistening mouth against her inner thigh, and standing. He leaned over her as he nudged his work slacks down, however, his tease only backfired as the wily Ms. Archer chewed on her thumbnail innocently, her long lashes batting as she nodded her head. He had seen *a lot* of porn, particularly in these last few lonely months, but seeing Ava sprawled naked on his desk, biting at her thumb and feigning innocence like a coy schoolgirl, shattered his chances of finding any corner of the internet that would satiate his primal urges.

Nate dropped his boxers to his ankles, the centrepiece of his thick and sinuous manhood pointing upward in a perfectly lazy arc against his stomach. He revelled in the way Ava's eyes widened upon seeing him in his true form, seeing the dark veins popping from his shaft with readiness across his smooth skin like a flexed muscle.

He didn't waste any more time, positioning himself between her legs and rubbing his violet crown up and down her wet slit, tickling her swollen button with each stroke and earning a series of mewls from her tasty mouth. Hot breaths left him as he felt the warmth of her most sensitive part on his own. She was so hot and wet, so aroused and ready, that he felt a surge of accomplishment knowing he had this effect on a woman of her calibre.

"Look at me," he said with a gasped breath, needing to see the expression on her face when their bodies became as one.

Forests met oceans as their lustful gaze found each other before finally, the well-lubed head of his sex pushed past her swollen lips and into the abyss. His thickness stretched her tight opening as he parted her petals, his chest heaving as he resisted the urge to buck his hips into her, and instead exercised restraint, gliding into her slowly and savouring the sensation of her clamping down and pushing against him.

"Na...Nate..." Ava released his name in a high-pitched

whine as she felt him tease her first by sliding his hardened length in and out, playfully spanking her bud with its heaviness and then repeating, pushing her towards delirium. "More," she demanded, tightening her legs around him and keeping him prisoner.

He answered her by rolling his hips into her at a steady pace, each stroke going deeper than the last in a rhythmic series of passes quickening to a crescendo. She could grip his hips with her legs all she wanted but he was in control, listening to her body and answering its demands as he varied the pace and depth with each of her moans and squeals.

However, the pressure was building in his balls, especially as he felt what could have been the start of her orgasm as her walls seemed to spasm and grip his cock. He was falling down the rabbit hole fast so he tossed her leg over his shoulder and hugged her thigh, pulling her tight little entrance closer to him as he filled her to the hilt. He desperately needed to quell his unsaturated hunger in his loins, painfully wanting Ava like nothing he had ever wanted in his life before.

In a moment of undiluted lust, Nate dropped her leg, grabbed the tie around her throat, and yanked her up against his chest where he kissed her longingly, a wet and messy kiss that was all tongues and exchanging of sensual breath. He was all logic and cool detachment until her lips were against his. She stirred something in him and overtook all sense. The rest of the world became an unimportant blur that was banished into the far recesses of his dark mind.

With a surge of endorphins, they clashed together in the ultimate of finales, shockwaves of pleasure exploding between their loins as they shared the high in harmony.

Slowly, all the grunts and groans, the profanities cursed

in God's name, the slapping of tangled limbs, now dispersed into silence as mini aftershocks rippled throughout their clenched bodies. Only the beating of two hearts and mixed breath could be heard as the illicit lovers held each other tightly, reluctant to let go of this moment, scared to let go of the illusion.

TWENTY-ONE

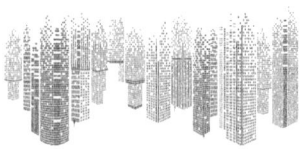

THE RED LIGHT passing through the slits in the blinds flashed, matching the tempo of the lovers' heartbeats. Nate and Ava lay bare upon the chesterfield sofa, their bodies glistening from sensual sweat as they came down from the third or fourth high in the last couple of hours. They were silent as they held hands, the soft feeling of touch bringing warmth and comfort as fingers idly glided between fingers, having conversations words could not convey and palms traced like roadmaps to the soul.

Nate admired her beautiful body lying against his, naked and breathless, golden tresses tumbling across her pert tits as she dreamily stared up at the ceiling with a just-fucked wetness between her legs.

He walked his fingertips up the ladders made by the shadowed black and red stripes on her thigh and continuing upwards, examining every inch of her flesh from the small scar on her arm that he knew was from the contraceptive implant to the purple kisses dotted across her tummy.

"What does this say?" Nate's voice was husky as his fingertips ran down the side of Ava's rib cage across white ink that he had first thought was a scar but upon closer inspection had realised it was a dainty white rose with words etched down along its stem.

"It's a quote by a poet," she replied softly, her face turning to nuzzle into the space beneath his chin as she spoke against his throat. "'Beauty is a curse the rose knows well; always picked first yet never a chance to grow.'"

Nate pondered the meaning behind this, wondering if Ava was that rose—chosen for her looks and body but never anything more than that. Had anyone ever touched more than this woman's body? However, then his mind drifted to their predicament. No matter how beautiful this moment felt, it would never have the chance to blossom for there was no place for Ava in his life. That slot was already taken.

"I think you should go now." Nate's voice was suddenly distant, colder than he had intended as he sat up and coaxed Ava to get off him.

"Yeah, can't be having any more sleepovers here; I doubt my neck could handle another night on this sofa." Ava chuckled, disregarding his melancholic tone as she stood up and stretched her long body upwards.

"No, we cannot," Nate uttered in agreement, his brow creasing over almost as though he had been wounded as he watched her perfect flesh stretch over muscle and bone. He wanted to grab her and pull her down to him just once more but resisted the urge.

The pair began getting dressed again, Nate helping pull the zip up on her dress as Ava played with the messy curls over her shoulder.

"I take it you're staying at the Beaufort Hotel?" Ava asked, her tone holding a slight insinuation that made Nate's eyebrows jump as did the zipper up on the nape of her neck.

"Yes," he stated with a dry tone, stepping back and shoving the red tie, which was stained with Ava's sultry aroma, into his suit jacket.

"Oh, it's just around the corner from me. You know I was think—"

"Ava, this won't happen again," Nate ruled, his words like a needle scratching across a record. He would give anything for her to fall asleep in his arms tonight but knew it was out of the question. He could have winced at the pained expression on her beautiful face when she snapped around to look at him.

"Excuse me?"

"I think you heard me; this cannot happen again. I don't have time for this arrangement, and quite frankly, you're a distraction that I don't need," Nate attested, standing up straight before turning his back to her, unable to bear another second of the hurt on her face that she was masking well. He needed control over this situation.

"A *distraction*?" Ava squawked, her heart beating faster for a second time this evening as she stood with her hands on her hips, glaring at the back of Nate's head. "I wasn't looking for roses and romance, Brooks."

"Good. Then you'll have no issue accepting that this was a one-time event."

"*Event*?" Ava's tone grew ice-cold and bitter. "Look, *mate*"—she bit the word in her thick accent—"I wasn't looking for anything out of this either, but you don't have to treat me like used goods."

"I meant no disrespect," Nate tossed, idly packing his briefcase without making eye contact. "I am just being clear on my standing and re-establishing a rapport between us. We already discussed the dangers of this type of engagement, Ms. Archer."

"Oh, I see," Ava scoffed, stood there with a scowl as she crossed her arms. "Fuck me like it's part of my role and responsibilities, like it's what you're *paying* me to do."

"Hardly." Nate finally peered up at her, his eyes narrowing slightly in annoyance before he stood and walked past her.

"You're not going to tidy the mess?" She pointed to the scattered and crumpled documents over the floor and his desk. "Wouldn't want anybody finding out your dirty little secret, *Mr. Brooks*."

"I'll sort it in the morning." Nate sighed a tired sound, waiting idly by the door with a key in his hand. "Ms. Archer, I'd like to go now, please."

"Ms. Archer," Ava repeated him, the use of his formal title for her causing a sting of offence deep in her belly as her teeth ground together.

He wants to act formal when his dick just informally fucked me?!

With arms crossed she breezed out of his office and gathered her belongings before marching to the elevator. The doors pinged open and Ava stepped inside but frowned when Nate remained grounded in place.

He doesn't want to be seen with me—got it, grreaaat!

Her finger punched the button on the wall, but Nate's suitcase stopped the doors from closing, giving her a pathetic fleeting feeling of hope.

"Ava," he said beseechingly, his eyes warming for a brief second and making her head tilt up expectantly. "Please... don't tell Sam."

AVA FAVOURED the one-night stand but never once had she felt like the person being tossed aside. Not until Nate. It sucked having that shift in power; it made her feel reduced to nothing more than a used cigarette. He had lit her up, burned her hot, took her high, and then tossed her aside like ash.

The following days twisted at her stomach and messed with her head as Nate blanked her like her existence was a fleeting thing. He avoided her and only contacted her when he required something at work. It made her feel cold, the warmth never managing to reach her bones, but in some twisted sense, it was whenever she looked up to see Nate that a flicker of heat licked at her skin only to be replaced by the arctic breeze of his shoulder.

To make matters worse, Nate was spending a lot of time with Charlotte Forbes. Sometimes the blinds would be shut but it was worse when they were open and Ava saw that snobby-mouthed woman laughing away, her eyes eating Nate up and making Ava snarl at the idea of all the flirtatious things she was saying to him. Why would Charlotte even be smiling when her stepson took his own life and the Murder Investigation Team was breathing down her neck? Oh, that's right...because with the second trustee out of the way she was the main executor to all her late husband's accounts. Life for her was peachy. For Ava, not so much.

"HELLO, EARTH TO TINKERBELL?" Sam waved her hand in front of Ava's face, making her slowly drag her dazed expression off the water drops trickling down the cafe window.

"Hi," Ava said after a moment, her lips feeling heavy as she pushed them up into a smile.

"Alright, what is going on with you this week?" Sam glared, sitting back in her chair and crossing her arms.

"I don't know what you mean."

"Oh, *aye right*, don't act the goat. What's happened?"

Looking up into her friend's ivy and amber orbs, Ava hated the fact that as much as she wanted to offload to her friend she couldn't. It wasn't as much trying to be faithful to Nate as it was fear of her friend's judgement. Would Sam be disgusted in her for sleeping with their boss?

"I hate men," Ava affirmed with a sigh and leaned forward to cup the warm tea on the table.

"What the fuck has he done?" Sam gasped, sitting upright in her chair, her rings tapping on the table as she grasped it. "I'll skin that ginger bellend if he's hurt you!"

For a fleeting moment, Ava dropped her jaw, about to ask how Sam knew about her and Nate, before quickly realising that her friend presumed it was Peter that she was referring to.

"We had sex, *amazing* sex, the best sex I've ever had really," Ava mumbled as though finally confessing this fact to herself, "and now, in the office, he's acting as though I don't exist."

"What a bloody bellend!" Sam cursed and Ava saw that fire burning in the amber in her gaze. "He was the one wanting to stay back for breakfast! Does he not want anything more now?"

"He called it off! The sex, he said it wouldn't happen again and now I just can't help but feel used," Ava fumed, her nostrils flaring as she shook her head. "And it doesn't help that he's now getting awfully cosy with that bloody Forbes woman."

"That wee arsehole! That explains why he came out of that meeting room all flustered with that Forbes woman that looks like she could crack a nut with a Kegel!" Sam growled, getting herself more worked up over Ava's situation than Ava herself. "You know, I reserve this word for the absolute crème de la crème but that man is a complete..." She hesitated for a second looking at Ava before blurting it out in the middle of the café, "A complete *cunt*."

"Samantha!" Ava flinched, the sharp word making her cover her ears.

"I know, I know, but he is! That is proper *cuntish* behaviour!" Sam attested before sending apologetic eyes to an older woman who tutted and shook her head at Sam before returning to her jammy scone. "If I were you, I'd get even."

"Get even? And how do I do that exactly?"

"Get the fancy knickers out, the short skirts, and make that *cu*—" Sam coughed on the naughty word before saying, "*man* realise just what he is missing out on."

TWENTY-TWO

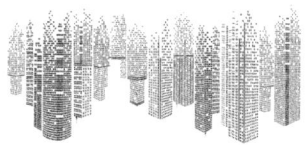

ALTHOUGH SAMANTHA DIDN'T REALISE at the time that she was actually referring to Nate and not Peter, Ava followed her advice and began dressing a lot more provocatively to work.

At first, she went easy on Nate, starting off with just some low-cut blouses and a couple of short skirts, but as the days went on with no attention received from her boss, her workwear got a lot more risqué to the point that Ava started to receive attention from some of the other gents in the office. It wasn't that she was invisible to Nate, she had noticed his jaw flex, the way he'd ball his hands under his desk, and could only imagine what she stirred in his pants. However, after a day or two of enticing him to utter more than two words to her, she began to get creative.

There were many ways to seduce a man in an office environment, for example: licking envelopes provocatively, bending over to fill the printer to expose your lingerie, sucking the spoon clean that you used to stir his coffee, but Ava's favourite had to be the filing in Nate's office. It was at the top of a tall set of shelves, so Ava had to stretch up so high that her short skirt rode up and exposed the fact she wasn't wearing any panties.

That was the day Nate ruined his shirt and burnt his cock with hot coffee.

And yet *still* he refused to acknowledge her, and nothing seemed to work. She'd put typos in her emails, left her desk messier than normal, and she even came into work late! Mr. Brooks was adamant that she didn't exist in his eyes other than as the good little assistant she was. He was avoiding her to the point of exile, and it drove Ava towards breaking point.

"The following images will be used as evidence in court, but also to spook you and shake your defence, Mrs. Forbes." Peter was leading the briefing and exhibiting things on the large screen at the front of the room while Ava, Charlotte, and Nate sat around a large conference table. "I must warn you now, they are of a highly explicit nature regarding Oliver's death."

"Very well, Peter. Go ahead, I'm ready." Charlotte sniffled behind a handkerchief, dressed in the most extravagant black dress that Ava had ever seen. She looked like she was attending a gala and not her attorney's office.

As Peter brought up the images on the PowerPoint presentation, Ava's gut lurched, and a churning mixture of stomach acid and her lunch filled her throat. She covered her mouth, catching Nate's concerned gaze. His brows creased together as if asking her if she was okay, and she nodded as she gulped down the bile and reluctantly looked at the screen.

Oliver Forbes's flimsy neck hung from the gym apparatus inside his art-deco-themed apartment. Even without blood flow, his skin was still slightly tanned, however, his face was a ghostly pale shade and his lips were stained a ghastly blue. He wore white silken pyjamas, flawless if not for the sunset-coral smear down his shoulder, a colour that wasn't quite the shade of blood and seemed out of place. His feet dangled like the rest of him, toes pointed towards the floor and only inches away from saving his life.

"As you know, Freya has been detained for being the main suspect in this case since there is hard proof of her being at the crime scene and having a motive for wanting her brother dead—to absorb his share of the inheritance," Peter explained as he continued on through the PowerPoint, bringing up images of evidence bags containing strands of Freya's hair upon the gym apparatus and Oliver's skin cells under her fingernails. "Her alibi is paper-thin, stating that although she was sleeping over at Oliver's apartment that night, she believes she was drugged during the auction event, having no recollection of the evening. While we wait on forensics to come back, the spotlight is then naturally turned to yourself, Charlotte." He held up a file and began flicking through it to produce a piece of paper that he slid in front of Mrs. Forbes. "During the night of your stepson's death, you claim to have been at a night spa in Wembley, a twenty-minute drive from Oliver's apartment..."

"I *was* there; I have booking receipts to prove it!"

"Yes, you clocked in at eight-thirty in the evening and we have CCTV footage showing you leave just before nine-thirty. However, Oliver died fifty minutes later..." Peter stated.

"Why do I feel like I am on trial right now?" Charlotte scowled at her lawyer.

"Mrs. Forbes, what Peter is trying to explain is that we have a void of time to fill with no hard proof to back up your alibi. Do you have any witnesses that can vouch for you?" Nate explained, the sound of his deep voice sending chills down Ava's arms. It was the first time in days that she had heard him say more than a few words, even if those words weren't directed at her.

"I'm sure the caterers would be able to confirm my whereabouts." Charlotte's demeanour softened as she glanced at Nate.

"Perfect, can you arrange a meeting?"

"Certainly, I'll do it the second I am home, Nate."

Nate? She was calling him Nate?! Ava fumed to herself.

As the meeting wrapped up, Charlotte and Peter began making their way outside as Nate stayed back typing something on his laptop. Ava saw her opportunity and leapt at it as she closed the door and watched Nate's head pop up from behind his laptop, his thick brows slanting down into his whisky-coloured eyes.

"Ms. Archer?"

"I think we're a bit past the *Ms. Archer* crap, Nate," Ava sniped, her red heels prowling towards him, relishing in the way his eyebrows jumped back up in surprise. "You've been avoiding me for days."

"No, I haven't," Nate said flippantly, his eyes glancing back down at his laptop. "It's impossible to avoid someone you work with." He shrugged, maintaining his cool composure despite Ava now standing a meter away from him with her knuckles pressed down against the large table and glaring daggers at him.

"Don't play coy with me, *sir*," she warned, prowling around the table like a scornful lioness. "You've been avoiding me, and I want to know why."

"I told you already, I've not been avoidi—"

"I am *not* some plaything you can toss aside just because you've had your fill! I was never looking for anything meaningful with you but that doesn't mean you can treat me like dirt on your shoe, Nathaniel Brooks!" Ava's voice cut across the room, dominating the space as her boss's face winced ever so slightly.

"Look, Ava, I'm sorry if I made you feel like that, but this is for the best," he sighed wearily, slumping in his chair as he dragged his hands down his face. "I don't want to make things complicated, but I just don't have room for you in my life... There's a lot you don't understand."

"Try explaining it to me then."

"Why can't you just accept that I can't get into this with you?" he snapped.

"Can't or *won't*?" she hissed, stood next to him now as her arms crossed over and inadvertently pushed her breasts up in the swooping neckline of her ruby blouse.

A moment passed where no words were uttered, Nate's eyes lingering on her chest before he suddenly barked, "*For fuck's sake*, will you please start dressing more appropriately for work!"

"Oh, what's wrong, Nate?" Ava feigned confusion as her fingertips ran down her cleavage. "See something you like?"

"Oh, come on!" he whined, pressing his thumbs into his eye sockets as his head hung back in exasperation.

However, the last thing he had expected was when Ava's leg suddenly appeared at the side of his thigh and her tight behind landed down upon his lap as she straddled him. His mouth fell ajar as he questioned, "What the hell are you do—"

"Nate," she cut him off with her finger pressed to his soft, plump lips, "I'll make this quite simple for you; if you really don't want me...push me away...and you'll *never* see me again..."

TWENTY-THREE

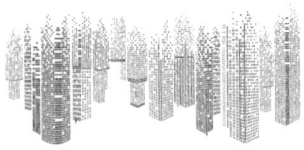

WHY DOES it turn me on when she's being such a brat?

Nate's moral compass was spinning out of control as he tried to move his hands and push the golden seductress off of him, but he couldn't find the conviction behind his actions. He craved her. She was honeycomb wrapped in velvet, her lips were rosebuds in spring, her nails were thorns, her eyes were oceans and he was drowning.

His self-control didn't just shatter, it exploded into a frenzy of lust as his hands tangled into her hair and tugged her forward.

Starved lips crashed upon each other as relief rushed through their bodies, greedy hands grabbing at any piece of flesh they could, two souls colliding as each breath built with subtle excitement on each exhale. Each kiss was wet and furious like a torrential downpour thrashing across the bare ground. He couldn't get enough of the liquid sunshine she poured into his mouth.

Ava needed this; she needed him. There was something about Nate that defined the meaning of *hitting the spot.*

Being touched by a man had never felt so good until she had found him.

He was spiralling into chaos. He knew it but damn if he could stop himself. Her nails grazing across his scalp had him losing his *shit* and made him turn primal as his hands yanked apart her blouse, not caring for the popped buttons as his mouth devoured her perfect tits. That spicy floral sweetness was concentrated upon her chest, sinfully delicious and making his teeth sink into her delicate skin and eliciting erotic gasps from her mouth.

"Stop that," he growled against her left mound as he felt her hands pry apart his belt buckle and reach for his zipper head. However, she continued tugging at his belt, not listening so he warned, "Ava, the door is unlocked, *stop.*" And yet, the defiant little minx yanked his head forward by his hair and kissed him rough and hard, stealing his breath.

"I don't care," she snarled like a feral kitten against his lips, her hand finding and wrapping around his arousal. "For the next ten minutes, you are mine."

"Sh-shit..." he hissed, groaning with her tongue dominating his mouth and her hand working him towards a mess that coated the curve between her thumb and index. How could a woman be so soft and feminine but so powerful and dominant? It was a complete mindfuck—the good kind.

With flushed cheeks, he hitched his hands up her short little skirt, that *fucking skirt* that had driven him to insanity these past few days. His fingers grazed her bare hip bone searching higher until the reality crashed into his loins hard. "*Christ*, you're not wearing any underwear..."

"Guilty as charged," Ava purred against her assault of kisses on his neck. "I know what I want." She pulled back, grinning devilishly before using his own words against him. "You."

That was the last straw for Nate, primal growls vibrating in his chest as he threw every last piece of caution to the wind and possessively gripped handfuls of her perfect ass, his nails biting into her flesh before he released and then abruptly brought his hands down, a sharp snap of skin on skin breaking through her moans. He grinned at the yelp she made for him, yanking her closer onto his lap until they crossed a wet line as he felt her beautiful slick centre kiss his shaft. However, as they both gasped, it wasn't from the intense pleasure they felt when reconnecting, but from the interrupting knock at the door.

"Hello? Is this room in use?"

"Get down!" Nate hissed at Ava's alarmed expression as he pushed her under the table in front of them.

Despite the panic rushing through her body along with the adrenaline, Ava couldn't help the small giggle that escaped her lips as she quietly clambered under the table and knelt between Nate's knees. She abruptly snapped her mouth shut as she looked behind her upon hearing the meeting room door creak open and saw the two sets of legs from beneath the table.

"Mr. Brooks, apologies, we didn't realise this meeting room was booked."

"Yes, I require this room for the rest of the morning," Nate answered casually, but Ava knew him well enough to hear the amount of restraint he was mustering.

He clenched the table with one hand, the other pointing a warning finger at the dirty little secret beneath it. Given Ava's immodest state, it wouldn't take a genius to come to the conclusion that he was fucking his assistant and if that got out all hell would break loose.

Nate was unlocking new sides of Ava, showing her that the danger of being caught thrilled her and brought on that fire low in her belly. As she sat there between his knees and stared at his twitching arousal, peeking through his work slacks, an idea sprung to her mind...and a very wicked one at that.

"No worries, we'll try the room down the hall," the suited gent at the door said as he turned to leave but then stopped and added, "Oh! I almost forgot, how is the Nolan case going?"

"Yeah, it's coming along," Nate answered with his jaw clenched in frustration but then suddenly shot upright when he felt the softest, warmest, and most succulent of lips wrap around the head of his member. Intense pleasure rippled down his length and burst in his balls making him suck in a breath.

Is she fucking kidding me right now?!

The lawyer stood at the door was luckily none the wiser as he glanced at his watch giving Nate enough time to swat his hand at Ava. However, this goddamn woman just sucked him harder and made every muscle in his body tighten to breaking point.

"Ah, good to hear! Hopefully another easy case to close off, right?"

"*Right.*" Nate strained, the muscles cording tightly in his neck as he clenched his hand on the table, his hand running into Ava's hair and fisting it tightly. "If you'll excuse me, gentlemen, I am in the middle of something here." The middle of something being her mouth as her expert tongue flicked against his tip.

After a few seconds that felt like a year in hell, the door finally clicked shut and Nate glared down at his lap, ready to roar hellfire at the idiotic woman who nearly cost him everything but then he saw her eyes. It felt like his birthday as two perfect bluebells peered up at him, her eyes like presents with long black velvet ribbons framing them. Then there were her lips, glistening with a silvery sheen as they locked around his manhood and reduced this man into nothing more than a boy—he was a goner.

"That feel good, boss?"

"You're unbelievable," he said with a deep groan at that filthy mouth, fisting the silk at her crown, a smirk climbing up his cheek as he watched her nod her head innocently. She was utterly perfect, everything about her from that fiery attitude problem to the way she expertly ground her tongue against the sensitive band of flesh running down the tip of his sex. "Fuck...your mouth... it's—" he groaned out, caught between the need to close his eyes and keep them on the two blue moons looking up at him.

"That's the idea, Brooks," she interrupted and guided his spare hand into her hair. "Fuck my mouth."

Nate responded, all but drooling for this woman, his hands bunching her hair at either side of her head, pulling her mouth down further while he thrust up into her. She obliged eagerly, the moans she made vibrating down deep into his balls and shooting up into his lower stomach. He had never met such a tenacious woman, yielding to her as his head fell back and his eyes rolling to see the stars at the back of his skull.

Ava was in her element, cutting this man down to size as her mouth stole his breath and claimed his soul. Her arms hooked under his thighs, hands grabbing his hips as she assertively tugged his ass off the seat, gripping him tight in her hold as she sucked him so hard that her cheeks hollowed.

Again, and again, she took her revenge, ensuring he'd never ignore her once more, bringing him to the edge of climax before dangling it just of reach. She watched him in awe, his face a kaleidoscope of pleasure, keeping up her torture until his thighs trembled, his face a shade of rose as the veins across his body bulged out in desperation.

"Av...Ava...*fuuuck!*" he ground out through shallow breaths, ecstasy filling his veins as his body finally lost control, falling silent as the pleasure climbed and climbed until bursting apart, his salt filling her mouth and throat while his teeth clamped down on his fist to stop him from screaming her name. Nate's hips bucked like a caged bull, his nostrils flaring angrily as his free hand held her head down to stave the explosion of fireworks in his loins until it eventually simmered down to sparklers.

Nate eventually gazed down at her oceans again, her smile the lighthouse guiding him back to safe land. He cupped her cheek as his thumb smeared away a single tear rolling down the blush of her cheek, her lipstick smudged from the aggressive treat she had given him.

It was in that moment that he felt something ache and stretch inside his chest as though his soul was trying to reach out for her but couldn't for being a prisoner of his own fate. That was the thing about destiny; it didn't give a crap about your plans. Nate had finally found the key to his happiness, but the real kicker was that fate decided to change the fucking locks.

Ava stood, buttoning her blouse while Nate opened windows inside the meeting room and made her chuckle to herself.

"Well, I certainly have never done *that* before," she quipped, wiggling her eyebrows at him as he shot her an unamused look over his shoulder.

"Well, I should certainly hope not." His eyes glowered possessively at her but there was a tease to his tone that only added to the good mood she was in.

Brushing down the creases in her skirt, they were both interrupted by the buzzing of Nate's phone sliding across the meeting table. Ava peered over and saw the caller ID and instantly frowned. A beautiful woman, with flawless olive skin and the type of chestnut hair that you could not buy out of a bottle, beamed Ava a cheery grin. However, the picture wasn't as alarming as the name across the screen.

"*Natalia* is calling you?" Ava squinted at the phone that Nate was now swiping off the table, silencing the device and placing it into his pocket. She brushed off his reaction but, something was nagging Ava...that name felt so familiar. It wasn't until Nate shut over his laptop that it sprung to her mind. "Natalia, that's the name of your yacht, right?"

"Right," Nate confirmed, his shortness with her causing her brows to crease further. "We should head back now," he said, clearing his throat.

"Is she family...?"

"No," Nate said through a clenched jaw.

"Friend?" she pressed, growing more suspicious.

"We need to get back *now*, Ava."

"I mean she's gotta' be pretty special considering you named a *boat* after her... My father told me you only name your boat after your daughter or your w—" She stopped short, staring at Nate. The frozen expression on his paling face was like that of a client put on trial, that moment when they knew they'd been caught. It was in that moment that Ava's brain, fuelled with women's intuition, put the pieces together with detective speed and her eyes fell upon his left hand. Ringless. She didn't want to ask it but forced the words out through the lump in her throat. "Nate...are you married?"

Her eyes bored into him and watched his mouth fall open, his silence speaking louder than words.

TWENTY-FOUR

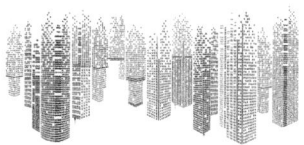

"OH, MY FUCKING GOD!" Ava squawked, recoiling back from him as her mind spun at a million miles per hour. It was in this moment of chaos that her mind was able to rationalise every detail of the last few weeks. "Dinner! You and my father were talking about *her* at dinner! I thought you both were talking about your boat sailing the Italian coast, not your bloody *wife!*" Bile was rising in her throat as she gripped her hair, her chest heaving with shallow breaths as the illusion between them wilted like a dying rose.

"Ava, if you'd just let me explain it's not as bad as—"

"Don't you bloody dare tell me it's not as bad as it seems!" she squealed, pointing a finger at him with a look that could kill.

"Will you keep your damn voice down!" Nate hissed, his hand grabbing hold of her elbow and yanking her away from the door. "Look, if you would just let me explain I—"

"Are you married, yes or no?" Ava cut to the chase, peeling his unworthy fingers off her elbow and socially distancing herself from the man she thought she knew.

"Yes, but it's not a serious marriage."

"So, you are legally separated then?"

"No...not exactly..." Nate hesitated, a deep frown setting into his forehead and creasing the bridge of his nose. His stomach sank and his guts twisted as he watched the betrayal steal the light from her eyes. He would give anything to ignite that fire again, so he stepped towards her but nearly felt his knees give way when she took a step away from him like his very presence repelled her.

"Do you *fuck* her?" Ava asked, her hands by her sides and balled into little fists. When Nate didn't answer straight away, she had her answer and snarled angrily as she stormed towards him and shoved his chest. "You vile man!"

"It's not like that! We haven't fucked in months, maybe even years—*I've lost count*! Just hear me out, please!" he pleaded, reaching for her again, his hands cupping her upper arms, desperately trying to calm her down so she could just hear him out. He *had* to make this right.

"Get your hands off of me!" Ava bit back, slapping his hands away from her body. "You'll *never* touch me again."

"Ava..." Nate implored her; the corners of his honey eyes turned down as he all but whimpered for her to just listen, but he knew that was impossible. She wasn't the type of woman to sit down and have a rational talk; she was chaos and fire suspended in flesh and bone. However, then she charged towards the door and yanked it open, instilling panic in him. "Where are you going?!"

"Home."

"*What?* Ava, wait!" But it was a useless feat as she stormed up the hallway towards the busy department. He wanted to rush after her to fix this, but he couldn't risk making any more of a scene and inevitably had to let her go. "*Fuck!*"

Ava knew if she didn't get out of this place right now,

she was going to throw up. Her mind ached as she grabbed her things in a hurry and rushed towards the elevators. It was her dramatic exit that caught her best friend's attention as a brown bob peeked up from their desk.

"Lass? Ye alright there?" Sam asked, her face a picture of concern.

"Yes, I'm fine, sorry you'll have to excuse me." Ava sniffled, stepping into the elevator, grateful that the doors pinged shut just as her best friend rose to her feet. She had had enough lies for one day and couldn't stand lying to Sam's face about the sin she had committed.

FOR AVA, the worst part about all of this wasn't that she felt foolish for not seeing the warning signs, but that she had been lied to. If she had known he was married, she would never have had such sinful intentions, but the choice was never given to her. He left her in the dark and hid the truth away from the light.

Her mind was a foggy turbulent sea, conflicted over the feeling of loss, and yet how could she grieve for such a thing? This wasn't the beginning of the end...there was never a beginning with Nate.

Ava did what any self-respecting woman would do in her situation—she turned to therapy.

The green bottle glugged as tasty burgundy licked up the sides of the large gin glass while she lowered into a squat to become eye level with her wine and get her money's worth.

Her grey onesie hugged around her body, her work attire out of sight and out of mind, although, there was a moment where she was tempted to toss her work clothes onto an open fire and burn the evidence of her ever touching a married man.

Padding her way into the living room, she set the bottle of wine down onto the coffee table and took comfort from the soft piano music filling her spacious apartment. However, just as Ava sat down and placed the glass to her lips, ready to embrace the fruity aromas, the front door rattled against its hinges as though the hordes of hell were trying to invade.

"Oh, fuck me," she groaned, setting the glass down next to the bottle and making her way to the front door. "I'm coming, for Christ's sake!"

When she opened the door, she realised it wasn't hell trying to invade, it was the Scottish.

"Can you not answer your bloody phone?!" Samantha shrieked in the hallway outside Ava's apartment before storming inside. Ava rubbed at her tired eyes, closed the door behind her, and followed an angry lass into her living room. "I tried everyone, even Trinny and Sue—*hell*, I even rang the bloody hair salon! You had me wanting to call Scotland Yard and put out a missing person rep—" Sam stopped short with her coat hanging off of her arms as she saw the bottle of wine on the coffee table and looked back to Ava with a grave expression on her face. "*Shit*...what's happened, hen?"

"Nothing," Ava mumbled, her eyes bloodshot, but that was from the wine and definitely not the three hours she spent crying like a drunken and emotional fool...

"Aye, like hell it's nothing!" Sam challenged, knowing her friend well enough that when she acted prim and proper with the "you'll have to excuse me" chat, that something was most definitely wrong. She sat down on the sofa and pointed up at Ava. "Your lips are stained and you're drinking wine out of a gin glass from a bottle that is..." She picked up the bottle and gawked at the label. "*Bloody Nora*! It's fifteen-and-a-half-percent strength! *Who the hell died*?!"

Despite Ava feeling numb from emotional exhaustion, she found herself chuffing at her friend's outburst as she slumped down onto the sofa beside her and buried her face into Sam's shoulder.

"No one died, only my tolerance for men," Ava whined into the thick knitted jumper she had more or less face-planted.

"Is this about Peter?"

That wasn't a name Ava had expected to hear, but as she looked up at Sam with glistening eyes, it wasn't because her friend had almost hit the nail on the head, but because Ava wanted nothing more than to pour her heart out to her friend but couldn't for her own shame and pride.

"Yeah..." Ava lied, hiding her face back into her friend's side and taking comfort from the warm amber notes of her perfume. "You know, I tried so hard this week, reduced myself to nothing more than an attention-seeking whore and it all just came back to bite me on the arse, and now I feel...I feel..." She tried but couldn't push the words past the bitter lump in her throat as her voice croaked. She felt degraded.

"Lovely, we don't have to talk about it right now," Sam soothed, her hand running down her friend's hair as concern creased the space between her brows.

"Thank you, I just want to get drunk and forget about everything."

"Aye-aye, captain! I have just what the doctor ordered." Sam beamed, pushing Ava back slightly and smirking down at her with a mischievous wiggle of her brows. "We're going *out-out*."

"No."

"Shut it, ya tit, we're going out! It's your birthday tomorrow"—Sam was interrupted with a whine that she ignored—"and in case you forgot, we still need to celebrate my promotion so we are getting dressed up tonight, no boys allowed, just dancing, cocktails, and bitching about menstruation!" she denounced but halted as she finally pulled out the object that had been prodding into her back for the past few minutes. From between the cushions of the sofa, she produced an empty bottle of red that made Ava give her a sheepish look. "And you call the Scottish a bunch ae alcoholics, ye wee fud!"

TWENTY-FIVE

"I'M TELLING YOU! When he hits from the back and pulls out too quickly, it's like a horse sneezing down there!" Sam blurted across the loud and bustling bar, her hands clapping together as she imitated a horse's mouth that sounded like a balloon deflating.

Ava couldn't breathe past the laughter, buckling over in her seat as tears lined her lashes. She had forgotten that only hours ago she was sat half-drunk on her couch with different types of tears in her eyes.

"Stop!" Ava pleaded through her chortles as a couple of gents looked at the pair oddly but still, her friend continued blowing raspberries. "Samantha Eastley, I'm going to wet myself, will you bloody stop?!"

"You know...that's a real problem when you reach thirty! Here, did I ever tell you about the time I went to a trampoline fitness class?"

"Bloody stop!" Ava howled as droplets of joy trickled down her cheeks, smearing her mascara under her eyes.

The night transpired into more wild tales from Sam, more hilarity, and more drunken banter. It really was just what the doctor ordered as Ava's mind was diverted away from the train wreck of her love life.

It was fast approaching midnight by the time the pair, arm in arm, strolled down the deserted cobbled street towards Ava's apartment. For claiming to have such a strong liver, her friend certainly couldn't walk in a straight line, although, that could be because Sam was barefoot in the middle of a cold Autumn. She claimed that the Scottish were immune to the cold.

"On the bonnie, bonnie banks of Loch Loooomond!" Sam howled as she sang for the entirety of London to hear, swinging a wine bottle back and forth before swigging down the substance she definitely did not need more of. The hilarious part was that the one Scottish person in a one-mile radius of them had heard Sam and chimed in.

"How they let you in past the borders, I will never know!" Ava laughed with a slight slur, shaking her head as she held her inebriated friend up. "You know, you really aren't doing your lot any favours. You're practically upholding the Scottish stereotype here!"

"Ack...could be worse... Could be English!"

"Oi!" Ava slapped at her friend's arm as they both burst out into playful laughter. However, the giggling banter was cut short as they both approached the front of her apartment building, she paused and blinked in confusion.

Stood outside the redbrick building, with white windowpanes and doors, was a man who was leaning against the black metal railing holding a beautiful bouquet of flowers.

"What are you doing here?" Ava asked with a deep frown cutting into her features.

"To wish you a happy birthday and to apologise," the auburn-headed gent replied.

"So, I may have done a *thing*..." Sam cut in, explaining she had texted Peter, and Ava would not be surprised if her friend yelled drunken caps lock at the poor man either. "I'll be off then, tah-tah!"

"Wait, *what*?" Ava blinked, snapping her eyes between Sam and Peter. "You can't leave, and no chance am I letting you walk home in that state!" However, as though her drunken friend had coordinated it perfectly, a black-cab taxi rolled up outside her apartment and Sam beamed her a smug but cheeky grin as she randomly pulled out a pair of sunglasses that she got God only knows where and placed them onto her face despite it being dark outside.

"I love you!" Sam gave her friend a sloppy kiss on the cheek and then retreated towards the taxi and all but falling into the back seat, but not before she yelled, "Oh, don't forget to try out the horse sneeze method!"

AVA PLACED the bouquet of white lilies, her favourite flower, into a white jug of water as Peter removed his jacket and hung it over the back of her kitchen chair.

"So, I must apologise..." Peter began, leaning against the kitchen counter now as he rolled the sleeves up on his green jumper.

"Apologise for what?" Ava quizzed with a scrunched nose as she poured herself a glass of water—she would need to be *a lot* more sober to get through this conversation.

"Sam said that you felt I was ignoring you for the past couple of weeks, and I honestly hadn't noticed... I've been so busy with Charlotte"—he cleared his throat awkwardly—"Mrs. Forbes, that I really have been neglecting you, ol' girl."

"Oh, no it's fine, I've just been stressed I guess," Ava brushed off the comment and jumped to sit up on her kitchen countertop, her legs dangling.

"Stressed?"

"Yes, just everything with my father and work being so busy...so many changes..." Ava sighed, her shoulders slumping as she rested her elbows on her knees and her chin on her hands. "It's been a hell of a month."

"Awh, my darling..." Peter's voice was suddenly in front of her as his hands came down upon her shoulders. "You need to relax, alright?" At first, Ava flinched from his touch, but the more his thumbs pressed into her tired shoulders and relieved the tension, the more she felt herself giving in to a little bit of TLC. "That's my girl, just close your eyes and relax," he cooed, running his thumbs up and down the sides of her neck as his fingers pressed deep into the supporting columns at the top of her spine.

A soft whine left Ava's lips as she closed her eyes but then felt Peter's touch on her inner thigh beneath her skirt, her blue orbs springing open. "What are you doing?"

"Relaxing you...if you'll let me?" He smirked such a dashingly handsome smile, his hands spreading her knees as his nails ran up and down the tops of her thighs and elicited goosebumps.

"I don't think that is a good idea. You should probably go..." Ava breathed a shaky breath, however, there was no commitment behind her words, a dark-rooted part of her craving intimacy.

"Go where? *Here*?" he breathed against her lips, running his fingertip over the lace covering her scantily dressed sex and evoking a small moan from her lips.

"Mmh, there," she whimpered, nodding her head, and

chewing on her bottom lip as his thumb pressed into her sensitive bud and massaged circles around it.

Peter began descending, his touch never once leaving where she needed it before his head disappeared beneath her red pleated midi skirt, his teeth nibbling up along her snowy thigh towards her sweet centre.

Ava's mind was a drunken mess, unable to think clearly from the pleasure his mouth brought as it latched over her heat and breathed fire down onto it. Her body shivered pleasantly, tingles of warmth oozing through her core as she gripped the counter and breathed heavy laboured breaths. His mouth had saturated her panties, his hands bunching her skirt up to her ample hips as she tipped her head back and closed her eyes.

This felt fucked up to her, an odd sense of guilt cutting through her as she peered down to tell him to stop. However, as she did, it wasn't Peter's red hair waiting for her, it was Nate's black locks. She gasped, blinking between the emerald and the hazel orbs coming in and out of focus.

"Peter...you should..." she moaned, staring down at Nate's sexy and dark smirk between her legs, his finger sliding into her underwear and hooking them to the side before his tongue laved a trail from her bridge to her clit. Her hands gripped dark tendrils, giving into this illicit fantasy as she pulled his face down against her ache.

Ava was certain she had lost her mind, that Nate had driven her to the brink of insanity and then shoved her over the edge, but she didn't care. Whatever had snapped inside her head, whatever fucked-up delusion this was, she never wanted it to end as long as it was Nate who was corrupting her thoughts.

Strong hands gripped her hips, tugging her ass off the counter until she was practically resting upon his mouth that was wrecking her into a sloppy and mewling mess. In one swift movement, Ava found herself wrapped around his waist and being carried, her mouth on his, tasting her sweet musk on his tongue as she clung close to her dark fantasy, scared to blink in case the illusion shattered.

She was in too deep and needed just one more hit of her poison, even though she knew it would never be enough.

The cold wood of the kitchen table nipped at her bottom as she was set down, lips worshipping her neck and making her sink deeper into the dark abyss of pleasure. She lost herself inside this perfect storm, her clumsy hands undoing his jeans as she kissed along his jaw and grew drunk on his sensual noises. She was coaxed into lying back across her table, hands gripping her hips before pleasure shot up through her, his length filling her to full, making her squeal out and arch her back. His movements were harsh but slow, skin on skin slapping as she pulled him down and sank her teeth into his shoulder to suppress her screams. Her mind was a million miles away, drifting back to that moment on his desk being fucked just like this.

Ava stared at the window next to them, watching them fuck, the distortion of reality more evident now as she watched his hair change from shades of red to black. She didn't care for the glitches in reality, wanting to turn up the volume on this bad dream.

If this was the only place where Nate could exist, she would lose herself just to find him.

TWENTY-SIX

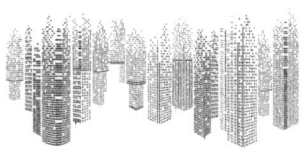

A THROBBING ACHED RAN across Ava's temples as she awoke to an empty bed, piercing white sunlight, and a terrible feeling in her gut. That feeling manifested itself into the form of Peter getting dressed at the end of her bed. Out of habit, Ava turned to her side, expecting an unwanted cup of coffee to be sat next to her bedside, but there wasn't one.

"Morning." Peter smiled, yanking his zipper up before slipping on his jumper.

"What time is it?" she croaked, her fingers touching her throat where it felt like she had gargled vodka and shards of glass.

"Seven in the morning, go back to sleep, you look a little delicate, petal." He chuckled as he rolled his top down over his modest abs.

"Mmh, you could say that again." Ava groaned, rubbing at her eyes and yawning as she sat up in bed. "Off so soon?"

"Yeah, I've got breakfast with some mates," Peter told her but there was something about his tone that made Ava doubt him.

"Oh, alright, I was going to see if you wanted breakfast

with me today..." Ava surprised even herself with this, but Peter's reaction was one of bewilderment as he blinked at her like she had just offered her hand in marriage.

Rubbing the back of his neck, he approached her with a sympathetic smile. "Look, Ava...what we have is really fun, but this isn't good for either of us. I can't keep doing this to myself, and honestly, I can't keep doing it to you too."

"Oh..."

"Workmates, yeah?" he asked, cupping the side of her face.

Ava couldn't understand the sinking feeling running through her. She honestly didn't care that Peter wanted to end their hook-ups, but something was aching inside of her at his rejection. She pushed a fake smile to her lips and said, "Of course," before watching Peter turn around to leave but stop as though he had suddenly remembered something.

"Actually, before I go"—he pulled out a document from his back pocket and approached Ava—"would you mind signing this?"

"What's that?"

"It's just the missives you typed up for me the other day, you forgot to sign them off and I'm on my way to post them today." He smiled, setting the folded piece of paper in front of her and handing her a pen.

"Yeah, no problem." Ava yawned, one hand rubbing her tired eyes as the other signed her name at the bottom of the document.

"Perfect, you're a legend, ol' girl!" He grinned and leaned in to press a kiss to her forehead. "I'll see you at work on Monday. Try to nurse that hangover, yeah?" Peter chuckled and soon left her apartment, thereafter leaving Ava feeling an odd sense of abandonment. Why did she suddenly feel like broken goods?

ALL WEEKEND, Monday had loomed like a lone dark cloud during a heatwave, time seeming to jump-cut like a buffering video until it arrived. Ava had been dreading this moment as she walked into the office and sat down at her desk. Her hangover was still lingering after a weekend of banishing her sisters from visiting due to the "flu" and instead lounging in bed watching *Friends* and avoiding the fact that she was another year closer to thirty with nothing to show for it.

She hadn't been sat at her desk for longer than a few minutes before the intercom beeped and Nate was summoning her into his office.

"Fuck off," she uttered under her breath before leaning forward and yanking the plug out of the machine. As expected, moments later, Nate was stood in front of her desk, and her eyes reluctantly peered up at the dishonest scumbag. Her stomach twisted as her eyes landed on him. His stubble looked grown out and there were dark crescents under his eyes, but he still looked more handsome than ever.

"Ms. Archer, I need you in my office."

"I'm busy," she clipped out and flicked through the paperwork on her desk.

"The filing can wait, I need to speak with you urgently in my office." Nate's tone was stone cold, his face an iceberg lost at sea as he walked back into his office and expected her to follow. However, that brat did anything but follow—she walked right past his damn door!

A frustrated snuff left his nostrils as he went after her, following her down the hallway, watching her struggle with her arms full of folders as she headed towards the archive. The moment she stepped inside what looked like a mini library with shelves lining the room, Nate shut the door behind them both.

"What the hell are you doing?" Ava jumped, startled by his presence as she peered over the top of the binders in her arms.

"Well, I need to talk to you and it's a bit hard when you won't answer your texts or calls!"

"It's almost as if I blocked your number for a reason," she chided sarcastically, her knee coming up to balance the folders but inevitably dropping them as they clattered to the ground.

"Leave them," Nate ordered when she started to fumble, but of course, she would ignore him and clumsily try to pick them up. He didn't have time for this shit and stormed over to her, yanking her up by the elbow as he reiterated, "I said leave them."

"You have three seconds to get your bloody hands off of me before I—"

"Why was Peter Taylor at your apartment on Saturday?"

A dumbfounded look slapped Ava across the face as she gawked up at Nate. "How the hell did you know about that?"

"Answer my question."

"I was *fucking* him," she said provocatively, leaning her face closer to his as a dark smile crept onto her red lips. A possessive growl snarled from Nate's nostrils, a sound that would have made Ava like putty in his hands, but that was before she found out he was a dishonest man. Scum, like the rest of them, hence why they weren't worth her time.

"That so?" he challenged, the anger evident on his reddening face as it was his tone, his thick American accent growing sharper and rougher. "Was he as good a fuck as me?"

"Careful, *sir*, your envy is showing."

"Oh, sweetheart"—Nate chuckled a deep, sardonic laugh—"it ain't envy. *Envy* implies I want something that someone already has." He yanked her elbow closer until he was pressed up to her front and inches away from her face. "I am *jealous* because that prick is tryna take what is already *mine*."

"I don't belong to anyone, certainly not you."

"Yeah? So, you just fuck whoever ya want, when ya want, like a little slut—that it?"

"Oh, because it's *always* the woman that is the slut, right?" Ava barked now as he nipped at a nerve of hers. "A guy can fuck whoever he wants, whenever he wants and he is seen as nothing more than playing the field, *a right lad!* But the second a woman wants her sexual freedom, she's what? *A common fucking whore?!*"

Nate saw that he had struck a nerve, but this conversation was going way off course and he had to steer it back. As nuclear as it made him to imagine another man's hands touching her porcelain skin, he knew she was right, and he knew he had no damn place getting mad at her for it, but he couldn't stop himself. That redheaded *punkass* didn't deserve to touch her goddess body...then again, neither did his own piece-of-shit ass.

"Did you like the lilies?" he asked, frowning when Ava's face twisted in confusion.

"Wait, *you* got me the flowers?"

"Yes, I left them on your doorstep as you weren't answering your door, and before you say it, yes I know breaching your privacy isn't ethical but I needed to speak to you and fix this."

Ava growled for one reason alone—all men were complete lying assholes it seems.

"There is nothing to fix; you're married, end of discussion," she seethed, finally yanking her elbow out of his grip and turning to leave.

But Nate wasn't taking no for an answer as he grabbed her wrists, spun her around, pinned her front against a filing cabinet, and restrained her arms behind her back.

"Seriously, is this the only way I can get you to listen to me?" he growled, pressing up behind her as she squirmed and threw a tantrum, demanding to be let go.

"I'll scream, you fucking demented, ignorant, stupid, lying, dishonest piece of—"

"Are you finished?" he interrupted, but that phrase seemed to pour gasoline over an open fire as she roared hellfire at him. "Oh, for fuck's sake," he groaned, adjusting his grip so both of her wrists were gripped in one of his large hands and his other came down over her mouth. However, as her teeth sank down upon his palm he recoiled and shook his hand, wanting to roar as she laughed at his pain.

Enough was enough.

His hand wrapped around her hair and pulled her head back as he moved his lips to her ear, trying to not let her scent make him drunk, his voice softer than that of his touch as he whispered, "I'm *begging* you, please just listen to me, Ava?"

Ava didn't know if she was just messed up in the head but a part of her was secretly excited by this sudden change in dynamic between them both. Her heart was racing, pushing the blood south as her breath hitched in her throat. She would never admit it, *but fuck* did she miss him. "You have one minute to bore me with your excuses."

TWENTY-SEVEN

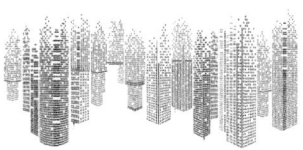

"THERE ARE NO EXCUSES," he sighed, reluctantly letting her go. "What I did was fucked up. I know that, *you* know that, and there is nothing I can say or do to actually fix it. I should have told you at the start, but I don't regret what we did."

"How many others have you fucked behind your wife's back?" she challenged, turning around to face him with a scornful expression frosting her face.

"No, it's not like that! I have never done anything like this before! Do you honestly think I was planning on coming to Europe and meeting someone like you who could destroy my entire career and flush my marriage down the drain?"

"Don't you *dare* blame this on me!"

"No, that's not what I meant. I'm not blaming you..." Nate groaned, taking a step back as his hands dragged down his face. "Look, my marriage isn't what you think it is. Natalia and I are just business partners. Our marriage is nothing more than a political fucking statement, a business deal that was practically arranged for me."

"An *arranged* marriage?"

"Pretty much." He shrugged his shoulders and leaned his back against one of the shelves. "Our parents hooked us up, said it would be a great way to increase our social status, that it was a great move financially for us combining our assets—and don't get me wrong, *it is*... but it's a loveless partnership. We are two completely different people living under this ridiculously large house, we barely speak to each other, and I wouldn't be surprised if Nat is fucking some guy behind my back...and *honestly?* I wouldn't care if she was."

"So...what? You don't fuck your wife, so your British mistress will do—is that it?" Ava snipped, not buying this story, and finding it twisted and messed up even if it were true.

"No, that's not it. Nat and I did fuck *a lot* at first, thought why the hell not mix business with pleasure, but it was just this senseless fucking day in and day out that—"

"Okay, okay, I get the picture, move on!"

"I don't *want* her, Ava. I haven't fucked her, or *anyone* for that matter, in months. Even then, there isn't any passion, no desire that consumes me, not like how it is when I am with...you." Nate stared at her like she was a shining beacon of hope and stepped towards her, his hands carefully slipping onto her waist.

"Nate...please d-don't..." Ava whimpered, music to Nate's ears as he saw it clear as day in her eyes—she felt it too. They fought and fucked with the same desire and craving for more.

"I will do *anything* to make this work. I will be whatever you want me to be, I'll give up *everything* for you, just don't let whatever *this* is go," he whispered, moving in closer to that aroma that made him high, his hand in her hair, cinching her body close as he ran his nose up the side of her neck. "I need you, Ava. I can't get you out of my head, I can't forget your touch. When I close my eyes all I see is you, beautiful, perfect you." His lips tenderly kissed along her jaw between words. "I want you to be my forever girl. You're everything—my desire, my weakness, my *obsession*..." He trailed off as his lips found hers and the pair melted into one another. All logic fell away from him as his lips chased after her soul, feeling more at home here than he did anywhere else. Within her touch all he found was peace. His body ran hot as he felt her warm palms sliding over his white shirt, reaching for his heart that he'd gladly rip out of his chest for her. But then, as he tasted the salt upon his tongue, a frown etched its way into his features before he was abruptly pushed away from his safe harbour. Pain sliced straight through his chest when he saw the tears sliding down her face like rain rolling down the sides of a perfect rose.

"I...I'm sorry, I just can't... It's too much—I—I don't feel the same way," she choked on the words before storming straight past him, but he couldn't move to chase after her. His feet felt as though they were cemented to the floor, his body turning to stone as her words echoed in his mind. Despair drowned him like darkness blanketing around his body, smothering him, forcing itself down his throat until his heart felt as though it was pumping thick tar. It wasn't until that moment that he realised he had given her the one thing he had no control over—his heart.

AFTER AVA HAD RUSHED out of work that day, it was the last he saw of her all week as she never showed up to the office. He took the hint and left her alone, but he'd be lying if he said it hadn't crippled him. Four days was all it took for him to reach insanity.

That week was hell, not only because her sunny face wasn't there to brighten his day, but because he struggled with the workload without his assistant.

It turned out Nate needed her in more ways than just one.

His true mistress was his work, each day blurring into the other, lacking colour and life, the same monotonous repetition as the last day. He never knew how deep her claws were in him until he was losing sleep over her. Every dream, there she was, a blissful escape, until he woke up and felt the pain of knowing it could never happen—she didn't feel the same way.

It was his own fault for plucking a rose from the earth oblivious to her hidden thorns. He was just flesh and bone to her, an expendable high.

Nate couldn't bear the dreams anymore, preferring the heavy feeling on his chest as though trying to breathe in but never filling his lungs. At least staying awake felt like he had control over something.

Nate was on his way back from a meeting when he stopped dead before turning the corner. The wet and breathy noise of a passionate exchange came from around the bend making his heart jump into his throat as images of Ava's and Peter's mouths invaded his brain. Rage ripped through his veins and curled his hands as he stormed around the corner.

"Mr. Brooks!" Charlotte Forbes gasped, jolting away from her stepson, Jenson, and making Nate's face screw up in confusion. "We were just discussing the trial next week."

She couldn't have looked any more caught if her hands were dipped in red paint.

"Right..." Nate's eyes squinted at this woman, seeing nothing more than a leech. It made sense; old man Forbes was dead so move on to his kid that's ages with her and suck him dry too? Money-draining leech. "As you were." He cleared his throat and plastered a polite smile onto his face as he walked up the hallway and finally sat down at his desk.

Nate was almost through with this week, Friday finishing time now on his doorstep, and yet, he took no solace from this. He rubbed his tired eyes and just as he looked up, Peter Taylor walked past his office door.

"*Punkass...*" Nate uttered, an annoyed snuff leaving his nostrils but suddenly the redhead swung into his office with a cheery grin on his face, the same smug expression that Nate had seen that day stood outside the elevator, the same one he now wanted to punch from his face to save his handkerchief getting spoiled.

"Hey, boss! You not finishing up for the ball tonight?" Peter asked, his hand cupping the door frame.

"Ball?" Nate asked, but then suddenly remembered the charity event he ought to attend to keep appearances and maintain professionalism. "*Ah, shit...* I forgot about it. I can't tonight." Truthfully, he had no plans, intending on drinking himself into a dreamless sleep, but even if he did want to go, he had nothing to wear to the black-tie event.

"Ah, that's a shame," Peter replied with a shrug before casually stepping into Nate's office uninvited. "Here, I meant to ask... Ava's been on annual leave all week but she's not answering her phone...do you know if she's alright?"

This was like music to Nate's ears knowing that the fiery golden goddess was ignoring not just him but this dick-for-brains as well. However, then it dawned on him that something could have happened to her and he felt sick for not being able to find out.

"I haven't heard from her, but I presume she is fine...why?"

"Oh, it's nothing...she's my arm candy for this evening was all," Peter chuckled, but Nate couldn't have been further from amused even if a clown was parading itself around his office as his jaw clenched and his hands fisted beneath his desk.

"I'll be sure to let Ms. Archer know that you're looking for her if I do hear anything," Nate lied, a practiced smile on his face as Red began to retreat out of his office. When he was finally gone, Nate let go of the breath he was holding. He would rather stick hot needles in his eyes than watch that redheaded idiot dance around with a lady who was far too much woman for that pathetic boy to handle. But then again, this was the pathetic man-child who allowed his girl to dangle by a noose at that auction.

His fingers drilled away at his keyboard before he whipped out his phone and pressed it to his ear. "Hi there, yes, I require a suit for this evening."

TWENTY-EIGHT

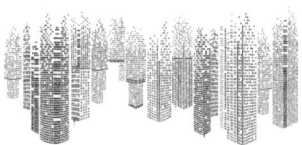

AVA COULDN'T BELIEVE she was going through with this as her heels clicked against the tarmac, her arm hooked in Peter's, peering up at the illuminated grand building of the Beaufort.

All week she had been throwing her very own pity party, her mind awash with the turbulence of her thoughts. Nate's confession had been too much. From the things he promised to the feelings he admitted—they hadn't known each other that long! She was wise to his cruel deception, having had many men before him go as far to claim they were in love with her, all just to bed her. Ava wasn't falling for his lies. She only had to wait for a couple more weeks before he would be shipped back to America and her life would return to normality again.

"Sam said there are no tables left," Peter advised, glancing down at his phone as he escorted Ava up the red carpet and inside the hotel. "Let me take your coat."

Ava peered around the opulent foyer in the hotel as she shrugged out of her black peacoat but glanced back at Peter when he suddenly gasped with his wide eyes dragging down her.

Crimson satin clung to Ava's petite frame, held up by two flimsy straps with a sweetheart neckline. The dress was longer on one side, cascading down one of her snowy thighs and stopping just below the knee. She added elegance to the ensemble by draping her voluptuous curls over one shoulder, a single glittering earring dangling from her lobe.

"Oh...shit..." Peter said, but his tone was not that of a compliment but of grave realisation.

"What's wrong?" Ava asked, turning around to see his grimacing face, her jaw dropping and stomach sinking as the reality of her surroundings sucker-punched her in the face.

Everyone at this event was wearing *black.*

"It's alright... It's not a big deal, they'll still let you in..." Peter didn't exactly sound confident, especially as his Adam's apple rose and dipped in his throat.

"*Not a big deal?!*" Ava yelled, her eyes glaring at his black tuxedo before hissing at him, "Why didn't you explicitly tell me it was a black-tie event?"

"I...I thought you knew?"

"I'm leaving!"

"No, wait!" He gripped her elbow and yanked her back with pleading eyes. "You promised you'd be my arm candy!"

"Yeah...no—fuck that." Ava shrugged, tugging against his grip. "I am not walking into that bloody ballroom like a red pariah!"

"Drinks on me tonight and I'll do all your archiving for a month!" He tried to negotiate like the good little lawyer he was.

"Bugger off!" Ava scowled, continuing to play tug of war with her elbow.

"I...I...I'll buy you and Sam the most expensive magnum on the menu!" he blurted desperately and finally caught Ava's attention, including two women stood next to them.

"Go on..."

"Oh, bloody heck, look here," he huffed, going into his suit pocket, and pulling out a key card, "you and Sam can even have the executive suite I rented for the night."

Ava wasn't even jealous knowing he had likely bought a room to impress and hook up with some woman who wasn't her. She just saw a fun sleepover for her and Sam.

"Deal," Ava stated, his shoulders slumping in relief before she challenged, "Why do you desperately need me on your arm anyway?"

"Some of London's biggest names in the industry are in that room and having a woman like you on my arm will work wonders for my reputation."

He was blunt but at least he was honest.

They both followed the sound of lively music before entering the main event. The grand ballroom was fit for Cinderella with glimmering chandeliers hanging from high ceilings, a majestic glass dome in its centre and white walls illuminated in a prosperous violet light. White cherry blossom trees decorated the tables surrounding the busy dance floor, and if not for the fact that everyone was wearing black, one could have mistaken the setting for a very expensive wedding or a casino event with the odd blackjack tables dotted around.

News of Ava's arrival began spreading like wildfire as people turned around and sent odd looks to the woman who didn't get the dress code memo. She felt her stomach twist as her nails dug into Peter's arm enough to make him wince.

When her face finally found a familiar pair of warm eyes, she felt a shred of relief...until that person decided to burst out laughing at her.

"*Omigod!*" Sam squealed as she burst into hysterics.

"Yes, *hilarious*—please can we get me royally blitzed so I can pretend this never happened," Ava said as she reached the tall standing table without any seats—her feet would not thank her later.

"Certainly. Samantha, will you help me carry the drinks?" Peter smirked, holding out his arm like the complete gentleman as Sam went along with it.

"Yep, great, just leave the pariah to stand here alone and fend for herself!" Ava chided.

"Just keep the table and I'll get you a bottle of wine." Sam patted Ava's shoulder as she passed her but not before winking as she teased, "A bottle of *red*, yeah?"

Ava glowered at her friend before huffing as she looked out to the dance floor, grimacing at the many people continuing to look her way before gossiping to one another. Still, even though this was social suicide, it was better than spending the best part of her week wallowing in self-pity over the death of her sex life. And then, just as though the gods were mocking her, her eyes landed upon the devil himself, dressed in a black tux and looking like the ultimate million-dollar man.

Stood on the other side of the dance floor next to an impressive ice sculpture, Nate was currently talking to a young redhead dressed in a glittering black gown. The vixen couldn't have been any older than twenty, with her pretty little hand resting on his shoulder as she laughed *with* him. They both looked like they were having a swell time, nice and familiar with one another, adding a tasteless new notch to his belt right next to his assistant's name.

Ava's hand curled around her temper beneath the table, her nails biting into her palm as her nostrils flared.

What a cunt.

"Who shat in your Coco Pops?" Sam cut through her thoughts as she dumped a large bottle of champagne on the table.

Ava let out a squeak, snapping her attention to her friend before asking, "Where's Peter?"

"Fuck knows, probably chatting up some bird with the 'I walked a million steps' patter, but *lookie hereeee...*" She fanned herself with his credit card and giggled in mischief. "Bloody idiot should know to *never* give his card to a lass at an event like this."

"I'll raise you that card for *these* bad boys." Ava winked, flashing a pair of key cards for the hotel room Peter had offered them both.

———

TWO HOURS. That's all it took for Ava to feel the buzz off of the bubbles as Sam and her spent most of the evening gambling at the pop-up roulette tables before finding themselves at the bar sipping Porn Star Martinis and doing shots.

"Naw, it's no spiking a man when you're just simply sneaking a Viagra into his complimentary muffin!" Sam slurred, dramatically waving her hands around before leaning her arm on the bar and pointing at Ava's face. "I'm *tellinggg* you...it was *the best* hour of my life!"

"Only an hour?!" Ava blurted as her hand covered her mouth to save spraying alcohol everywhere.

"Well...I had been drinking Porn Star Martinis all night so...I passed out after the first round." Sam said it so matter-of-a-fact that Ava lost it and began howling with laughter, buckled over until small snorts escaped her nostrils. "He was fifty shades though! Had handcuffs, those wee vibrator thingies, and even had lube in his top drawer!"

"Never trust a man with lube in his top drawer, Sam," Ava said through tears of laughter.

"Aye, why's that then?"

"Because a real man shouldn't need lube. If he doesn't intend on making his lady's wax drip for him then he shouldn't expect her to light his flame." Ava hid her cheeky smirk behind her glass as she added, "Unless, of course, the front door is locked..."

"True, but lucky for him it was Porn Star Martini–flavoured lube so I didnae ken the difference!"

Ava's laughter fluttered above the noise of the lively disco behind them, carrying across the dance floor like bird-song. When she opened her eyes to wipe the tears, something possessed her to peer over her exposed shoulder, a type of magnetism. There she saw him, the dark figure cutting through the dancing bodies and headed straight for her at the bar.

Nate.

TWENTY-NINE

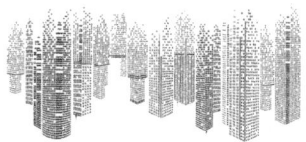

"LET'S GO DANCE, YEAH?" Ava said, grabbing hold of Sam's arm and yanking her.

"But this isn't 'Proud Mary'!" Sam protested, already dragged onto the dance floor as Ava steered them far away from the asteroid heading towards them.

The energy of the music flooded the crowded dance floor as the bass kicked Ava in her chest and fuelled her feet to the tempo of the song. If it wasn't for the grand evening gowns and tuxedos, with her eyes closed she could imagine being in a club, the colourful lasers dancing behind her eyelids as the music and atmosphere made her synapses jump and sparkle with life.

Sam hooked an arm around Ava's petite waist, yelling the lyrics of the song into her face as the pair laughed and moshed their heads to the song. For just a few blissful moments, Ava wasn't at a work function, her hormones and heart weren't at war, and everything in life made perfect sense. She would have complete control over everything again—well, other than her inebriated brain as she danced with her best friend.

However, that moment came crumbling down when Sam pulled her close and yelled into her ear, "Prince Charming is staring at your arse...wanna show him what he's missing?" *Nate*.

Ava didn't know what possessed her, whether it was the lies Nate told her or seeing him move on to another woman so quickly after confessing his false feelings for her, but suddenly her inner freak let loose as she pushed Sam back just enough to flick her sunny hair and sumptuous hips in unison.

"Snoop Doggy Dogg it!" Sam cheered.

"You *what*?" Ava squinted and momentarily paused.

"Drop it like it's hotttt..." Sam sang, making Ava scrunch up her nose further before Sam hollered, "Will you just bloody *slut drop* already!"

Tipping her head back and laughing, Ava parted her knees as much as her tight dress would allow and did Snoop Dogg proud by dropping into the provocative dance pose. She pushed her peach out, rolling her body in a sensual wave as she straightened and stood back up.

"Mission accomplished, lass—six o'clock incoming!" Sam slowly backed away from her with a sniggering expression.

The moment Ava felt strong hands grip her hips from behind, her stomach flip-flopped. His hands pulled her bum up against his hard front, encouraging her movements to grind against his hipbones as her arms laced their way up and around his neck.

Intoxicated or not, as his fingertips brushed down the sides of her thighs, her legs couldn't wait to hear what his hands had to say.

"*Taylor, get your damn hands off of her!*" Nate's voice boomed across the dance floor, shattering the moment like a rock being tossed at a window as people gasped and turned towards the commotion.

Ava's stomach tightened into a ball of nerves as she snapped around to the origin of his voice—not behind her as she had expected but next to her. It wasn't a second later that Peter was ripped off her as she spun around to see Nate growling at him like a territorial wolf.

"What the bloody hell, mate?" Peter gawked at Nate like he had lost his mind.

"You touch her again—"

"What are you doing?!" Ava interrupted Nate with little blue dots for eyes. She watched as his stare cut to hers, a fleeting look slicing across his honey orbs before he reluctantly looked away.

"Uh...can someone explain to me what is going on?" Sam chimed in, swaying slightly on her feet in her drunken state.

"This is a work event. I won't have my employees conducting themselves in such a debased way." Although Nate's words were professional, his heavy breathing and that wild look in his eyes was anything but. He looked animalistic.

"Oh, but it's okay for you to flirt with little miss red over there?" Ava snapped, her hand flying off to the side and nearly slapping someone in the face.

"*What?*" Nate squinted, his head snapping around him to try and locate whoever she was talking about. "Ava, I wasn't flirting with—"

"Err...is there something going between you two?" Peter cut in, his face creased in confusion, making Ava's and Sam's eyes widen in sync at the accusation.

Ava tried to make her tongue connect behind her teeth, to push the vocalisation out of her lips, but it felt like her tongue had turned to sandpaper and was stuck to the roof of her mouth.

"Don't be absurd!" Nate cut across the silence, his voice the epitome of authority as it shut down any of Peter's speculations.

However, if there was one person who could see right through Ava, it was her friend. Sam was squinting at Ava's guilty face before her jaw dropped, realisation causing her hand to clamp over her gasping mouth.

Ava stared at that look in Sam's eyes, that betrayed look furrowing across her brows that made Ava's stomach sink low. She didn't feel sick because she had been caught, but rather that she had lied to her best friend.

"Sam…" she began, but her friend shook her head and parted her lips in shock. Ava peered around her between the confused expression on Peter's face and some of the bystanders around her before the naked shame finally snapped inside of her.

If ever she wanted her Cinderella moment, it was now.

Ava bolted from the dance floor, bumping shoulders with people who hollered offence at her as she did. She had to get out of here, her world spinning out of control as her terrible sin likely spread like wildfire and would soon reach her father. It felt like her life was crumbling—her career, the networks she had built, her reputation, her womanhood, the trust she had with her father, and her friendship with Sam.

Panting after running out of the ballroom and down the hallway, she reached the elevators and jabbed the button. She was grateful to hold the key to her quick escape—the hotel room Peter had given her access to. At least no one would find her there, drowning herself in the minibar before all hell broke loose the next day and she'd have to face the horrible reality.

Stepping into the elevator, she peered up at hearing feet pounding against the carpeted flooring.

"Ava, wait!" Nate boomed, his voice echoing down the hallway as he pumped his legs faster into an all-out sprint.

Panic tightened Ava's stomach as she punched at the button and sighed in relief as the doors pinged closed and the elevator began ascending. She slumped her back against the wall, ready to burst into angry floods of tears when suddenly the doors sprung open at the next floor and a hand slammed against the metal to keep them open.

Her mouth fell open with a gasp as Nate stood hunched over, his shoulders rising and falling heavily as he huffed for breath and the curls of his hair dangled in front of his eyes.

THIRTY

HIS BLACK TAILORED jacket hung open over his white shirt with dark buttons, a red pocket square tucked into the chest piece as Nate pushed his way into the elevator beside her.

"What the hell do you think you're doing?" Ava pushed off of the wall and went to move past him, but he had other ideas as his arm hooked her waist and pushed her back inside. "Have you lost your damn mind, Brooks?!"

He didn't answer her as his finger jabbed the up button, his hand pulling at the black bowtie strangling his neck and popping a button on his collar so he could catch his breath after sprinting up a flight of stairs.

"I've let you walk away from me more than once. I ain't letting you do it again." Nate took shallow breaths, his eyes squinting as sweat glistened upon his creased brow.

"You can't hold me here against my will!"

"Wanna bet?" he challenged, stepping closer to her but stopping short as the walls of the elevator changed. As they ascended, London's skyline came into view, the city lights dotted around in a bokeh haze against the glass.

That was when it dawned on Nate: elevators and heights, his two biggest fears.

"Are you okay?" Ava frowned, watching him take a step back as though he were wounded, his hand gripping the metal railing for support.

"Yeah," he ground out through his teeth as his hands attempted to bend the rail. "I just hate elevators...and heights." His face grew paler, adrenaline coursing through his veins like ice, making him light-headed. The fight or flight kicked in, making him feel like a caged bull stuck inside this metal deathtrap. However, then his worst nightmare unfolded as the elevator stopped short and made a whirring powering-down noise that made his stomach sink. He breathed out as though he had been punched in the gut, his first instinct to reach for Ava, but then he saw what she was doing...her finger was pressed against the red button on the control panel. "*What are you doing?!*"

"What? You clearly wanted to talk so let's talk." Ava shrugged, feigning innocence.

"Yeah, not in here!" Nate's voice cracked in panic, and he felt as though if he tried to step towards her right now, that his jelly legs would surely collapse.

"Oh, look, you can see Big Ben!" she chirped, peering out the window.

"Ava, *stop*." Nate gawked at her, having no idea why she was being so twisted, his heart thudding inside his throat as he clenched his eyes shut and panted for the air they were running out of in this confined metal coffin.

"What? Is it not fun being held against your will, Nathaniel?" Her voice was sweeter than sugar but colder than ice.

"Okay, you've made your fucking point!" he said, reluctantly opening his eyes and nodding towards the control panel, pleading with her to release him from this hell.

However, she made no attempt to move, crossing her arms as she rested her back against the glass.

"Why did you do that?" she asked with a cold and detached voice. "Making such a godawful scene and putting me in a position that could ruin *everything* for me?"

She seriously wanted to do this right now?

His legs were beginning to shake as the blood left his limbs and a cold clamminess spread across his body. "He had his hands all over your body!" he said after sucking in a deep breath to try to rationalise the anxiety flooding his system.

"We were *dancing*, Nate!"

"You were *provoking* me!" he barked back at her, his voice rattling the tin can they were suspended in. "You weren't just dancing, you were making a fucking point!"

"I thought he was you!" Ava blurted, throwing her hands in the air and shrugging her shoulders.

"Oh, like hell ya did!" he seethed, channelling his fear into anger as the veins pulsed at his temples and bulged upon his neck. He could see himself in the reflection of the glass, looking unhinged with his bowtie hanging loosely around his neck, his dark hair curlier from the dampness of sweat clinging to his scalp.

"And what about you, hm? It's alright for *you* to provoke *me* when flirting with a woman who is half your age!"

"That *woman* is running the pop-up casino to raise money for charity! I was making a fucking donation, Ava!" Nate attempted to push himself off of the railing but faltered when his knees trembled. "Why the hell would ya even care if I did flirt with her? You made it clear you wanted *nothing* to do with me!"

"Th-that's not the fucking point!" Ava screeched, her nails clawing through her hair as her blue orbs sliced into him and she quickly fumbled to steer the conversation back on track. "I could ask *you* the same bloody question; why the hell would you care if I flirt or even *fuck* Peter? Why would that even matter to you—*you're married!*"

"*Because I don't fucking love my wife, I love you!*" Nate erupted, the words bursting from his mouth as though they had been pressurised beneath the surface for weeks, his fist rattling the glass cage as he struck the window.

It took a lot to render Ava speechless. She wasn't one to bite her tongue in a heavy conversation, but Nate had just obliterated all rational thoughts from her mind and left her with fewer words than a mime artist.

She stared at him slumped against the glass and gripping the rail behind him, barely recognisable from that day in the office where they first met. His dishevelled demeanour now revealed the vulnerability he did well to hide behind his masquerade of dominance and cool resolve. Somehow, she had reduced his iron fortress into transparent and fragile glass, a mirror that reflected her own vulnerability.

Ava always pushed herself away from what made her uncomfortable, her biggest fear being that of loneliness. She realised early in life when watching loneliness cripple her father that in order to conquer her fear, she simply had to embrace it, and from that moment on, she never let anyone get close enough to use her weakness against her.

Now her mind was fighting a losing battle between her head and heart as not one ounce of her didn't believe the rawness of his confession. The only part she struggled to trust was his marriage; his description of it felt farfetched and immoral. Why would anyone stay trapped in a union that didn't make them happy? Money could only buy you so much joy, it was something she knew well.

The man before her look crippled but not from sadness or fear, but from the very thing that Ava had avoided her whole life. Nate was crippled by the loneliness he had made for himself.

Call it weakness, call it primal urges, desire, lust, or downright drunken intoxication, but married or not, Ava didn't just *want* Nathaniel Brooks, she *needed* him. She needed him to fill the void of loneliness that only made itself known when he walked into her life.

Ava's guard didn't drop, it crumbled like a detonating building as she crossed the line and dived into sin. Her hands grasped the face of a married man and let go of her morals as her lips greedily stole his.

Nate blinked, his brain taking a second to register what was happening. All fear dissolved from his body through the kiss as his hands wrapped around the only thing that gave him strength. Kissing her was like a butterfly landing on your shoulder or a small bird eating out of your palm.

As she stretched up and looped her arms around his neck, his own wrapped around her body and brought her close to him as though trying to knit her soul into his. He no longer cared for his fears, feeling infinite in this moment with her as he pressed Ava against the glass window and allowed his heart to speak its truth through the kiss.

They knew right from wrong, but the problem now was that as their lips moulded together...wrong suddenly felt so incredibly right.

THIRTY-ONE

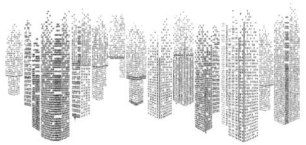

ONE MINUTE they were inside the elevator and the next, Ava's body was pressed up against the hotel room door in the hallway. She swore her breath had turned to steam as Nate's frenzied hands ran across her body, his lips seeking any exposed piece of flesh on her.

The door clicked open as they tumbled into the suite like a hurricane of passion, tangled in one another and uncaring of the objects they knocked over on their way.

Nate heard his suit jacket drop in a puddled heap behind him before feeling her hands claw and rip apart the buttons on his crisp linen shirt, exposing his bare chest to the kiss of cool air. He attacked her neck in a series of devouring wet kisses, his teeth grazing her skin primally. Suddenly, his neck was yanked forward as she tugged upon either side of his loosened bow tie and brought their mouths together again, his groans muffled by her fleshy explorer delving in and out of his eager mouth.

Truly, he couldn't get enough of her, the kiss growing intense and making him burn hotter and hotter until he was sure he would reach supernova. He struggled out of his shirt before tossing it aside, his mouth never daring to leave hers, becoming intoxicated upon the opulent champagne staining her tongue.

Her back pressed against the wall-length mirror, a fog of condensation silhouetted around her, goosebumps rising upon her milk flesh as she clenched her legs together like pressed flowers, her thighs like a rosebud waiting to bloom.

Nate gripped the hem of her satin dress and rolled it slowly up over her curves before discarding it, puddles of white, black, and red on the floor.

"You're so goddamn beautiful..." His heavy brows creased together as though he were trying to decipher a piece of art, his honey eyes drinking in her red lace bra and panties adorning her snowy bodice. Red really was this woman's colour, contrasting against her skin a shade of moonlight, her tresses like fields of barley, black rings around those sapphire eyes, and lips painted crimson. She brought the colour to life; danger, passion, fire, power...*love*.

His mouth meticulously covered her chest in adoring kisses, feeding off every little gasp and whine she made for him. He skimmed his nose down her supple cleavage before his teeth yanked apart the clasp between her perfect tits, freeing them from the red lace holding them hostage.

With her hands tangled in his dark tufts, she guided his mouth to the destination they both shared as his teeth sunk upon her pert pink bud and sucked the moans straight out of her.

He had never tasted flesh so sweet, his fingernails brushing down the ridges on her sides as he lowered while trailing his lips down her smooth tummy, his stubble tickling her flesh.

Ava was convinced he was stealing her air which made no sense since oxygen was required to start a fire and right now there was so much heat surging inside her chest, she felt as though she were about to implode.

Her lashes unfurled as she peered down to see him staring intently up at her while his lips ghosted down over the top of her thigh. She could barely keep herself upright as he delicately lifted and draped her leg over his shoulder, the anticipation crashing through her, and yet, she couldn't tear her eyes away from his, waiting for him to unravel the last thread of decency she possessed.

Nate's large hands grasped her thick curves, tugging her towards him as his nose skimmed up the lace covering her flower, her sweet and earthy scent making him sigh in relief before his tongue ground against her most fragile and quaking part.

"Agh..." she moaned, tipping her head back with her fingers twisting in his unruly mop. He breathed against her slit and sent liquid fire pouring down her thighs, weakening her stance as her back squeaked down the mirror.

With a sharp intake through her teeth, Ava found both of her legs suddenly draped over his shoulders as he lifted her hips, straightening himself and pushing her up against the glass. She gripped his hair tightly, mewling like a kitten in catnip as she stared down at his tongue snaking in past her panties and wrecking her saturated arousal.

The moment her icing coated his tongue, Nate's arms surrounded her lower back as he groaned loudly into her pussy, feasting on her like she was a banquet for one and keeping her tight body held up against the mirror with ease.

Seconds that could have been hours passed before Nate finally lowered her body, now glistening with sensual sweat, down his front, her legs securing around his waist as he carried her through his spacious penthouse suite. He laid her down upon the large bed as though she were made from crystal, delicately removing her panties along with her strappy high heels.

She stared up at him in awe, watching as he held her foot and tenderly pecked her instep before standing there admiring her naked body as he slowly undid his belt and slacks, freeing his arousal. Without taking his eyes from hers, he leaned over slightly, his hand upon the base of his angry girth before he spat a single drop of fluid down onto his crown. He was lust incarnate, his movements building the tension between Ava's legs. Her eyes were black with desire as she watched him pleasure himself until she could take no more of his teasing, growing restless as her impatient hands grabbed a hold of him. However, before she could get a grip, Nate suddenly flipped her onto her stomach and tutted his tongue.

"No, tonight I'm going to need you to go slow." He chuckled a husky noise with his mouth against her peach, his teeth dragging across it and instantly silencing her. "No smart-mouthed comebacks? Really?" He couldn't help the smirk etching its way onto his face as he heard her suck in a breath to fire out a snide remark but bet her to the finish line as he dived his face in between her cheeks and thrust his tongue inside her.

"*Fuck me!*" Ava squealed in shock, her palms slapping against the mattress as Nate grinned against her wet mess, loving that little expression she used whenever he caught her off guard.

His arms slid under her thighs and his hands hooked her hips, fingers pressing into her pale skin as he pulled her ass higher and sank her face deeper into the sheets, muffling her beautiful begging for more of his ruthless kisses. He released one arm so that he could let his digit wander through her dewy petals, coating it in her nectar before easing inside her and curling down so it dragged against her swollen walls.

His tongue wrote a love letter in cursive circles around her swollen clit, untangling her insecurities and rationalising her feelings for her until they were reading from the same page.

On and on he kept up this euphoric cycle: a little lick here, a stroke of one or two of his fingers there, until he felt the slight spasm of an impending orgasm and abruptly stopped, pulling her back from the edge and making her whimper in protest.

"No, you don't get to cum just yet, sweetheart," Nate grunted as the front of his body pressed down against her back, his hand securing around the front of her dainty neck and craning her head back to look at him. "*Slow*," he ordered, leaning over here and kissing her passionately from their reversed positions. There was no chance he was giving her what she wanted after she deprived him for so long. He was a fickle man who held a grudge, something he wasn't proud of, but in this moment he revelled in his flaw.

Ava whined against his lips, her elbows struggling to keep her upright as she felt his bare manhood prod into her soft cheek. Whatever it was about him, it had a hold of her, his touch taking control of her mind, body, and soul.

"*Please...*" she whimpered against his lips, the first time she truly ever begged a man, but for some reason, with Nate, it didn't feel as demeaning as she thought it would...it felt *empowering*.

Nate heard her voice split apart, saw the need in her azure galaxies, and felt the splintering crack through her resolve. He wasn't going to push her any further so angled his hips forward and in one swift motion, slipped inside of her. His long drawn-out groan harmonised with the high-pitched whine leaving her lips as their flesh melted into one.

"Holy...shit..." He almost sounded like he was in pain as intense pleasure gripped a hold of his balls and squeezed. It had never felt so good. With a steady, slow gait, he rolled in and out of her, his face buried into the side of her neck as his humid breath tickled the shell of her ear. He kept himself up with one hand as his other continued to hold her throat, his groans turning into growls as he felt her push back onto him, meeting him thrust for thrust as her hand tangled in his hair.

Losing himself inside her, his knees parted further as he allowed his mass to sink down on top of her, both of his hands now masking hers as their fingers entwined and fisted the bedsheets.

"Nate...I...I want..." Ava said breathlessly, no sense in the words coming from her lips, their bodies rolling in a sensual and intimate wave against one another as she nuzzled her cheek into the side of his damp hair that smelled like the seaside.

"Give me *all* of you, Ava," he groaned into her ear as he continued to pin her down with his weight, "every last piece." Nate didn't just want to make love to her body, he wanted to make love to her thoughts, undressing her conscience wall by wall until he was fully inside of her.

This didn't feel like fucking to Ava, it felt more intimate and savouring as though the couple had all the time in the world to consume one another, as though what they were doing was a completely moral act.

She found herself wanting to reach inside of herself and give her lover a unique part of her that no one else had—she wanted to give him the best of her.

Ava didn't just finally submit to him, she took a

flamethrower to those protective thorny vines she had wrapped around herself for all this time.

Nate listened to her body, the way it sang for him, the way it trembled as though walls were coming down inside of her. With desperate movements, he flipped her onto her back, his arms hooking under her shoulders as his hands cradled the back of her head. His eyes swam in restless pools of blue, watching her come undone as his hips found hers again and her legs hung over his ass. She secured her arms around his neck, pulling him towards his oasis as their mouths met in a union of adoration and their bodies gorgeously tangled in one another.

Her soft cries grew louder as she hit her crescendo and Nate tightened his grip on her so he could speed up his pace, growing rougher and more impactful. He stared down at her, watching her face crease, a sight to behold in the throes of pleasure as she struggled to remain focused on him.

"I...I fucking adore you," Nate grunted in between the harsh swing of his hips and felt her hold back, felt her resist the high as though her orgasm would finally admit what she was terrified to. He pulled her head up so he could press his forehead to hers, his gaze was fiery and intense as he growled, "Don't you dare hold back, don't you dare fucking hold back. Give me all of you, Ava."

Her mouth crashed up against his as pleasure burst apart at the seams, her core imploding in on itself. Rhythmic convulsions rippled against his length, gripping him tight as her screams were muffled by his tongue claiming her mouth and swallowing her cries.

The feeling of her coming undone around him didn't just tip him over the edge, it catapulted him as his stomach pulled tight, his balls ready to erupt as he finally let go of all that emotion built up inside of him over these past few weeks. Hot spurts coated her walls, bathing her insides with his silk as he emptied all the love his heart had to offer into her.

Whether it was moral or not, and whether she chose to admit it, Ava knew one thing for certain in that moment... she needed his love.

THIRTY-TWO

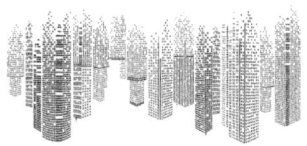

THE MOON YAWNED as it rose from slumber and stretched across the lovers' bodies, the sun now kissing the cotton candy wisps in the sky as it dances across tangled limbs laid bare upon crisp white sheets.

Nate and Ava woke to face each other's tender embrace and even in the brief state of sleep their bodies found one another. One small sigh from smiling lips led to one small moan from kissing mouths, slowly burning for each other like the sticky hot wax trickling down the side of a candle.

A shadow danced sensually back and forth across the thick carpet that was burnt orange by the sunrise flooding into the suite. Ava mounted Nate's lap, her hips rolling on and off his manhood, every movement fuelled by desire and nothing else.

"That's my girl...just...like...*that.*" Nate groaned long and deep, just like his cock that dragged against her silken humid walls.

With fingers entwined like their souls, Ava pinned his hands against the headboard, a dark giggle leaving her lips as she peered down and shook her head coyly. "Oh, I'm not your girl," she purred, her golden hair on fire as it curtained her face, "I'm your *woman*." She adored the burning look in his gaze that her words elicited, cherished the way his biceps tensed and pushed the network of veins to the surface. Her back arched as she used his hands as purchase, her ripened peach now twerking on his sensitive tip and taking claim on his body.

"Sh-*shit*," hissed Nate, his arms shaking as he tried to keep his composure, but she was making it impossible with the way her wet little cunt was fucking his rock hard crown. "Slow down, you're gonna make me...*fu*—!" His voice broke apart as she cut him off by abruptly sinking down onto him. Skin slapped upon skin, her breath fanning across his face as she moaned against his length stretching her out deep inside.

"Gonna make you *what*, sir?" Her lips grinned dirtily down at him making him want to fuck that filthy mouth all over again.

"Ava..." he growled a warning, but she paid no notice to it, speeding up her movements until sweat began to saturate the roots of her golden nest. Nate couldn't take it anymore; he reversed the grip of their hands, taking both of hers in his right as his left abruptly clamped her pretty throat. "You naughty little brat"—he tightened the grip on both of his hands—"you wanna act like a petulant child?" Nate brought her face close to his and watched that beautiful masochistic smile light up her face as she innocently nodded her head. "Then you're gonna fuck Daddy's dick until you remember how to behave."

Ava's eyes sprung wide at his words. She had never heard such a term in the bedroom, and was confused and conflicted by the level of arousal it stirred within her. Nothing short of a squeal left her lips as he rocked up into her with the force of a freight train, one short stab before slowly dragging himself out of her.

"More," she whined, eyes closing and lips opening in slow motion. He answered her with hands suddenly appearing on her plump derrière, nails biting into her flesh as he took a tight grip, released, and then suddenly swatted her flesh before gripping her again. "God, yes!" Ava squealed as strong hands gripped her slim hips, holding her down as he drove up inside of her, hard and fast to make her cry out again and again for more.

"Suck," he ordered, placing his digit into her mouth, groaning loudly as she did as told, swirling her hot little tongue around him and mimicking that day in the board room. His finger popped out of her mouth only to pop straight into her puckered star.

"*Gah!*" The foreign object inside her rear was a pleasurable intrusion as she tensed and gripped his finger.

An erotic symphony filled the morning air: skin slapping skin, blended moans, the headboard rattling against the wall, and the springs in the mattress begging for mercy. They both melted into one another with a grip of hair here, a scratch and bite there.

Ava had never experienced such aggressive sex before and despite the sunlight shining upon their glistening bodies, it was a darkness that was creeping out of both of them, their sinful fantasies being shared. It felt like they were taking their frustrations and jealousy out on each other —the fact that they didn't belong to each other and morally shouldn't.

All morning, every corner of Nate's hotel suite was baptised in their unholy union of flesh on flesh, dancing around the elephant in the room. They both knew they were destined to fail—the complications of work, marriage, and the inevitable distance that would be put between them —but neither of them could stop.

"I can't tell you the number of times I've stood in this shower and dreamt of having you in here with me." Nate smirked against her ear, stood behind her in a soapy embrace.

"Oh? Pray tell, Brooks."

"A gentleman could never reveal such derogatory thoughts."

"If you tell me...I'll make sure it happens..."

"You're like the Energizer Bunny!" Nate laughed as his arms wrapped around her middle and pulled her back close to him. It never failed to amaze him how she fitted his body perfectly, the epitome of a missing puzzle piece. He couldn't help but wonder what kind of sick joke God was playing on him by giving him his other half at the wrong time.

"What's wrong?" Ava asked, feeling his arms tighten around her tummy as though he never wanted to let go.

"It should have been you..."

"What?"

"Nothing," he sighed softly and leaned down to kiss her shoulder. "Finish getting cleaned up, sweetheart." He spanked her bottom to cut the conversation short, chuckling as she jumped from the unexpected sting upon her blushing rear. As he stepped out of the shower, he allowed himself a moment to watch the stream of hot water meander down her gorgeous figure, the steam misting around her as though she were a walking shampoo commercial.

"Are you going to stand there and perv on me all day?" Ava teased, her back to him as she lathered soap into her hair.

"You say that like it'd be a bad thing," Nate chuckled,

wrapping a towel around his waist before making his way out of the luxurious bathroom.

When Ava eventually joined him in the room again, a towel wrapped around her body, the nutty aroma of coffee filled the air.

"What do ya British call it...a 'cuppa' is on the side table for you," Nate said with a wink as he pulled a tight pair of black boxers up around his package.

"I don't drink coffee." Ava rolled her eyes at the small white mug placed upon her bedside, wondering why every man she had slept with felt the need to make her coffee the morning after.

"I know. That's why I made you tea." When Ava stopped short to look up at him, his eyebrows creased together in confusion at the look on her face. "What? You didn't think I'd forget the coffee machine fiasco, did ya?"

She couldn't help but feel a warmth seep throughout her chest and stomach, different from when his hands wandered between her legs. This feeling was different, more deep rooted within her. Whatever it was, it pushed her to ask, "Would you like to get breakfast with me?"

"Can't."

"Oh..." She couldn't help but slump her shoulders in defeat.

"It's too late for breakfast so I've already arranged brunch." As soon as the words left his mouth that look appeared on her face again. "What is that look?" Nate couldn't help but laugh.

"Oh, nothing..." Ava grinned as she dropped her towel and walked towards the only man who could ever steal her heart.

THIRTY-THREE

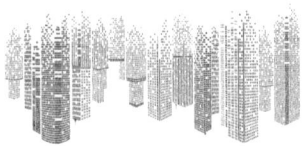

THERE WAS no walk of shame as Ava strode down the hotel hallway in the afternoon dressed for the evening prior. It was clear that she was not attending some charity event or gala today, her makeup long gone, and her hair tossed up into a messy bun of sorts. Despite the train wreck of her life and her whole ensemble, she felt an odd sense of wholeness as she almost skipped away from Nate's suite with a dreamy smile on her face. That was until she saw a flash of messy ombre curls.

"Sam...?" Ava called out towards the woman dressed in a black jumpsuit, clutching her head and slowly turning to look. Sam's eyes widened as she dropped her purse, scattering vodka miniatures and complimentary toiletries. She quickly grabbed what she could before darting towards the elevator, her finger mashing the button. "Samantha?!" Ava yelled and began running down the long hallway towards her friend. The elevator doors pinged opened and Sam rushed inside, but Ava wasn't taking no for an answer as she quickly removed her red high heel and launched it at the closing elevator doors.

"*Jesus, Mary, and Joseph!*" Sam exclaimed from inside as the red stiletto wedged between the doors in the nick of time before springing them open.

"Good morning," Ava chirped a little breathlessly as she retrieved her shoe and stepped in beside her friend.

"Afternoon."

"Good evening?" Ava asked, placing her heel back on.

"No, it's afternoon," Sam corrected.

"No, I meant did you *have* a good evening?"

"Aye, 'twas eventful." Sam tilted her chin upwards, refusing to meet Ava's eye as she sniffed her nose and crossed her arms.

"How was Peter's suite?"

"Aye, 'twas braw." Sam turned to face Ava with her eyebrows raised. "Are we honestly going to ignore the pirouetting elephant in this lift with us?"

"No, of course not." Ava sighed, turning to face Sam as well. "Can we just go for a cuppa and I'll explain everything?"

"What's there to explain? You're knobbin' the boss that just so happens to have a wife."

"How did you know he was married?!" Ava's stomach sank despite the bile rocketing up her throat.

"Facebook, hen! See, this is why I keep telling you to get it!"

"Oh God." Ava turned away, her palm against her hot cheek as she shook her head. This wasn't how she wanted to come clean to her friend. "I swear at the beginning I didn't know he was married, Sam."

"So you're telling me you're coming out of that man's hotel room today despite *knowing* he's married?" The elevator doors pinged open as an elderly couple stepped in, but Ava's silence spoke loud and clear of her sin. "You know, lass," Sam hissed down to her side, "I know you've been dipped more times than a chip and that you're a bit of a top shagger and all but this is low...*very frickin' low.*"

"It's not like that, Samantha! It's complicated!" Ava hissed back, growing angry at her friend's judgemental tone.

"Oh, it is, aye? So complicated you couldnae tell yer best friend about it?"

"I didn't want you to think less of me!" Ava fired back loudly, ignoring the little hunched over couple that was nervously glancing at each other before looking at the pair of squabbling idiots behind them from over the silver rim of their glasses.

"You had me message Peter like a complete tit that night and then you went and fucked him *anyway* even though you were probably, at that point, involved with a *married* man *who also happens to be our boss!*" Sam trilled, the old couple gasping as they turned and looked at Ava, the woman with her frail hand upon the cross pendant of her necklace.

"That isn't what happened!"

"Isn't it?"

Ava felt like the steam fuelling her veins had finally run out as she slumped against the mirrored wall of the elevator and hung her head.

"I didn't mean for *any* of it to happen. It just did," Ava croaked, her eyes unable to lift from her feet. "I didn't tell you because, of all the people, I cannot bear for my best friend to see me as I currently see myself...as a home-wrecking *cunt.*"

Sam's eyes widened along with the old couple as they gawked at Ava's language. A moment of silence passed in the elevator as her friend gnawed on her bottom lip, deep in thought, before releasing an exasperated sigh and throwing her hands into the air.

"C'mere, lass," Sam huffed, stepping forward to wrap her arms around Ava as she gave an awkward smile towards the *aww*ing couple in front of them.

That was the thing about best friends; they never judged you for your fuckups in life, no matter how much of a mess you made. True friends were your ride or die and would take your secrets, flaws, and fuckups to the grave with them.

———

"I'M SO SORRY, I wish I had just told you everything at the start," Ava huffed as she sunk back into Sam's bed wearing the matching onesie she kept at her house.

"Well, aye, that would have been helpful!" Sam laughed, sitting next to Ava with her infamous llama mug poised at her lips. "We've known each other since we had to start wearing bras. You're more than just a pal to me, we're practically family, and you should know you can tell me anything. I'm not angry at you I'm just—"

"Please don't say you're just disappointed," Ava whined as she hid under the pillow.

"No!" Sam laughed, grabbing the pillow off her. "I'm just *annoyed* that you lied to me in the first place, but I understand why you did. If I was in your shoes, I dare say I'd no have the backbone to fess up to my mate either."

"I know. I was just so ashamed because first of all, he's my boss, and if Dad finds out I'm done for, and second of all, no matter Nate's circumstance he is still married." Ava let out a long-exhausted groan as she stared up at the ceiling and dragged her hands down her face.

"So...just walk away then! There's plenty mare dick in the sea!" Sam chuckled, jabbing Ava in the ribs and cursing when her tea spilt onto the bedsheets.

"I wish it were as simple... I can't explain it but every time I try to stop and walk away something just pulls me right back in as though I am somehow tethered to him. I see every red flag and still I choose to ignore them because when I'm with Nate I feel like I have all the missing puzzle pieces in my arms, but one wrong move and I drop them all. It is completely disconcerting to feel so secure and yet on the edge of losing everything at the same time."

Ava wished she could explain the difficulty of hiding her feelings for this man, how their delicate relationship fed off stolen glances, disguised touches, and secret encounters.

"Holy fuck..." Sam gaped, ignoring the stain on her white linen sheets as she stared at the confused look on Ava's face. "Ava, are you in love with him?"

"What?!" Ava blurted, sitting upright and scoffing, "Of course I'm not!"

"You bloody are, aren't you?"

"No!"

"Ye ken yer blushing, aye?"

"It's just the tea, it's hot!" Ava shot back as she pulled at the pillow.

"You love him, don't you?" Sam pressed, putting her mug down as the pair played tug-of-war with the pillow that Ava hid behind. The pillow finally snapped from Ava's grip and she was able to see the tormented expression on Sam's face. "Ye ken I hate to ask this, lass, but what are you going to do?"

"There's nothing I can do. In a week's time he's going back to America...back to his wife and back to his real life."

Ava pushed the words past the lump in her throat. "And I'll simply fade away from his existence and prove to be nothing more than a very silly and very unfortunate mistake. We will forever remain oceans apart."

"Yup, and you'll end up alone forever with spaniel ears for tits and surrounded by the cats that will one day eat ye," Sam teased, the pair screaming as Ava shoved her friend out of bed, but in doing so, sent burning hot tea flying as Sam clattered to the floor with an almighty thump. "Oh my God, are ye alright?"

"No! I just bloody burnt my—" Ava stopped, realising Sam wasn't talking to her.

"There's been a fatality!" Sam's head popped up from the side of the bed, the llama mug presented to Ava with one ear now missing. "Barry...his ear..." She pouted with a sniff before glaring at her friend. "What are you laughing at? It's naw funny! He's gonna be made fun of now by all the other mugs!"

"You're right," Ava said, struggling to compose herself. "He'll look like a right mug now."

"Dick," Sam hissed.

"Fanny," Ava shot back.

"Tit!"

"Mug fucker."

"Husband fucker," Sam blurted before immediately covering her mouth as Ava's jaw dropped with her tongue in cheek as she suppressed laughter. "*Hey*! Where are you going?"

"I told you earlier, Nate is coming over tonight for dinner." Ava chuckled as she began changing into her dress from the night prior.

"What are you cooking?"

"Steak," she replied, struggling to pull the tight dress down over her stomach.

"Hear that, Barry?" Sam said, earning an eye roll from her friend as she looked down at her mug while her tongue repeatedly prodded the inside of her cheek.

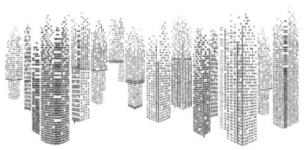

THIRTY-FOUR

"OH, *FUCK MEEEE!*" Ava whined, standing in front of the hob as she stirred one pot only for the other to throw a tantrum. To add insult to serious injury, the door buzzer went meaning that Nate had arrived on time for their dinner date. "Bugger!" she squealed before buzzing him into the building.

She was nowhere near ready considering her hair was still tossed up into a messy knot and she hadn't yet changed out of her housework clothes—an unflattering baggy white tee sporting some elegant food splatters hung from her shoulders and her favourite pair of skinny jeans from three years ago that were frayed at the thighs.

"Hello...?" Nate called out in her hallway, his head peeking through the red door, fearing he had gotten the wrong apartment.

"Just come in! I'm in the kitchen!"

He sighed with relief as he heard Ava's sweet voice that sounded a little flustered. A smirk lit up his face as he stepped inside the warmly lit apartment and paused to take his shoes off—a habit drummed into him by his mother.

Following the melody of gentle guitar, he placed a bottle of wine down onto the table and stopped behind Ava with his jaw resting upon the floor as his eyes dropped to her perfect peach wrapped in tight denim.

"Don't worry, I'll be changing in a moment," she said over her shoulder as she saw the horror on his face. "I lost track of time!" However, while she was turning the steaks over, giggles escaped her lips as she felt Nate stand directly behind her, his fingernails grazing up the backs of her thighs before his hands dipped into her rear pockets.

"Don't. I like the jeans...*a lot.*" He chuckled huskily with his lips skimming down the side of her neck as he palmed the sumptuous curve of her ass.

"Nate, I'm *attempting* to cook dinner here," she bubbled, her head automatically tilting to the side as she felt his teeth nip and tease at that spot below her ear that had a direct link to that spot between her thighs.

"My apologies..." he whispered between the kisses planted across her exposed shoulder before moving back up to nibble upon her lobe. "Am I distracting you, ma'am?"

Ava's lashes fluttered as her heart trembled inside her chest. This man had a way of sending shivers down her spine that felt both hot and cold. He was a fever that left her needing to be fed.

"Yes, now bugger off before I ruin dinner!" She laughed breathlessly, chewing down on her lip to stop herself from caving and releasing the moan that was upon the tip of her tongue.

However, Nate wasn't taking no for an answer, his hands still in her jeans pockets as he abruptly spun her around and pinched her chin to focus her attention up on him.

"Good," he said in a gravelly tone with a dirty smile on his lips that pressed down against hers. His hazel orbs remained opened to witness her reaction, revelling in the way she melted into his kiss as her lips parted eagerly against his own. He tickled her upper lip, but upon feeling her bratty little tongue trying to force its way into his mouth, he abruptly pulled back.

"What are you doing?" She gasped, her face paling as she watched Nate casually back away and begin to open random drawers in her kitchen.

"What does it look like I'm doing, sweetheart?" he retorted plainly over his shoulder as he pulled out some cutlery.

"Giving me a blue bean by the looks of it!" Ava ridiculed, huffing as she turned around to tend to the dinner again and trying to ignore the bemused noises Nate made as he set the dining table.

DESPITE HAVING SPENT the afternoon preparing a meal from scratch, Ava had barely eaten her dinner, her appetite much stronger for something else in the way of American cuisine.

"This is nice," Nate sighed, sinking back into her sofa as she sat upon the opposite end with her ankles crossed over his lap.

"What? Drinking wine out of a regular wine glass instead of a coffee mug for a change?"

"No." He laughed, reaching forward to place his glass on the table. "This...just like...sitting on a sofa with you talking. It's a luxury I don't really get back home."

"Do you not spend any time with Natalia..." Saying her

name out loud made Ava feel like the worst woman alive, as though she were betraying womankind.

"Nope, not really. We're passing ships in that house. She comes home, we sit at opposite ends of the table to eat, and then when we're done, we go our separate ways."

"But that sounds absolutely miserable!"

"It is! I haven't heard Nat laugh since our wedding day and even then, I think she did it for the camera," he sighed, his head falling back as he stared up at the ceiling. "It's not like I haven't spoken to her about all of this or even tried to make us more compatible. It's just that each time I have, I am very bluntly told to suck it up and think of the bigger picture, the real incentive behind why we're together. I'm told that we're just simply happier apart than we are when we're together."

"Oh, *fucking hell* that is tragic..." Ava huffed, sipping on her wine as she rubbed at her forehead.

"Do you believe me?" Nate frowned, looking at her with his stomach in knots. He knew all she had to go on was his word and even that looked like a flimsy piece of paper considering the nature of his character when he was around her.

"I honestly do but what I don't understand is...if you're both that unhappy...why stay together just for the sake of money and social status?" She watched as a pained look creased at Nate's features and sent her stomach dropping. "I'm sorry, that's really not my place to ask that considering I am 'the other woman' and all."

"Hey, no... don't label yourself that," Nate admonished as his hands subconsciously began rubbing her feet. "It's easy for anyone on the outside looking in to label us what-ever shitty thing they want to but they ain't us...they don't share the same emotions or struggles as we do and they sure as shit don't understand that just because you aren't alone doesn't mean you aren't crippled by loneliness on a daily basis.

"Now, I ain't tryna excuse my less-than-honourable actions here... I know that what I'm doing to Nat ain't fair... but I have spent years of my life putting everyone else's happiness before my own, so *sometimes*...you just can't worry about whose feelings are gonna get hurt in the pursuit of your own happiness. A good life ain't one without problems, Ava. A good life is one with *good* problems." If there was one lesson learned for Nate, it was that a person in one month could make you feel what a person in one year could not because time meant nothing —character did.

Ava felt as though a heavy weight had been sat upon her shoulders, staring at this man who was living in her own hell. He was the one thing she feared above all else: lonely.

"So, you've never just Netflix and chilled with any of the long list of women that have thrown themselves at you?" she asked with a smirk, deciding to lighten the mood.

"The list ain't long!" he scoffed.

"Oh, really?" Ava said dubiously with lowered brows. "What's your number?"

"My number?"

"You know...the number of people you've *been* with."

"Oh, let's see..." Nate's thick brows pulled together as he stuck his tongue in his cheek and recalled his pitiful sex life that was mostly active during his college years. "Twenty-five-*ish*, give or take."

"Th-that's it?" she asked, choking on her wine.

"Why, is that bad?"

"Not at all, I just presumed that the sexy, serious, and perfect Nathaniel Brooks would have more notches on his belt!"

"I'm not as perfect as you think, sweetheart!" He laughed, shaking his head as he pinched the bridge of his nose.

"Oh yeah? Show me *one* defect, Brooks," Ava challenged, grinning as he sat upright.

"Alright, see this tooth?" He pointed to one of his incisors. "*Fake.* Lost it tryna impress a girl at college."

"What, like in a fight?" Ava's eyes widened like a drama-thirsty vampire.

"No...more like me tryna bust open a beer cap with my tooth and then, *pop!*"

"Oh my God, that is tragic!" she squealed, her hand covering her mouth as she burst out laughing so hard that gentle snorts left her nostrils. "You're a closet dork!"

"Yeah, well, never judge a book by its cover!" Nate laughed with her.

"Mhm, a very tall, dark, and sexy book at that!"

"Alright, alright, what's your number?" Nate asked, taking her wine glass off of her before she ruined her sofa—that after all, was a very Ava thing to do. However, when her laughter fell short and she made a move to stand up, he gripped her ankles and pinned them down to his lap. "Oh, no you don't. Spill!"

"Do you promise not to judge me?"

"Scout's honour," he swore, adoring the sweet blush on her cheeks and the adorable pout of her lip.

Damn, I gotta bite that lip soon.

"Well...I, uhm...kind of...lost count after...the hundred mark...?"

"Hundred?!" Nate's eyes nearly popped out of his skull.

"Yeah okay, look, I know what you're thinking," Ava whined, pulling her knees up as she hid her face behind them. "'Oh, what a slut, never been in a relationship in all her twenty-eight years, what a complete waste of a wom—'"

"Actually, no, that's not what I'm thinking at all," Nate interrupted and reached across the sofa to pry her face away from her legs. "I'm thinking it's kinda devastating that you've never been cherished by a man in the way that you deserve. At least...not until now."

Ava shyly met his eyes, and felt for the first time in her life, as though her black-and-white heart was made to be coloured in his colours. She slowly crawled her way over to him, straddling his lap carefully as she cupped his face. In his embrace she felt so safe and at home.

"We should really talk about our situation..." Nate whispered against her lips that were brushing against his own as his hands wandered up her white shirt and skimmed down her curvaceous figure.

"Not right now...right now, I just...I need you closer."

THIRTY-FIVE

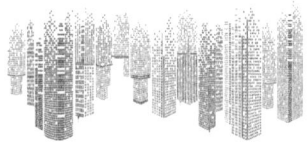

MONDAY HAD CREPT up on Ava before she had a chance to rationalise the predicament she was in. No matter how bitter the pill was going to be to swallow, she had to somehow approach Nate and end the affair before it was too late. She was already in far too deep with him.

Tired and drained of motivation, she leaned forward in the staff kitchen and placed her lunch into the fridge. However, when a hand abruptly smacked across her behind, she shot upright with a sharp yelp as she whipped around to face the culprit.

"Nate!" Ava swatted his arm, pointing a warning finger at the dark and mischievous smile he beamed down at her. "Have you lost your mind?" she hissed, pulling him aside away from the doorway that looked out onto the busy department. "Not at work!"

"Good morning to you too, Ms. Archer." He chuckled a husky noise by her ear, his breath tickling her helix and sending pleasurable shivers down her spine that she tried and failed to ignore. "I haven't stopped thinking about you all weekend." It was the truth. Even after their countless rounds of sex during the weekend, his brain refused to switch off from her.

"That's lovely," Ava faltered as she was cornered up against the kitchen counter by him. "However, can we *not* do this here?" Her blues darted back and forth between the doorway and Nate's earthy eyes that were turning into dark forests.

"Did you miss me?" he asked as he placed two hands on either side of her onto the counter, boxing her into his embrace and obscuring the exit from her line of sight.

"What?" She squinted up at his whimsical expression that held a genuine level of curiosity to it. "Yes, of course I did, but we should really talk later wh—"

"I missed *this*." Nate's hands grasping her peach interrupted all words and thoughts as she sucked in a gasp of air. "God, do you have any idea how much I want to fuck you on this counter right now?" He felt recklessly out of control, caring not who would see this debase display between a boss and his assistant. His nose ran up along her carotid as he inhaled long and deep to savour her floral sweetness upon the back of his throat. It amazed him how her pheromones alone had the power to make his cock twitch inside his pants.

Ava couldn't resist temptation, her back arching as she pressed her stomach up against his grey blazer and silently cursed herself for choosing to wear her tailored suit and not a dress or skirt today. Excited breaths left her lips as she trailed her fingertips down his stomach over each button and then to the buckle of his belt until she finally felt his hard and aching need pushing against his zipper. It aroused her to no end the effect she had on him.

"Down boy," she breathlessly giggled against his lips, her heart pounding against his own as she pressed closer and cut off any morsel of space between them. Her cheek turned in to his touch as he cupped her face, his eyes running across her in such an intimate manner that it made her forget the function of breathing.

"I love you," he whispered against her perfect lips as he paused to stare beseechingly into her eyes. He meant every word of it so brutally candidly that he felt like a damn fool for selling himself short to a woman back across the Atlantic who never made him feel a drop of devotion as he did with Ava. Staring into her blue diamonds, Nate finally knew what love was.

Ava froze on the spot, those three words having the power to grip her heart in a vice-strong hold and squeezing a droplet of fear from her. However, as she stared back into his eyes, it felt as though her jigsaw was finally complete, no matter if a puff of air could shatter such a fragile piece of art. "Nate, I—"

"Yeah, Kensington told me he filled the retraction yesterday, can you believe it?"

Nate and Ava turned their attention to the voices approaching the small kitchen before jolting apart in the space of a heartbeat. Despite their nonchalant appearance of leaning against opposite ends of the kitchen, their hearts were pulsing amongst *other* areas of their body.

Ava gave the two suits a tight smile and a nod of her head as they entered the kitchen before glancing back at Nate's stoic expression, watching his lips twitch as he struggled to hide his amusement. When the two gents were preoccupied with the fridge, Nate wiped his brow, readjusted his awkward crotch situation, and huffed in relief, causing Ava to cover her mouth to suppress her amusement.

AVA SPENT the rest of her day digging her way out of her workload and avoiding any further near misses with Nate. She was currently sat at her desk tasked with the *glamorous* job of balancing the remainder of the late Oliver Forbes's inheritance between the remaining Forbes family members. It was a very mundane task to undertake but involved a lot of time-consuming paperwork and auditing. However, as her finger jabbed the enter key to complete the transfer from Oliver's escrow account, a large error popped up like a big dirty mark on her screen. One side of Ava's nose scrunched up in confusion as her finger stabbed away at the enter key, again and again, willing the pop-up error to die until she huffed in defeat and slumped back in her chair. She pinched the bridge of her nose, knowing she was burnt out from being chained to her computer all morning, and decided to take a break.

As Ava stared into the office's bathroom mirror, her thumbs pressed under the purple crescent welts staining the delicate flesh beneath her eyes. It was perhaps the worst thing about being so pale, the fact that every little blemish and imperfection showed up like the Blackpool Illuminations.

"Oh, Ms. Archer!" boomed the ostentatious voice of Charlotte Forbes as the cubicle door banged open behind her and caused Ava to jump like a spooked kitten. "My apologies, did I frighten you?"

"It's fine," Ava croaked with a hand against her fleeting heart. "And please, call me Ava."

"Ava," Charlotte agreed with a gracious nod of her head as she joined her by the sinks and turned to notice her dabbing a cold paper towel beneath her eyes. "Oh my...busy weekend, dear?"

"Is it that obvious?" She chuckled, looking at Charlotte

before back at her reflection. "I swear there isn't a facial out there that could rejuvenate the hours of overtime these eyes have undergone!"

"Pish-posh! All you need is a top-quality eye cream and the best concealer on the market, my dear!" Charlotte denounced as she opened her clutch bag and pulled out a few tubes of various beauty products. "Please, do allow me?"

Ava was taken aback by the woman's generosity as she let Mrs. Forbes dab makeup upon the unsightly blemishes. "That's very kind of you, thank you, Mrs. Forbes."

"Oh, anytime, and please do call me Charlotte." She finished smudging in the mixture with Ava's skin before announcing, "There, good as new!"

"My God! That really is a fabulous concoction you've got there!" Ava marvelled at the non-existent stains under her eyes.

"My secret is that I add a tiny amount of tanning pigment to it, works wonders!" Charlotte said from the side of her mouth and chuckled.

As Charlotte began putting away her makeup, Ava glanced down into her purse, noticing a lipstick in an oddly familiar shade of orange that she couldn't pinpoint where she recognised it from, however, the colour made her stomach sink deep into her stomach and fill it with dread—for what reason, she did not know.

"Lovely shade isn't it?" Charlotte said, noticing Ava's stare.

"It's a very unique colour..."

"Yes, it was a gift from my beloved Oliver... Anyway, best be off, my dear. Remember to get some beauty sleep!" Mrs. Forbes abruptly breezed out of the ladies' toilets leaving Ava wondering if her first impression of the woman had been too hasty.

When Ava was back at her desk, the brief time away from her computer had given her a new sense of motivation as she rolled up her sleeves, ready to tackle the dreaded system error still upon her screen.

"Let's have a look then, Oliver...why is your account blocking me..." she murmured to herself as she clicked her tongue thoughtfully in time with the clicking of her mouse. "What in the hell?" Her eyes widened as she clicked onto his inheritance fund that the firm was safeguarding until a settlement was made. "No...no...no, that can't be right..."

Where the balance had once shown the amount of £250,000 now showed as *nil*.

Panic gripped a hold of her gut as she frantically treaded through the entire system, desperately searching the audit trail to see who released those funds from his account, but every lead came up blank as though a phantom had come in and wiped Oliver's account clean. She left no file unturned, flicking through every financial document she could find, seeking an explanation to the quarter of a million pounds that had ludicrously vanished.

It didn't matter who Ava's father was, if she didn't find that money her arse was on fire.

"*Fuck me,*" she croaked with a hand covering her mouth, anxiety creeping up her throat as she took a deep breath and wiped her palms on her legs. Many people would bury their heads in the sand at this point and wait until some other unfortunate soul spotted the error, but that wasn't Ava. Whether she buggered up the system or not, she would put her hand up and own up to her error.

She gathered all the documentation on Oliver's

accounts and pushed her legs one in front of the other until she reached Nate's office with a polite knock on his door.

"Sorry to disturb, but the weirdest thing just hap—" Ava stopped short with a gasp, gawking at the silver set of eyes that were cutting through her like shards of ice.

Sat upon the ledge of the large mahogany desk, Mr. Archer glared so furiously at his daughter that Ava didn't need to question why he was here. Her eyes glanced down at Nate, who was peering sheepishly over his shoulder, sat on one of the chairs in front of her father.

"Ava," Tom seethed her name through his teeth as his fists gripped around his cane. "Shut that door and get in here now. You have a lot of explaining to do, young lady."

THIRTY-SIX

"DAD?" Ava shut the door behind her and treaded carefully towards him and Nate. "Wh-what are you doing h—"

"*Sit!*" Tom boomed with the authority of a magistrate, the type of commanding aura that cut through the thick air and made Nate's shoulders jump and Ava's legs collapse into the seat.

"Dad, just let me explain, the account it—"

"Do you realise how many security cameras I have around this department?" Tom asked, stalling Ava's train of thought as her lips attempted to manifest the confusion she felt into words. "Twenty-six cameras, Ava. Twenty-six cameras *including...*" His cane lifted and stabbed the air pointing to an object behind her.

Ava turned around and glanced up at the small black box mounted above the office door, a red light blinking down at her as Nate's hands dragged down his face.

"I don't understand..." she faltered, turning around to see the reddening face of her father.

"That camera safeguards not only our clients' assets but

this firm's as well." Tom pushed off the desk, his walking stick slamming down onto the floor near Ava's feet as he spat, "What it does not safeguard is *my daughter fucking my business associate!*"

Twice in her life had Ava heard her father swear: once when he found out about the young gentleman her mother was having an affair with, and now this moment right here. Her brain stuttered, her eyes taking in more light than expected as every part of her went on pause while her thoughts played catch up. She felt like a camera flash, stuck in time and unable to connect with the world that was spinning out of control, her perfect jigsaw puzzle falling in slow motion to the floor.

Nate's stomach was so tight with dread that he doubted he'd feel a fist to his gut right now. He turned to look at Ava, her frozen pale expression was similar to that of his own when Tom had busted into his office not long before Ava had shown up.

"This isn't her fault," Nate said, reaching for her and almost flinching as he felt the ice cool of her frail hand. "This is on me. I take full responsibility for—"

"Shut your damn mouth, Nathaniel!" Tom snapped, running a hand through his thin wintery hairline. "To think of what you've done behind your poor wife's ba—"

"Oh, come on, Tom," Nate ridiculed, sitting upright in his seat as he threw his hands in the air before leaning upon his knee. "You of all people know that what me and Nat have isn't as black and white as it is on paper!"

"Perhaps not, but do you not both realise the gravity of the situation you have forced me into? That footage was not something I stumbled onto by mere chance; it was presented to me by the head of security!"

"*Mike?*" Ava finally snapped out of her catatonic state

as she looked up at her father who gave a sharp nod of his head. Burning hot betrayal ran through Ava. Mike, the sweet security man who had wished her good morning for the past few years, and sure, likely had a crush on her, had now just grassed her into her father for no gain of his own other than to boost his own selfish ego.

"And since we are not the only people to know about your ludicrous relations, word will spread like wildfire. I cannot be seen to let this scandal be brushed under the carpet. I am forced to discipline you both for this!" Tom stumbled backwards, his hand clutching the sharp twinge in his chest as Ava instantly jumped to her feet with concern creasing her face. He swatted away her fretting hand and sighed, "What were you both thinking?"

"I *wasn't* thinking, it just happened, Dad!" Ava wailed past her heart lodged inside her throat like a piece of glass. "And I swear it won't happen again."

Nate's eyes widened at Ava, and he felt as though she had just blown out the flicker of hope inside of him. She couldn't have meant that, could she?

"You're correct, it will not happen again," Tom attested, straightening himself against his walking stick and clearing his throat. "Ava, you are suspended until further notice, and Nathaniel, you will return to the firm back in Manhattan—effective immediately."

"*What*?!" Nate shot up out of his seat as Ava's jaw shattered on the floor.

"Dad, you are in no state to come back here yet, let alone run this department by yourself!"

"*You will not speak of my state!* I have run this firm for many years, most of which were spent without much of your aid, and I will continue to do so. Do not forget your position in this department, Ava—you are but a simple assistant to me," Tom fumed down at Ava, his expression softening for a fleeting moment before turning to stone as he snapped his attention away from her. "Now get out of my sight."

Nate's heart was pounding so fast inside his chest, this loss of control making him feel like he was falling down a very dark and lonely rabbit hole. He turned and watched Ava cover her mouth as she darted out of the office, a look of pain twisting her perfect features.

"You're a damn fool, Tom," Nate growled with his fists clenched. He couldn't stand by and let Tom pound down on her like that; it was unfair after the part Nate had played in all of this. He was getting off far too easy.

"I beg your pardon?" Mr. Archer sputtered as though someone had slapped him with a wet fish across the face.

"She practically ran this firm while you were away! You have her sit at that desk looking pretty and quietly filing away your shit when you have no idea what that woman is actually capable of!"

"Oh, and you do? Disgracing this firm, my daughter, and your damn marriage by frolicking around this department and using Ava like a cheap whore that—"

"I am in love with your daughter!" Nate boomed for the whole department to hear and didn't give a crap about the repercussions. "And she is *not* a whore." He pointed a finger directly into his business partner's face. "I have made many monumental mistakes in my life, but that woman out there, she ain't one of them."

As Ava's finger mashed the elevator button, she wished that Sam had turned up for work today, needing just one person in this department to not be burning their eyes into the back of her skull right now. The doors pinged open and she rushed inside to escape the shame clouding her but just before the doors began to shut, Nate dived in beside her.

"Nate, please don't," Ava whimpered as the metal doors slid shut behind him but gasped as his fist suddenly smacked against the red stop button. "What are you doing?!"

His fear of heights and confined spaces was nothing compared to the fear of losing his everything.

"Look, I like control in every aspect of my life but some things I just can't control. Like the way I feel for you, Ava. However, I can control my circumstance which is why when I am home, I am explaining to Natalia that we don't belong together." Nate spoke with the conviction of a priest, reaching his hands out and wincing when she took a step back and shook her head.

"You cannot do that! You ca-can't just move your life over here for me!"

"Sure, I can!"

"No, you cannot and will not, I won't allow it." Ava moved away from him, her eyes welling with regret. "We aren't a love story, not after what we have done. There is no happily ever after for us."

She utterly detested the crushed look on his face, the way the hope drained from his expression, the sweetness of honey turning bitter in his eyes. But then his head lifted, his face lighting up like a warrior mustering the strength for one last stand.

"Then how about a happily ever *now*?" He gave her a weak smile, a small attempt at lightening a shitty situation— like hell he was giving up on her just because shit got real.

"Nate, I'm so sorry but I—"

"No, no, no," Nate cut across her and closed off the distance between them as he held her face in his hands and made her look at him. "*I'm* sorry. I am sorry for getting you into this mess, I'm sorry for pushing you away, I'm sorry for ever lying to you in the first place. But what I am *not* sorry for is for ever meeting you and falling madly and uncontrollably in love with you, Ava Archer."

Words failed Ava as she stared up at the man who made everything feel so incredibly right in the world. She hated how pathetic she felt when trying to say those three words, feeling as though there was a flaw in her code that blocked her from conveying such things.

Three little words, two joining of hearts, and one monumental insecurity were all that stood in her way.

To the ordinary person, that simple phrase could be exchanged as easily as a *thank you* or *hello*, but to Ava, it was a mountain that had to be climbed slowly with a clear and promised view of the top.

"It's okay, I don't need you to say it out loud," Nate chuckled softly as his thumb swiped across her lower lip. "I just need to know...do you feel *anything* for me?"

Ava knew she could lie right now and make her life so much easier. Yes, it would be painful upfront like pulling off a plaster, but then all her problems would disappear, and everything would return to normal. However, she wasn't much of a liar and ever since lying to her best friend, and everyone else for that matter, she silently vowed to never do it again.

Nate stared down at the shy nod of her head, his eyebrows jumping in bewilderment as his lips failed to hide his glee. There was a chance of her loving him back? Hell, he'd take it!

"But I need some time to think...please, this is all so much so soon."

"Of course, look"—Nate took a step away from her to

give her some room to breathe, not wishing to push his luck any more than he had—"I'll come over in a few hours, we can talk properly then and take this at your own pace. Will that be alright?" He knew what they had was chaotic and fast, but it didn't feel rushed, it felt raw and real, something that he didn't want to wait the rest of his life to experience. He wanted it right now and with her.

"That is more than alright," she gushed as she reached out for him, her arms securing around his waist as she embraced his comforting scent and pressed her cheek against the heart that was slowly helping her to climb that mountain. "I'll be waiting."

AVA'S MIND was like a storm at sea, having no idea what she was going to do now that the cat was out of the bag and tearing up everything around it. She had no idea how she was going to handle her father nor how much damage this affair was going to do to her reputation. Her career would certainly be up shit creek once word got out. And then, of course, there was the matter of Nate being willing to give up absolutely everything for her and not knowing if it was just infatuation or genuine love that guided him.

One thing was for sure and that was that Nate wasn't thinking with his head. She had never met a man like him, driven by passion, and not just physical passion, but a fierceness to seize life and go after what he desired. Being with Nathaniel Brooks made Ava feel like she was inside some romance book sat gathering dust upon a shelf with a wrinkled binder and dog-eared pages. But unlike those stories, his love didn't burn slow like an ember, it burned hot and fast like a firework. In every sense, Nate was her American dream, her fourth of July.

She dragged herself up the stairs leading to her apartment, her phone pinging inside her coat pocket as she pulled it out and frowned down at the screen.

1 New Message, RBE BANK ALERT:

Ms. Archer, the funds have been secured and are ready for collection in branch at your earliest convenience.

AVA ROLLED her eyes at the scam attempt and placed her phone back in her pocket as her heels echoed down the long hallway towards the red door at the end. When she reached her apartment, her hand hesitated upon the brass doorknob, her eyes squinting down at it. The weirdest sensation overcame her, a chill prickling its way up her spine as she reached forward and opened her door that she didn't remember leaving unlocked.

"Hello...?" she called out as she cautiously stepped into her silent apartment, the only noise coming from the tap dripping into the sink, each one reverberating around the spacious apartment like a cymbal. "Sam...are you in here?"

Something wasn't right and she couldn't place what. The air was so brittle that it could snap, and if it didn't, Ava knew she surely would. Walking down her small hallway, she stopped inside her tidy living room, but something felt out of place as though someone had been through here and disturbed it, a single ripple deviating a calm lake.

Apart from family, there was only one other person who

knew Ava kept a spare key under her doormat and that person was—*bang!*

Ava let out a squeal as her apartment door was slammed shut behind her, spinning her heels in a one-eighty to turn around and face the culprit.

THIRTY-SEVEN

"WHAT IN HEAVEN'S name are you doing here?!" Ava shrieked as she peeled herself down from the ceiling, her heart pounding so fast that her ribs ached from the battering.

"I suggest you take a seat, ol' girl." There was no hint of humour nor apology in which Peter Taylor addressed her.

"What?" Her brows knitted together.

"Sit."

"You know what? I'm a bit fed up of the men in my life telling me to 'sit' today so you have about three seconds to tell me why the bloody hell you are in my apartment right now because I've had it up to here wi—"

"I said *sit*, Ava." The distinct noise of metal cocking against metal prickled the air as Peter pulled back the steel hammer of the revolver and extended his arm.

Fear sat like a cushion across Ava's mouth and nose, her vision turning vignette as she stared down the barrel of a gun.

"Is that—I—I mean how do you have a—"

"Do you have the money?" he cut across her and saw

the look of dumb confusion on her face. "You should have received a call or text from the bank this morning."

The penny dropped in her stomach like a missile of dread as Ava recalled the text, she had received from the bank moments ago. "Peter, what have you done?"

"I haven't got time to explain—check your online banking now," he clipped out, stepping towards her with the gun still pointed at her face. "Do it!"

Ava's shoulders jumped as he barked his commands, her hand fumbling inside her pocket for her phone as she shakily did as she was told in a state of blind confusion. When her eyes dropped onto the most recent bank transaction, all the air escaped her lungs as though someone had sucker-punched her in the gut.

"How is this possible?" Ava sputtered, staring down at the chilling and unsettling £250,000 sat in her account that she knew belonged to the late Oliver Forbes. "I never agreed to release those funds. I...I never signed anything...I never..."

The reality abruptly sat down upon her chest like a ton of crushing bricks as she recalled the morning of her birthday.

"Actually, before I go"—Peter pulled out a document from his back pocket and approached her—"would you mind signing this?"

"What's that?" Ava asked.

"It's just the missives you typed up for me the other day, you forgot to sign them off and I'm on my way to post them today." He smiled, setting the folded piece of paper in front of her and handing her a pen.

"You...you set me up! You tricked me!" She felt as though her legs were going to give way from the betrayal as she stumbled back and gripped on to the dining table.

"We work in law, Ava. Deception is our art." He

lowered the gun, closing the distance between them, his voice stern as he stated, "You're going to take a trip to the bank with me and withdraw that money right now."

"Like bloody hell I am! Are you *crazy*?!" Her eyes nearly popped from their sockets as she shook her head and tried to rationalise this insanity. "Look, if you're struggling for money, I can help you in *other* ways, Peter, but this is wrong, it's misappropriation of funds, you could go to ja—"

"Oh, no, gorgeous!" He laughed the type of sardonic laugh that made Ava's gut clench and twist in on itself. "You see, it isn't *my* name or signature on the records so if there is anyone that's going to be locked up behind bars..." He raised the revolver, causing her to flinch as he used the barrel to sweep away a stray curl over her shoulder as he whispered, "It's going to be you, ol' girl."

The overuse of that pet name had always irked Ava, but the use of it just then made her mouth fill with disgust as she gulped down the bitterness of his betrayal. She felt like a damn fool for ever letting this disgusting man climb between her legs.

"Let me make myself clear," Ava ground out from between her teeth as she tilted her chin up defiantly and ignored the weapon pointed at her. "I will take *no part* in these illicit affairs with you, Peter."

"Oh, but you will unless you want Daddy finding out what a *cheap nasty slut* his little girl is by fucking his business partner on the side," he sneered, but faltered when Ava scoffed at him, her palms leaning back on the table as her eyes scanned the room as if searching for the fuck she did not have.

"Do it! Be my goddamn guest, you pathetic sack of testosterone!" She shrugged.

"You want to do this the hard way?" he growled, flicking

his tongue over his lip, and chuffing at her unperturbed bratty face scrunching up before pulling out his phone.

"What are you doing? Who are you phoning?!"

"Put her on." His tone was glacial as he held up his phone for Ava to see the pixelated images of what appeared to be a warehouse of some kind.

"I...I don't understand, what is th—" She stopped short gasping, her trembling fingers covering her mouth. The scene was unbelievable and sent Ava's mind reeling, unable to comprehend or process the images being sent by her wide eyes. She looked away, then looked back to see if the scene of her best friend gagged and bound, mascara running down her horrified face was still there. It was.

"*Sam! Where is she? What the fuck have you done to her?!*" The fear split apart in her voice as she jolted forward only to be shoved back against the dining room table.

"She's fine, for now," Peter stated as he ended the video call and swiftly placed his phone in the top pocket of his green peacoat. "And you have my word that no harm will come to her as long as you keep your pretty mouth shut, and for once in your life, do as you're told, Ava Archer."

———

AVA'S HEELS pattered along the marble floors of the grand atrium inside the bank. The sandstone building had seen many eras and its interior decor gave off a type of art gallery vibe—if the artists lacked soul and passion, that was.

She peered along the aisles of brass counters, paying no notice to the lifeless suits that stood behind them, her eyes counting the many chandeliers lining the walkway, and her neck craning back at the intimidating archways and the golden ceiling that rose into a stained-glass dome.

On the outside, Ava was very much like a duck drifting peacefully on water, but beneath the surface, her legs were frantically trying to keep her buoyant. The last thing she wanted was to assist Peter with his fraudulent intentions, but she didn't see any other option when her best friend was held at gunpoint God only knows where. The very thought of something happening to Sam made Ava stall on the spot, fear gripping her throat and turning her heart to winter.

"Madam? Can I assist you at all?"

Ava's head snapped out of her trance, her heart rattling inside its porcelain cage as she nodded her head too quickly and gulped down the sick inside her throat.

"Yes." Her voice trembled and the older woman stood before her frowned at Ava's nervous disposition. She couldn't afford to mess this up since Peter made it quite clear what would happen if she didn't return with the money so she forced her posture to relax and plastered on a fake smile as she explained, "I am here to collect the funds I arranged. My name is Ava Archer."

The moment her name left her lips, the banker's eyebrows popped up, her frail hands straightening her grey uniform as several others turned around to look at the surprisingly young blonde withdrawing a large sum of money today.

Everything about this situation raised alarm bells.

"Ah, Ms. Archer... Yes, we were expecting you. My name is Adeline and I'll be assisting you today," she said with a tight professional smile, one that highlighted the creases at the corners of her silver eyes brought on by the repetitive expression. "Come right this way!" Her hand motioned forward before she led the way down a side corridor, the clicking of their heels echoing and matching the cadence of Ava's erratic heart.

She was escorted into a small office, one that felt more like an interrogation room if not for the small withering plant on the desk and the picture frame of two children.

"Oh, don't mind them, madam," Adeline chuckled as she saw Ava flinch at the two security guards stood by the door. "It is common procedure that they are here when we are dealing with this type of transaction."

Yeah, the illegal kind?

"Of course," Ava said with a sheepish smile and a polite nod of her head to the armoured guards before finally taking a seat at the desk.

"So…" Adeline sighed the type of sigh that came at the end of a long workday as she sat down behind her computer. "I shan't keep you long, Ms. Archer. However, there are some necessary checks and routine paperwork we must get out of the way first before we can approve the withdrawal. I do hope that is quite alright with yourself?" When she received a tight smile and nod from the young woman she continued, "Very well! First is the matter of identification?"

Ava didn't feel like she was walking on eggshells—it was a minefield she was tiptoeing around. She pulled out her purse, her fingers ice cold, and the pads of which were numb as she fumbled for her ID card. The card, along with some coins, clumsily scattered to the floor as Ava squeaked and bent down to pick the mess up with a series of flustered curses under her breath before passing over her ID.

"That's quite alright," Adeline soothed as she ran her identification through the system.

Ava had nothing to hide with her identity, however, she felt as though wanted posters of her face were stuck to the lamp posts lining the streets of London as she waited for those tense few seconds before Adeline approved it.

"Next is just to run through some of the security questions you answered a few days ago, Ms. Archer." At this, Ava's ears pinned back as she recalled the cover story that Peter had carefully fed her before going inside the bank. "Can you confirm the amount you are withdrawing today?"

"Two hundred and fifty thousand."

God, that is a disgusting amount of money to say aloud.

"And the reason for this withdrawal?"

Not a fucking clue.

"I am purchasing some estate abroad," Ava stated, gulping down bile as every muscle in her body clenched from the lie that would put her behind bars.

"And where does this estate reside?"

"Mexico," Ava answered automatically, her stomach sinking as Adeline frowned at the computer before Ava blurted, "No, sorry! It's...it's *New* Mexico." Her shoulders barely relaxed as Adeline smiled and struck the enter button on her keyboard.

Minutes that felt like hours in hell passed by as more gut-probing questions were asked until the blessed announcement came that Ava had passed the checks and that Adeline would now go collect her money from the vault.

It was when Ava was finally left alone that she clutched her chest feeling as though her heart was going to derail. Sweat tickled at her hairline as she took calming breaths to try to rationalise her anxiety and this madness.

She had no idea why Peter desperately needed that money, her only theories being that of his greed for wealth or that he found himself in a bind with bad people. However, the truth was, she could come up with a million excuses to try to defend his choice but at the end of the day, he was still breaking the law and still had a gun held to her friend's head.

He betrayed her and for that Ava would ensure he'd pay the price.

As she chewed at her nails and tried to think of a way out of this situation, her get-out-of-jail free card presented itself by way of a mobile phone that sat charging on Adeline's desk. Footsteps suddenly began echoing down the corridor behind her so acting upon impulse alone, Ava dived across the desk and swiped the phone, placing it inside her jacket pocket before calmly sitting back in the chair.

"Your money, madam." Adeline motioned towards the black box that one of the guards carried. "There's just one more thing to..." She frowned, staring at her desk before darting around it and began pulling open drawers causing the breath to hitch inside Ava's throat. "It was here earlier, I'm sure... Ah, here it is!" She pulled out an e-signature pad and slid it across the desk. "If you could just sign anywhere in the box to confirm you've received the funds today, please."

Ava exhaled through her nose as she reached across and quickly scribbled her name down on the pad before asking, "Is that all?"

Please for the love of God say yes.

"I believe so, however, do you have transportation arranged, Ms. Archer?"

"Yes, my driver is waiting outside." Ava cleared her throat and stood up too quickly, her head rushing as she stumbled but caught herself on the back of her chair. "Weak ankle," she brushed off with a small laugh before anyone could make a fuss.

Once the awkward pleasantries were out of the way,

Ava was escorted outside by the two guards who placed the money box in the trunk of the blacked-out Range Rover before Ava climbed into the back seat.

"Everything in place?" Peter asked without turning around in the driver's seat but before Ava could answer, a chap at her window made her startle as she turned and slowly lowered the window.

"Ms. Archer," one of the guards said as he passed her an envelope, "the code for the box is inside." However, as Ava tried to snatch the envelope from him too quickly, he pulled it back, frowning through the plastic visor of his helmet. "Is everything alright, miss?"

Ava's head snapped towards Peter, her eyes glancing down at his side whereby the silver tip of his gun peeked through his arm and body, fear gripping hold of her throat.

"Perfectly fine," Ava croaked, swiping the envelope through the window before the engine roared and tires cried for the help that Ava could not.

THIRTY-EIGHT

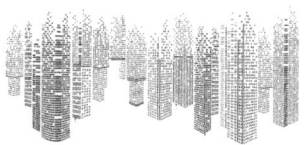

THE SUN HAD long set as they drove for the better part of an hour, darkness engulfing the country roads they took and sheets of rain distorting the view from the windshield as the wipers struggled to keep up.

Ava's nails had been chewed down to the quicks, her anxiety pulsing through her veins like steam as her stomach remained knotted since her apartment. However, it wasn't fearful thoughts consuming her mind; it was anger. It was the burning resentment she felt for the man who sat in the driver's seat, his blatant lack of respect as they sat in silence without any explanation of where they were going or why. She wanted to go through every memory spent with him and take a flame thrower to them. Peter's betrayal was the worst kind of all. He was her silent assassin, an inside job where he had earned her respect only to shatter it by threatening not only her but her best friend too.

Ava's icebergs burned a hole into the back of his curly red mop as she glanced down at the mobile she had obtained. Taking nervous glances between it and Peter, she swiped her thumb across the screen and blessed relief rushed through her, grateful that the older generation was not as tech-savvy to have adequate safeguarding—ironic considering the woman worked *in a bank*!

In the darkness of the cabin, Ava panicked realising her face was illuminated in white and concealed the phone in the nick of time as Peter looked up at her in the rear-view mirror and finally broke breath.

"For what it's worth, I truly am sorry for all of this," he sighed but frowned as the blonde scoffed and shook her head. "I hope you understand that I had no choice, ol' girl."

Ava had been fed enough bullshit by the men in her life to last her a lifetime.

"Two things," she clipped out, sitting upright to meet his gaze in the mirror. "One: I am not your 'old girl', and two: we *always* have a choice. Whether we make the right one or not is down to us."

"That's easy for *you* to say with your cosy apartment down on *Mayfair* and your bloody membership at the country club—all thanks to Daddy's deep pockets!" he barked, tightening his grip on the steering wheel until his knuckles turned pale.

"You know I work *damn hard* to earn my place in this world!" Ava seethed through her teeth, her face a picture of offence as the muscles corded tightly in her neck. She took a deep breath and sat back in her seat. "We may have walked different paths to reach the same point in our lives but I am a firm believer that it is not the *environment* in which we grow but *the people* in our lives that shape us into who we become. And right now, you have kidnapped someone that helped me become the woman I am today, the one person that I cherish more than *any* worthless piece of material or asset. And I can promise you..." Ava leaned forward with her hands balled around her fury as her eyes sliced into the back of his skull. "If *any* harm comes to my Samantha...no amount of money will *ever* be able to fix the carnage I will unleash on your life. I swear to you if you hurt her, I will *destroy you*, Peter."

Although she could not see his face, she heard how her lethal promise had affected him in the way of him gulping down his nerves. She bit back her smile knowing that if Sam had heard her, she would have likely cracked a Liam Neeson joke at this point. However, even Sam knew that there was one thing that mattered to Ava above all the rest and that was family.

He would learn the hard way to never come between two sisters, not joined by blood but by spirit.

Eventually, the car pulled up onto a set of docks east of London. Shipping containers were stacked high above them like badly packed Tetris blocks, cranes towering over them like giant watchmen. Seagulls squawked, circling around Ava's head like vultures as she stepped out of the car and peered up at the warehouse sat upon the sea bank, the water stormy against two white beams from the headlights.

"Move," Peter ordered, carrying the money and leading Ava by gunpoint towards the two sliding doors left ajar in the warehouse.

Inside, aisle after aisle was stacked the height of the large building with pallets and containers. Ava struggled to orientate herself with where they were, her only clues coming from the salty air that was tainted by the odd sting of alcohol and the seagulls' song that echoed around the corrugated building.

She felt like a lamb being led to slaughter as they walked down one of the aisles, her eyes desperately trying to pick some information from the storage boxes until they turned a corner and her legs seized as though the cement they walked on had spread up into her limbs.

Between several stacked pallets, Sam sat on the ground in front of a forklift, her hands bound in rope and a dirty rag gagging her. The moment she noticed Ava, her eyes lit up with hope as muffled squeals left her lips.

"Sam!" Ava sprinted towards her, skidding to a stop as she peered down and saw the state of her friend. The whites of her eyes were red, her pale cheeks glistening from fresh tears, and dried brown blood sat crustily upon her temple. "What did he do to you?!" she shrilled, dropping to her knees in front of Sam and pulling down the gag from between her teeth.

"*You!*" Sam seethed, tugging against her restraints as she looked to the side of Ava, her finger pointed at Peter. "You ginger-headed cunt! I shoulda maxed out that fucking credit card when I had the cha—"

"Oh, shut your fat gob," he blustered, suddenly appearing behind Ava with the revolver clicking harshly by her ear. "Envelope. Hand it over."

"Take it then." Ava held out the envelope and waited until he bent forward to retrieve it before spitting up into his face with a spiteful scowl on her face.

"*Hah!* Classic, Archer!" guffawed Sam. Ava would have cracked a smug smile if not for the cool steel colliding with the side of her head and knocking her face-first to the ground. "You fucking dick! I'm gonna rip yer balls to yer gullet, you twisted sick son of a—"

"Can someone please gag that loud-mouthed Scotswoman already!"

Everyone stopped and turned to the latest arrival to the shitshow. Mrs. Charlotte Forbes emerged out of the darkness like an emerald dressing in dollar bills.

With her cheek pressed to the ground, Ava gawked up at the woman who had shown her only kindness that day and squinted at her in bewilderment as she sauntered towards Peter, her arms wrapping around his neck before her coral lips met his.

"What is going on?" Ava looked at Sam as she sat up.

"Nae clue, hen." Sam shrugged and pointed to Charlotte. "Her twatty driver knobbed me on the side of the head and the next thing I knew I was in this shithole!"

"You are lucky that that was all that Henry did, dear," Charlotte remarked as she pushed Peter's auburn curls away from his eyes that were staring at her like a brainwashed and lovesick zombie.

"Oh, wait! I had it here a second ago..." Sam stated, gathering everyone's attention as she awkwardly searched her jacket pockets with her wrists still bound. "Aye, here it is!" She pulled out nothing from her pocket apart from her middle finger primed and flipping off Charlotte, much to the Forbes woman's non-amusement.

Ava's mind was reeling as she tried to piece together the puzzle. It was no secret that Charlotte reeked of the title gold digger, but what didn't make sense was why she was having relations with Peter if it was money that she was after. Women like her utilised the men in their life, usually for power and money, so why did she need her defence attorney?

That was when it hit her like a bag of gold to the head.

"You're using him," Ava gasped, staring up at two sets of squinting eyes.

"I beg your pardon," Charlotte said with her nose turned up.

"That explains why you were trying to seduce Nate that day in the meeting room. You needed someone high up with enough clearance to release Oliver's inheritance from his escrow account!" However, then it dawned on her that Charlotte had seduced Nate prior to Oliver's death which meant... "Oliver didn't kill himself, did he, Charlotte?"

Peter's attention snapped to Charlotte, his thick brows creased together as Ava's theory began to make sense.

"I have no idea what you are talking about but for you to accuse me of such things is indeed an offence! It is bad enough that they detained poor Freya for it!" Charlotte hissed before composing herself and turning to Peter, her paw cupping his cheek as she scratched the underside of his beard. "I thought I knew what love was with my Holden, but I realise now that I was just a young pretty thing for him to admire, just another collectable on his shelf. Peter is the love of my life and we are going to have our happily ever after, isn't that right, my love?"

Peter squinted at Charlotte for a moment as if weighing up both stories but eventually his shoulders relaxed as he nodded and turned his cheek into her touch, causing Ava's stomach to plummet.

"You can't possibly believe her, Peter!" Ava bleated.

"Guy's a fud, thinking with his dick like every other yin oot there."

"Why would you do this?" Ava croaked, her eyes pleading with Peter to see sense.

"*Why*?!" he barked incredulously as his arm looped around Charlotte's waist. "Why would I choose a woman that wants *more* than just a quick fuck to fill the lonely, sad, and pathetic void in her life? Come on, Ava."

His words struck Ava like a knife straight to the gut as her eyes dropped to the ground. Trust a man to play on a woman's insecurities. That was when an idea came to mind as her chin tilted up defiantly and she decided to play with his ego.

"So, you're just going to run away into the sunset together and avoid the law. *That's* your master plan?"

Ava knew it would warrant a rant from Peter, but truthfully, she wasn't listening, especially as the corrupted pair professed their undying love for one another. Sitting in front of Sam, she discreetly passed the mobile phone back to her, praying that her Hail Mary would save them both.

"My love, I do have to confess one thing..." Charlotte sighed, her lips pouting as she stared down at Ava. "Seeing *her*, your prior lover...it does irk me."

"Darling, she means nothing to me. She is nothing but collateral damage with a pretty face."

Ava felt her throat tighten, her eyes sting with the threat of tears, but she balled her fists refusing to let this disgusting couple get the better of her.

"Regardless, her existence bothers me." Charlotte moved to stand behind Peter, her chin resting upon his shoulder as she whispered in his ear, "Get rid of her."

"*What?*" Peter and Sam gasped in unison.

"Prove your loyalty and love to me—kill her."

"You said no one would get hurt..." Peter challenged over his shoulder.

"Yes, but a woman with a pretty face and a sharp mind is a dangerous thing. I don't want her ruining everything for us..." She planted her lips at the spot behind his ear, the spot that Ava knew he adored to be kissed. "You love me, do you not?"

"Of course, I do!"

"Then..." She raised his hand that held the gun and pointed it towards Ava's paling face.

"Peter..." Ava's eyes were full of regret and fear, her

head shaking as her lips trembled to make words. "D-don't do this...p-please."

"Aye, listen to her, man! You're naw seeing sense! This is Ava!" Sam roared, tugging at her rope as she pulled at Ava's shoulders to desperately try to pull her into safety.

"I'm...I'm sorry...ol' girl," he croaked, the gun rattling as it pointed to the spot between her brows.

Ava stared down the dark tunnel leading her to death, waiting for the images of her life flashing before her eyes, but no such thing happened. She couldn't fight nor flee, a caged bird that was frozen in a state of blind panic. Her brain had stalled and all she could think about in that moment wasn't that she was going to die, it was that she was meant to meet Nate tonight and now would never get a chance to say goodbye.

It was odd that when faced with death, how your brain went from blind denial of your fatal reality to accepting your fate in a matter of seconds.

Ava didn't close her eyes, bravely staring up into the eyes of her killer and wanting him to be haunted by the colour blue for the rest of his undeserving days. "Do it," she sneered with a dry mouth. "Do it, you goddamn foul *ma—*"

Bang!

Sam's screams tore through the air above the gunshot that reverberated around the warehouse. Her wrists were raw as she fought against the rope, trying and failing to catch Ava as her friend went tumbling down to her side like a dead tree and lay in a pool of crimson.

THIRTY-NINE

EARLIER THAT NIGHT...

NATE WAS glad to have finished up the gruelling process of handing over his workload to Tom Archer. The experience was up there with getting teeth pulled at the dentist. His business partner was keen to ship him back to the States as soon as possible and was in an ass of a mood all afternoon —not that Nate could blame him. Not after what he did to the guy's daughter on his office sofa...coffee table...desk.

Yeah, okay—dick move.

"Nathaniel, you're not in love with her," Tom had said as Nate was leaving the office. "You have not known her long enough to profess such feelings and I won't have you make a homewrecker out of my little girl."

"Perhaps I've not." Nate smiled at the floor before looking up at Tom. "But I know that what I feel for Ava is that deep-in-your-gut feeling that is both familiar as it is uncharted. She is the first woman to know every piece of me and accept everything that I am, everything that I have done, and everything I will one day do. What I feel for her is unapologetically chaotic and if that ain't love then...I don't want to know what the damn thing is." He chuffed through his nose before heading out of the office knowing that he will never have that man's blessing until the day he made things right by his daughter and filed for a messy divorce.

However, none of that seemed to matter now that he was bounding down the sidewalk with pip in his stride. The molten-silver sky grumbled with the promise of rain, but Nate couldn't care less as he swung his briefcase by his side. It was funny how with everything blown to shrapnel that he saw order within the disarray and that the problems he had feared from the start were actually the solution to everything.

He was going to make this right.

They were going to find a way to make this work, and for the first time, his happiness wouldn't be the front cover of the brand that the people in his life created for him.

Nate skipped his way up the stairs leading to Ava's apartment block, his finger pressing down on the silver call button. After a few moments without answer, his brows knitted together as he tried again before finally trying her on her cell phone.

Straight to voicemail.

"She wouldn't have forgotten...would she?" he uttered to himself before retreating down the steps and staring up at the building to see that her lights were the only ones out. With a heavy sigh, he found himself sat down on the bottom step seeing no other option than to wait on her return.

And wait he did.

After an hour of sitting in the evening chill, in nothing but his suit, he finally heard the door open behind him and snapped upright like a dog waiting on their owner's return before slumping as an elderly woman trotted towards him.

"You alright, love?" she asked with a frail Welsh accent, frowning down at Nate. "Locked yourself out?"

"No, I'm actually waiting on a lady—tall, blonde, incredibly beautiful...her name's Ava?"

"Oh, Ms. Archer!" The woman beamed fondly of *his* girl and he couldn't help but beam a hopeful smile at her. "She left a little over an hour ago with a gentleman."

"A gentleman?" Nate's smile fell flat as he slowly rose to his feet.

"Yes, the redheaded gent—he's often round at the weekends. Terrible racket they make," she chuckled, pulling her rain bonnet up over her head.

Nate had only been punched a few times in his life, but none of those times compared to the sucker punch given by this old lady. Ava knew they had only tonight to sort things out and that he was leaving for New York in the morning. *Why would she leave with Peter?*

The sinking feeling in his chest answered that question; she wanted to give him a message and what better way to tell him there was no room for him in her life than *this*?

"Thank you," Nate said with a bittersweet smile as he looked down at the scuff marks on his polished Italian shoes.

"Are you alright, m'love?"

He looked up at the woman's pale teal eyes and with a feigned smile said, "Nope. Not even a little bit."

The lady opened her mouth to speak but before she could, Nate had already turned away from her, briefcase in hand as he began walking down the crescent-shaped street that was shaded by crimson trees.

With slouched shoulders, his body felt heavy, legs like lead pins, and with each step, he felt the warmth evaporate from him. Every memory with her was a burning Polaroid being held up to his face. The time spent with her lit up his life. She set his soul on fire with words that breathed oxygen into him and with a touch that brought heat to the gasoline in his veins. But now his soul felt like a dying ember.

The reality sunk deep inside him until the heartache left him feeling frozen as though concrete were drying in his chest.

I'm not enough for her.

His feet came to a stop as he turned around and stared down the street he had just walked. Nate hardly ever thought with his heart, but as his mind made up a million reasons why Ava would have left with Peter and not him, he couldn't help but wonder if it was his brain or his heart trying to find excuses for her actions.

As he lifted his foot to retreat to her apartment, a flash of light shredded the sky before an almighty clap boomed from one side of London to the next. He peered up at the dark clouds as pellets of water stung his face and made his stormy eyes blink.

Nate wasn't a superstitious man by any means, but as the rain saturated his hair and suit, he knew this was the universe trying to give him a sign. It was the one thing that Ava had been trying to tell him all along. Not all romances are love stories.

"ANOTHER." Nate raised his empty glass to some barmaid inside some crappy bar that sold crappy booze with crappy clientele—himself included in that remit.

"You sure about that, mate?" she replied, frowning down at the several empty glasses in front of him, grimacing at the way his brows lowered and his nostrils flared. "Another coming right up!" Her palms rose defensively as she cleared the empty glasses and poured him a fresh scotch.

Nate huffed his thanks to her, running a hand through his wet hair before rubbing at red bleary eyes. His suit jacket hung in a drenched heap over the back of his barstool, his pants clinging uncomfortably to his legs, and his damp white shirt rolled up at the sleeves. People were giving him concerned looks but he couldn't give a damn and instead sneered at them with a nod of his glass like the drunken idiot he was.

Everything about his situation sucked: having to go home to the States, having to return to a life-sucking succubus, having to go back to his mundane job with his mundane assistant that wasn't *her*.

How the hell was he meant to go back to the strict structure of the real world when she had come into his life like a goddamn hurricane and disrupted everything about it like the most chaotic and perfect storm?

One last shot, he thought to himself as he pulled out his cell and tried calling her for the hundredth time in the past hour. As expected, her voicemail greeted him, his fist almost managing to bend the metal pressed to his ear as he imagined her arm around that redhead instead of him. He slammed his phone down on the bar before knocking back the burn of alcohol along with the sting of rejection.

He knew Ava was afraid of commitment and terrified of abandonment—any guy with half a brain could figure that one out. But did he really mean so little to her that he wasn't worth an explanation or even a *goodbye*? Just phase him out of her life because it didn't matter anyway since he would be out of her hair soon enough, was that it?

The worst part was being ghosted by someone who already haunted your every waking and sleeping thought.

Taking out his wallet, he pulled out a silver ring and stared at it as he slid it onto his finger. Natalia only wanted the rings for the wedding pictures that would forever be published in some tacky tabloid somewhere. She said that it spoke a louder message to not wear their rings, that it would tell people they didn't need some expensive piece of metal to bind their love and marriage. *What a fake fucking message*, he thought before taking it off and dropping it into his empty glass.

He remembered watching Nat come down the aisle on their wedding day. Damn, she was beautiful. Her long dark hair was tied up, showing off the perfect curve of her long neck, and all he could think of was kissing it. Her skin was a flawless and deep honeyed brown that stood out against the ivory dress that stuck to all the right places. She was the definition of beautiful and what every man on this earth desired in a woman, but not a wife. Nat's beauty was only skin deep, like a golden apple that was rotten at the core. The only things she valued in this life was social status and money.

Nate hung his head in his hands as the alcohol seeped into his bloodstream, slowly starting to realise that sometimes the safest choices in life are the ones most detrimental to your heart. He knew then that he couldn't do it anymore. He could not continue the facade with Natalia and knew that the second he got home, he was filing for a divorce, even if it meant trudging through hellish financial lawsuits. Even if it meant being alone.

"*Omigod*, is it real?!"

Nate heard a woman gasp next to him, her high-pitched voice enough to bring on an early hangover as he rubbed at his bloodshot eyes.

"No idea, but look, it's streaming live right now!"

Another woman answered, holding up her phone as they both gawked like bloodthirsty vampires at the latest scandal on the internet and caused Nate to stand up and move further down the bar.

"Holy shit! It's going viral! Look at the views!"

"This is Ava!" Sam's brazen accent cut across the phone's tiny speakers and caught Nate's attention as he paused and snapped his gaze to the two women. He couldn't make out what was going on from the jumping images on the screen, unsure if he was so drunk that he was conjuring up scenarios in his head.

"I'm sorry, ol' girl..."

"Do it." He knew that voice.

Staggering towards the two women, he pushed himself between them and snatched their phone.

"Oi! What the heck do you think you're doing?" the woman protested as she tried to get her phone back, but Nate was glued to it as he saw the familiar sunny glow of Ava's hair. His stomach dropped with confusion and dread when he saw her knelt before Peter.

"Where is this?" Nate roared at the woman.

"I don't bloody know! It's live on Facebook!" she shot back at the disorderly stranger.

"Oh, my actual God, he's got a gun!" the other woman said, gawking and pointing down at the screen where Peter held a silver revolver to Ava's head.

"Do it, you goddamn foul ma—" The bang that cut off Ava's sentence had crackled the speakers and made Nate's shoulders jump. He stared down at the screen that turned black, his heart throbbing like it was about to derail.

"Ava?!" He heard Samantha Eastley cry out, his lungs taking sharp breaths to try to rationalise this madness as he watched with helpless desperation at the black screen flick-

ering through flashes of light, the speakers sputtering before an error message popped up and the live-stream ended.

"What happened? Where did it go?!" Nate barked at the woman with a murderous glare, thrusting the phone towards her. *"Bring it back, right now!"*

"I—I can't, they've taken it down!" She gaped at the drunken idiot, stumbling back into her friend as people began to pay notice to the commotion at the bar.

"Right, mate, I think you've had enough. Go on, out you go," said the barmaid, pointing a stern finger at the door as Nate gave her a dismissive wave, his brain scattered. He felt like his whole world was spinning out of control as he staggered towards his seat and picked up his phone to see a notification on the screen.

Facebook: Samantha Eastley is sharing her LIVE location with you.

FORTY

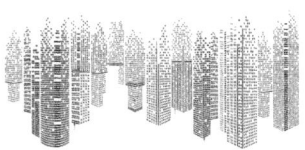

AVA'S EYES were wilder than a deer caught in a trap as warm speckles of crimson splattered across her face like poppies peering through a snowy field. Her bluebells stared at Peter with her cheek pressed to the cold hard ground.

She had always marvelled at how his eyes could change from twinkling emerald cities to vast forests of moss-covered trees. However, now staring into his eyes, his gaze was vacant as though those cities had been diminished to ghost towns, and those forests had long been ripped out and burnt down to deadwood.

Some would see the bullet hole in the centre of his fore-head, but Ava saw the person around it. The person who jested with her daily, who had the most obnoxious sneeze she had ever heard, who always cradled her after they finished having sex, and the person who had betrayed her the most. The person who was now gone.

Time froze still as she lay on her side feeling her world spin on its axis. Her brain refused the picture her eyes sent it, disbelieving that he was dead even as blood trickled down his nose and cheek. She ignored the echoes of panic happening somewhere in the distance until Sam's boot jabbed her in the ribs and snapped her back to reality with a winded gasp.

"Oh, thank Christ!" Sam huffed in relief and awkwardly reached forward to help her coughing friend sit upright. Peering down at Peter she gulped and asked, "Is he...?"

Ava sputtered and nodded her head before craning her neck back to stare down the barrel of the gun that saved her life. However, it was not relief that she felt when she saw her saviour but alarm.

"Jenson Forbes?" Ava gasped as her eyes darted between Charlotte and the man dressed in an off-white suit, his blonde hair flawlessly gelled away from his steel-blue eyes. She glanced down at Peter and back to the gun Jenson held before rasping, "You...*you killed him!*"

"Simply tidying up a loose end, my dear," Charlotte sneered, caring not for the life taken of a man who only moments ago she professed her undying love for. The viperous woman was too preoccupied with her appearance as she casually applied lipstick.

It was at that moment that Ava suddenly realised why that particular shade of orange lipstick had made her stomach drop earlier that day in the work toilets with Charlotte.

The image of Oliver's lifeless body dangling by his neck was something that would forever be burnt into her memory. Even now, if she were to close her eyes, she could detail the whole scene down to the purple pattern left by the noose around his neck and especially the orange smear on the lapel of his white silken pyjamas.

"It *was* you!" Ava gasped up at the Forbes woman and felt chilled to the bone. "But you couldn't have possibly pulled that off alone..." Even if Charlotte was nearly six foot in height, she couldn't have possibly mounted Oliver to that gym apparatus herself. She turned to look at Jenson just as his jaw twitched and rasped, "You killed your own brother?!"

"My brother had it coming. He was forever putting his nose where it shouldn't have been," Jenson gibed with his nose turning upwards. "I could not very well stand by and watch him destroy Lottie. I would not allow him to ruin everything for us." He lowered the gun from Ava's face as he took the hand of his stepmother, his attention dropping down as he intimately entwined their fingers.

"Help ma boab!" Sam's exclamation suddenly cut through the tension in the air like an airhorn at a funeral. "So your first payout expires and pops their clogs so you move onto the guy's son?"

"No, you delinquent," Charlotte hissed down at Sam, her face only softening as it turned to Jenson with her hand tenderly cupping his square face. "It was always Jenson and me right from the start. Holden was simply a means to an end."

"Wait...you *planned* all of this?" Ava choked on her disgust for this vile and twisted woman. "You're telling me you married that poor man, not for love, but for his *money*?!"

"Why of course, dear," Charlotte stated as a matter of fact before her jaw clenched as she looked back to Jenson again. "Four torturous years of staring at a wretched clock waiting on that decrepit old fool's heart to finally give out."

"But *why*?" Ava asked.

"It was meant to be simple..." Jenson sighed, pressing a kiss to the back of Charlotte's hand. "At the time, my father wasn't meant to have long left, certainly not *four years*.

When he finally died, we were going to take the family fortune and leave peacefully. *But no.*" He turned his attention down to Ava with scornfully narrowed eyes. "Ollie just had to put a spanner in the works. My *entitled* little brother had never welcomed Lottie into our home, so of course, he was never going to allow her any part of my father's legacy. However, we never imagined he sought to *destroy* and leave her with absolutely *nothing.*" His nostrils flared as he gripped the handle of the gun and released a heavy sigh. "We had almost managed to strike a deal with the bastard when he bloody walked in on us at the auction and figured everything out. He no longer wanted to simply cast aside Charlotte; he wanted vengeance upon me. I couldn't let him ruin all of our plans, not after how far we've come..."

"So, you went to his apartment that night after the auction and killed him."

Jenson shook his head at Ava and fretted, "No. We were reasonable. We begged him to reconsider our offer, but he refused. He was as vindictive as my old man once was and wanted to impoverish both of us. So yes, we did get into a heated debate and one thing led to another and...I...I—"

"You did what you had to, my love," Charlotte soothed, embracing his side, and leaning up to plant a kiss on his lips. "He can no longer meddle in our affairs and we can finally be happy together after all this time."

"But what about Freya? How is your sister deserving of being framed for this murder?! I have met that girl and she is timider than a mouse!" Ava screeched at the wicked pair.

"I absolutely agree," Charlotte denounced, letting go of her lover and crouching down to meet Ava's height. "But love isn't always easy and sometimes we simply cannot care about the feelings of everyone when trying to chase our own bliss. Dear Freya understands what she must do, and the spotlight is already off of her and onto *this* unfortunate excuse of a man." She scrunched up her nose distastefully and stood upright as her stiletto prodded Peter's side.

"Now, just hold on. Ma heid's mince!" Sam blurted, signalling the two criminals to wait with her tied hands. "You're telling me that yous orchestrated this whole *ruddy* mess for all those years," she awkwardly began listing things off on her fingers as her eyes glanced between them both, "married an old geezer, became your *stepmother*, started a fake affair with your attorney, got them to embezzle money in the firm handling your lawsuit whilst screwing over little blondie here, made the murder of your brother look like a suicide, framed your wee sister, and now killed your attorney *all so you can both have a wee bit of cash behind ye*?!"

"Tell me, Ms. Eastley...how far would you go for the one you love?" Jenson retorted.

"Naw far enough to watch ma Mrs shag ma da for four years and then kill ma wee bro because he was quite rightly tryna protect his own and his family's rear end!"

"I don't expect someone of your *class* to be able to grasp that we did what was necessary!" Charlotte barked at her.

"Aye, and I don't expect a couple of snobby wee eejits to grasp the length ae time they'll be locked up behind bars for this pish!" Sam shot back, clumsily raising the mobile phone with her bounded hands. "Wave hiya to yer fans then," she said with a smug grin before turning the camera around towards herself to see the hundreds of thousands of views her live stream on Facebook was racking up. "And they woulda gotten away with it too, if it weren't for this meddling lass, kids!"

Ava's jaw dropped as she gasped with a triumphant grin lighting up her face. Just like that, her best friend had single-handedly caught two criminals in their confession. She turned her attention towards the gobsmacked Forbeses, one of which had turned into a living strawberry.

"I have had enough of this bitch!" Charlotte roared as she dived for Jenson's handgun.

Ava's eyes burst into small dots as they darted between the gun pointed behind her and to her friend's grave expression. She watched as Sam dropped the phone and struggled against the rope binding her to the forklift. Acting solely on instinct, Ava scrambled to her feet, tackling her shoulder into Charlotte's stomach, and causing the woman to splutter as she tumbled back into her lover and sent him onto his rear with a loud *umph!* Her hands wrapped desperately around the barrel of Charlotte's gun, grappling for the weapon, and pointing it to the corrugated ceiling just in time for an almighty bang to rattle her eardrums and sting her hands. Both women snarled and grunted as they fought over the revolver until a second bang shattered against the four walls of the warehouse and left an eerie silence in its wake.

Ava felt nothing as she plummeted towards the ground.

It was as though her left leg could no longer bear the weight of gravity or as if gravity itself had kicked her leg out from under her. She squawked as her elbow collided with the concrete and stared in confusion as an oddly numb, yet hot and wet sensation sprawled across her thigh. Her fingertips touched the blood saturating her left trouser leg and all she could do was stare at the bullet wound in confusion. Then came the fire—burning, shredding, vivid pain that ripped through her flesh and ached deep inside her splintered bone. Her pain receptors sang a loud operatic song as agony shot up and down one side of her body forcing her to choke on a scream.

"Ava! *Ava?*!" Sam shrieked both a cry for help and in concern of her friend's well-being, but with Charlotte recovering from the wrestle, the gun was back to being pointed at her face. Her blood turned to ice as she watched the sneering devil dressed in green hitch her thumb back on the hammer of the gun.

"I am doing the world a great justice by ridding you from it!" Charlotte jeered as her finger pulled on the trigger and another thunderous shot banged through the air.

For the first time, Ava's friend didn't have a smart retort. Instead, Sam's eyes clenched shut upon the bang of the gun as though she was waiting to register the pain of a bullet wound. Whimpering and wailing came from a woman but it was not Sam. It was the bitch who tried to take a shot at her best friend. Charlotte was currently curled up over her lover on the ground.

Ava's heart was beating so fast that she was sure it could be seen protruding from her chest. Her fingers and arms tingled as Peter's gun trembled in her hand. She had meant to hit Charlotte, but truthfully, she shot blind due to a mixture of adrenaline and pain fogging her mind.

"You shot him!" Charlotte screeched at Ava before looking down at Jenson. "No...no...no, darling stay with me!" she whimpered, cradling his limp body in her arms and palmed his cheek, leaving a red smear behind from the blood pouring freely from the hole in his chest. "Come back!" Charlotte wailed as Jenson's eyes fluttered and his lips quivered, struggling to say his goodbye as incoherent sounds tumbled from his mouth.

Ava didn't have time to feel guilt or shock at the heinous act she had just committed. Her body was in survival mode as blood leaked from her leg. Already her vision had blackened like a vignette filter, so she wasted no time as she dropped the gun and feebly dragged herself towards her best friend.

"I know you're waiting for some wise-arse comment but I..." Sam began to say, her lips failing to make words as she struggled to grasp that her friend literally took a bullet for her.

"You owe me a drink," Ava croaked through the pain with a faint smirk on her lips as she clumsily undid Sam's wrists.

"You saved my life! I think I'll put Scotland into a drought with the amount of drinks I'll be buying you, doll!" Sam scoffed as she tossed the rope aside and dived in to hug her friend, easing off when Ava hissed and cursed in pain. "Soz...?" she said with a sheepish smile.

"*You've taken everything for me!*" Charlotte screeched like a vengeful witch rising from the pits of hell, her high heels clicking quickly as she charged at Ava with the gun primed and ready to avenge her beloved Jenson.

Adrenaline burnt away the anxiety Ava felt as her mind sharpened to a tack and any pain she felt was numbed down to a subtle ache. She dived towards the gun lying a few feet from her, squawking as Charlotte's stiletto sent the metal scraping across the ground, kicking away her only hope.

"Charlotte, you don't want to do this..." Ava warned with her palms raised defensively.

"Oh, but I *really* do," Charlotte croaked through the tears streaming down her face. "I should have known from day one that you were a problematic blonde bitch that needed to be eradicated!" With only a small distance between her and Ava, she aimed the gun directly between Ava's brows and snarled, "Say hello to Peter for me..."

"*NO!!*" Sam screamed.

If there was one thing that Ava had to be grateful for, it

was the loss of blood that now clouded her vision and made her whole body feel like it was filled with fuzz, desensitising her to any further pain. It was the end of the line for her and she wasn't ready or able to make her peace with that fact. She still had so much left to do in this world, so much left of herself to offer and so many things she wanted to conquer. In that moment between the blink of life and death, there was no reel of her life flashing before her eyes but just the sad realisation that she had barely lived at all. Years were wasted hiding away from love and it took the hardest offer of commitment, made by a married man, and to be held at gunpoint for Ava to finally realise just what her biggest regret was in life—never telling the man of her dreams just how madly in love with him she was.

As the gunfire pierced her ears and splintered her heart, it robbed her of the life she took for granted and should have cherished more.

FORTY-ONE

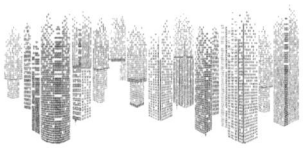

ONE WEEK LATER...

THE CEMETERY WAS LITTERED with brown frosted leaves, the many glittering fragments shining brilliantly in the wintry light. Today there was no wind, no rain, nor cloud, just sub-zero temperatures. Even the stems of the leaves laid white and sharp. The path meandering throughout the well-kept grass glistened in the early morning sun like white quartz, the concrete dusted in shimmering ice crystals.

All that beauty over everything dead.

Clouds of white rose into the air from Nate's lips as he gathered with a crowd of people around a grave and stared down at the casket being lowered into the earth. His expression was stoic, feeling nothing inside apart from the gaping void in his chest, while others visibly showed their raw pain. The two Archer girls, Heather and Suzannah, embraced one another in silent screams of anguish and there wasn't a single dry face—not even from Mr. Archer as he stood before the mourners to give his goodbye speech.

"As many of you know, the woman being buried here today wasn't just my co-worker," Tom spoke loud and clear despite the obvious quiver to his voice. "In every sense, she was what a father wanted in a daughter. She was someone that brought joy into every one of our lives and will forever remain in our hearts." With cheeks glistening with tears, he tossed a single rose on top of the coffin before his two girls followed suit by dropping their own in as well.

As little Archer's trembling hand covered her sobs, Nate's jaw twitched as he tried to remain composed. He wanted to stay strong and be a supportive rock today, but it was hard not to think of the lively and tenacious woman lying at rest in that black box. It wasn't sadness that plagued him as much as it was the vengeful anger at the innocent woman being taken far too soon.

She didn't deserve this.

His nostrils flared with emotion just as icy fingers laced through his own, pulling him back from the brink of an outburst and reaffirming that he had to keep it together today.

"You don't have to say anything if you feel you can't," he whispered down to the best friend in mourning, however, the woman was already strutting awkwardly towards the side of the grave upon two crutches, defiant as ever and mustering strength from God only knew where.

"Samantha Eastley was more than just my friend," Ava announced with a splitting voice as she sniffed back the tears that ran down her face like two waterfalls and gathered in the seam of her pale, cracked lips. "Most people believe that they are given one soul mate in life, one person they are destined to meet that will complete and guide them. She was it for me. Samantha completed me in ways that transcends words, she was my north star. In every sense of the meaning, Sam was my soul sister." She looked up at Nate with red bleary eyes, taking strength from his encouraging nod that helped her to push the words out of her trembling lips that twitched into a melancholic smile. "If Sam were here today, she would have wanted me to say something *wholly* inappropriate right now," she scoffed, her throat feeling tight as though splinters of her heart were forever lodged there. "But I wasn't the funny one in our relationship. She was the one always making people laugh, whether that be with some rude Scottish turn of phrase, some crude innuendo or anecdote, she always brought joy to everyone's day.

"I believe that when good people pass, they leave in us a part of their goodness, and in that way, forever live on in us. Even today, a day of pain and sadness, of frustration and anger, we can all feel it and want to reach out for that goodness, and to have the memory of our Sam keep our broken souls burning bright." Her words brought on sad smiles from the small crowd as she turned her attention down to the grave. "So, I'm sorry, Sammy, but I can't do you justice by making some wise-crack comment today. All I can say is that I will forever be grateful for everything you have done for me and you'll be sorely missed." She tossed a single pink peony flower, her friend's favourite, into the grave and wept. "Goodbye, my lass, I will *always* love you."

Long after the funeral had ended and the crowd had dispersed, Ava remained in place, alone by her friend's grave, peering down at the letters etched into the white stone.

She had spent days in denial over the unspeakable events that had transpired. It sickened Ava that she was the one who got to live, that even Charlotte Forbes got to see the sunrise every morning, albeit through bars, while Sam rotted in the ground.

All that pain and suffering plagued Ava every single

night with the same reoccurring nightmare of her best friend dying in her arms only to wake up and realise she was living this hell. The dream itself was a memory, vividly crafted down to the minutest of details to torture Ava, and it always started and ended the same way as it did in real life.

I CAN HEAR the wail of sirens echo far into the distance, painfully aware of the gun being pointed to my forehead and knowing that any hope for my soul was just that little bit too late and out of reach. My eyes are scrunched up so tightly that the twinkling of stars blinks across the black canvas of my vision.

The bang of gunfire cracks the air in front of me and penetrates my ears, rattling my skull as my breath hitches in my throat before a mass of weight suddenly tumbles down in front of me. Confusion twists my stomach as I nervously open my eyes and look down at my best friend curled up in a ball.

Why is Sammy on my lap?

When I peer up at Charlotte, the lack of certainty increases as I see the alarm on her face, the gun she is holding still pointed straight at me. I don't feel fear, nor do I even flinch as the woman's finger aimlessly begins curling back on the trigger only for it to click repeatedly against an empty cylinder. All I feel is confusion and I'm not sure if that has anything to do with the amount of blood leaking through the hole in my leg.

"S-Sam?" I falter, dread turning my bones to winter and my blood to ice as I carefully peel my friend's arms away from her body. "Sammy?!" A flash of red covers her chest,

blood seeping from the bullet hole and spreading like wildfire over her shirt.

"H-hurts..." she croaks, her chest trembling every time she inhales as though her body was rejecting oxygen.

"Why did you do that? You shouldn't have done that! Why?!" I yap with panic thrashing my insides as I compress the wound to reduce the blood loss, but as I look up, I see Charlotte picking up Peter's gun and aiming it at us again. All I want to do is open my mouth and scream vengeance from my lungs until this woman shatters into a million pieces and leaves us alone. However, before I can, the thunder of several feet running towards us grows louder until the law enforcement rounds the corner of pallets and barks at Charlotte to lower her weapon.

"Ye ken...yer ma...best pal, ae?" Sam struggles, stealing my attention as I hold her close in my arms like a mother swaddling their child, but there is so much blood, warm and watery as it slips between my fingers like the grains of sand in an hourglass.

"Last warning, drop it now!"

Gunfire opens, a series of short sharp bursts that brings Charlotte to her knees before her face meets the ground.

"Do you think...the NHS will give me a free...boob job... for this?" The words splutter from Sam's lips, wheezes of air struggling to pass through her lips that are turning an alarming shade of blue.

"Only you would crack jokes at a time like this, you cunt!" I blurt out through nervous laughter that brings on clear domes of emotion to well up on the surface of my eyes.

"Scottish cunt," she corrects me, however, suddenly begins convulsing in my arms as blood splutters from her lips.

"Sam?!" I shriek, quickly turning her onto her side to

stop her choking, but as I do, liquid life is pouring also from the exit hole in her back and her eyes are beginning to flutter as though her consciousness was slipping. "Why are you just standing there? I need a medic now!" I scream at the officers through my tears before pulling my best friend closer to my body as if that will somehow protect her. "Don't you bloody dare leave me! Come on, Sam, hang in there, just a little longer!" And she does, my determined wee lass opens her eyes and looks up at me even if the blood continued to splutter from her cold lips. "You can't leave me, I need you. We're soul sisters for life, remember?"

The worst feeling in the world is feeling helpless, to feel all hope drain from your body, that sinking feeling in your stomach as your brain logically decides the odds are not in your favour.

Despair was all I felt as Sam opened her eyes for the last time, her trembling lips stained like two rose petals sat upon a frozen blue lake. It was then that my best friend uttered one word with her last breath. One word that would forever be etched into my soul and haunt me until my dying day.

"Always."

FORTY-TWO

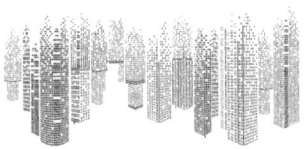

WEEKS WENT by like the turning of a page for Nate. Autumn had faded into a cold winter as snow blanketed the ground and stripped the remaining life clinging to the trees.

In that time, he had stayed at Ava's apartment, caring for her as she mourned the loss of her friend and struggled with daily tasks due to her leg injury.

He believed that when Sam died, she took with her a part of Ava. It killed him to see her like this, a walking shell of a woman, a ghost that spent her days silently in front of her bay window staring outside or down at her cell phone replaying videos of her friend's laugh.

He could never fully understand the pain and torment she felt, how hard it must have been for her with the daily reminders on the news about her friend's death, the goddamn media banging at her door for a statement from the blonde girl in the Facebook video.

God, it must have been hell for her.

The worst part was feeling completely useless, trying everything in his power to ease her discomfort such as helping her into a bath every night, preparing her hot meals, and then encouraging her to actually *eat* those meals. He supported her throughout the gruelling physiotherapy even when her outlook was poor and that she'd likely remain on a walking stick for the rest of her days—a walking stick that she *refused* to use despite his incessant nagging.

It wasn't lost on him that in those few weeks he had cared for her in a way that any husband should care for their wife—another sick joke made by the universe.

He was patient with her healing, not just physical but mental healing. She needed a friend, God did she need a friend right now, and his shoulder was there no matter the time of day or night. Nate gave her space, crashing on her couch and suffering the neck ache for it.

Each night, he found himself falling into the same routine: running into her room at exactly 3 a.m. as she cried out for her friend. His body had become so used to it that it naturally woke him up just before the clock struck three.

However, tonight was different. There was no crying, no screaming, only an unsettling silence that shrouded the apartment. He lay awake staring at the clock on the fireplace reading 03:26 just as the floorboards creaked behind him as bare feet stumbled towards him on the couch.

"Ava, is everything alright?" He shot upright, ripping the blanket from him as he turned to see her, his heart melting on the spot. Ava wandered closer to him, her casted leg dragging behind her and her hair a bird's nest of unruly golden curls. She looked adorable with that comforter swaddled around her, so tiny and innocent, childlike. "Did you have a bad dream again?" he asked and frowned when she shook her head. "Then what's wrong?"

"I didn't see her tonight," she mumbled with her bottom lip trembling.

Nate knew straightaway what she meant. She would

rather the painful experience of dreaming of her friend dying than not seeing her at all.

"Come here, sweetheart," he sighed softly, coaxing her to lie down on top of him and grimacing at the noise of discomfort her leg gave her. She never admitted she was in pain, but he knew better. As she nestled her face into his white cotton tee his heart sang a symphony for it was the most intimate they had been in weeks.

"It should have been me."

"What?" He craned his head back to peer down at her.

"This is my fault. Sam received the death penalty and all I suffered was nerve damage and a fractured femur. She didn't deserve this. She wasn't even closely involved in the Forbes mess."

"No one deserved any of this, Ava," he sighed with his arm wrapping around her small frame as he smoothed her hair.

"Did I ever tell you what Jenson Forbes asked Sam just before she died, Nate?" He knew it was a rhetorical question so remained silent and waited on her to continue. "He asked her how far she would go for love..." She peeked her head up to look at him, tears trickling down her face that he caught with his thumb. "But I never thought she would go as far as *this* and I can't live with it, Nate. I can't live knowing she's gone, and I get to stay!"

After all this time, Nate thought that seeing Ava cry would get easier, but it still managed to reach inside his chest and squeeze the life out of his heart.

"No, beautiful. You're looking at it the wrong way," he soothed, cupping her face with both hands so she looked at him. "You're right, you *do* get to live, and that isn't a burden but a *gift*, Ava. If Sam were here, you know for a fact that she would tell you to get up and start living your life to the fullest. She'd want you to live the shit outta each and every day."

"Oh, I know what she'd tell me. She'd tell me to stop being a dramatic cow and get off my tinky arse and wear something other than her onesie!" Ava laughed through her misery.

"Yeah, she'd no doubt have something to say about you sniffing her dirty laundry as well," Nate chuckled, his face lighting up for the first time in weeks to see her attempt to let the joy back into her life. It was like he had managed to find a flicker of light trying to break through all of the darkness his girl was drowning in.

"I miss her so fucking much, Nate."

"I know, sweetheart. I didn't know her as well as you, but I miss her too."

"The worst part isn't the fact that my friend died in my arms...it was seeing her *suffer*. It's knowing that her future will forever be an unwritten chapter, that she will never receive her promotion at work, never laugh again, and cease to exist in this world."

"I can't imagine what you're going through. I feel like a fool for how I acted that night. I should have got to you sooner," Nate confessed and watched her face twist in confusion. "That night...I went to your apartment looking for you when your neighbour told me you left with Peter. I've never felt heartbreak as bad as that. I thought you didn't want me—"

"That's not—"

"It's fine, I know...but I didn't at the time and I ended up in a bar drinking my problems and I found out all too late just how goddamn foolish I was," he groaned, slumping back onto the sofa as he stared at the ceiling.

"You couldn't have possibly known," she protested, her

legs straddling his side as she sat up and reached for his face to look at her. "Tell me you don't blame yourself for *any* of this."

"I..."

"Nate, none of this is your fault! It's *no one's* fault! Who could have possibly known how twisted and wicked those fucking Forbeses were, or how manipulative and convincing that redheaded cunt was! If it is anyone's fault it is *theirs*!" she attested, receiving raised eyebrows from him and suddenly realising that what she just said applied to herself as well.

"You should take your own advice..." He gave her a sweet smile, reaching up to brush her curls from her face before pulling her down so he could plant a loving kiss on her forehead. "Get some sleep."

Ava nodded and settled back down onto his chest, taking comfort from the soothing song of his heart echoing in her ears. She realised that all the tears she cried kept her soul alive in the furnace of this pain, but they also helped clean and repair the soul. The only problem was...Sam was the other half of her soul, and no amount of time nor healing could ever make her feel whole again.

NATE AWOKE the next morning to the smell of burning that caused him to jump upright and look around for Ava, who was nowhere to be found.

"Ava?!" he called out in alarm as he rushed towards the source of the smell.

"Sorry...I'm not really the best at baking..." Ava fretted, stood in front of the stove, fully dressed in clothes for the first time in nearly a month.

For a moment, Nate just stood there gawking at the grey knitted dress fitted to her curvaceous figure. Even with the white cast wrapped around her leg, she still managed to knock him on his ass with her beauty.

"Baking? What are you...*oh*—" He paused, seeing the black circle stuck to the frying pan and laughed. "I wouldn't qualify pancakes as baking, sweetheart."

"Well it is, *look*! Eggs, flour, sugar, and one of these whisk thingies!"

"An eggbeater, yes." He covered his smirk with his hand and watched as she grew more and more flustered.

"Oh, bugger off, you know what I mean!" Ava huffed, flicking the utensil at him, and gasping as pancake batter flicked across his face in creamy splatters. "I am so sorry, let me clean that up for y*aah*—!" she shrieked as Nate suddenly picked her up and set her down on the kitchen counter.

"*That* was incredibly naughty, Ms. Archer," he tutted, running the tip of his finger through the batter before licking it off and waving his index back and forth in front of her face.

"It was an accident..."

"Oh, *really*?" He smirked, standing between her legs as his knuckles pressed down on the counter.

"Yep, but *this* isn't!" she blurted as she blew flour into his face, her hair tumbling down her back as she tipped her head back and laughed.

"Oh, you're dead..." Nate growled as he gripped her hips tight and tugged.

"*No-no-no!* Invalid remember!" she protested as she pointed down to her thigh, watching his eyes soften from their scowl.

"*Fineeee...* I'll let you milk that excuse a couple more times," he warned, pointing a finger in her face before winking. "Let the *Yank* show the Brit how to *properly* make pancakes, eh?"

FORTY-THREE

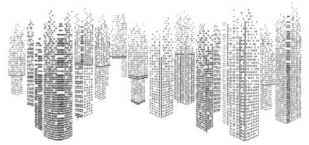

"NO, I kid you not, she ended up in a wheelie-bin *drunk as a skunk* singing 'Proud Mary' at the top of her lungs and demanding that I push her!" Ava laughed, running her finger along her watering lash line as she sat at the dining table with not a single bite left of the best pancakes she had ever eaten.

"But why in the hell was she is the trash in the first place?!" Nate chortled, sipping on his coffee as they spent the last hour reminiscing about her late best friend.

"Who knows, but Sam claimed that because the bin had wheels, I had to help the 'big wheels keep on turning'!"

Grief came in waves that, to begin with, were so strong they swept you away with the tide. They came at such random moments, replacing any semblance of normality with tears that set fire to your soul. However, in time, those waves soon lessen and eventually allow the happy memories to flood in instead. In time, the pain and sadness, the anger and despair, is soon replaced by waves of smiles and warmth, those funny and sweet things that were said. And one day, you wake up no longer crippled by the sting of loss but remember it as a single missing puzzle piece from your soul.

Nate could see that Ava was trying hard to allow the joy back into her life. He had never met a woman so strong and was forever dazzled by her willpower.

"I should probably tidy all of this up now," Nate said with a groan as he rolled his neck and stood, making his way over to the mess left behind in the kitchen.

"Oh no! I'll get that, you sit down!" Ava insisted, getting up from her seat and standing upon her weak leg which refused to take her weight as she went tumbling with a squeal.

"Whoa there!" Nate rushed over and only just managed to catch her as his arm snaked around her waist and pulled her to safety. "You alright?"

This is why you need your damn walking aid.

With her back swooped down low, Ava peered up at him with damsel's eyes and felt her heart wake up from a month of slumber. It was as though her body was trying to remind her of the effects that this painstakingly gorgeous man had on her.

Every wall she had wrapped around herself for the past few weeks began crumbling to ash as her heart screamed out for the love of her life. With her arm around his neck, she pulled herself towards his lips and whined with relief as their mouths mated and his arms cinched her body tight against his chest, finally reuniting their hearts. It was as though he had the power to breathe life back into her as she parted her lips and tasted home.

Nate hadn't realised just how starved he was until her lips were against his. He poured all the love in his heart into this kiss, willing it to heal and take all of her pain away. Both of his arms squeezed her tiny waist as though he were terrified to ever let this woman go again before carefully picking her up into a bridal lift and carrying her towards the sofa. He laid her down delicately, never once interrupting the kiss as he hovered over her and planted a trail of adoration down the side of her neck.

Shivers ran down Ava's spine like waves of pleasure trickling inside her body as her soul finally accepted the light back in. She whined softly as his fingertips ran up under her dress, bringing their bodies closer touch by touch. The only frustrating thing was how weak her thigh was, feeling heavy and awkwardly wrapped in the unflattering cast. Her good leg wrapped easily around his side as her other failed miserably. However, as if he somehow knew of her struggle, his palm found her thigh and glided up to her knee. She wanted to scream at the hard fabric blocking his touch until she felt him bring her leg slowly up to his side and hold it there for her. Moans escaped from her lips, her back arching for more as she felt him press down between her legs.

"Take this off," Ava whimpered, fingers tugging at the hem of his white cotton tee. When he obliged, she didn't waste a second as her lips brushed across his collarbone and down over each pectoral, lavishing his flesh with kisses. There was a time, not so long ago, that she thought she'd never get this again so made sure to worship every inch of him in this moment.

There was something different about her and Nate couldn't figure out what. Each brush of her lips on his chest, every caress of her fingertips on his sides, the way she held him close, it was softer and less demanding than before. She was savouring this. Savouring him.

Nate slowly peeled her knitted dress over her head before running his lips down her bare chest. As his lips glided over each of her pink buds, it wasn't solely to give pleasure, although the sweet noises leaving her lips were welcomed. He too wanted to savour her.

This was uncharted territory for Ava. Her body was on fire but in ways it never had been.

Everything she felt for Nate was smouldering inside the furnace of her heart that pumped molten emotion around her body. She *burned* for him. For the first time, she experienced pleasure through emotion more than she did through feeling.

As their clothes came off and they embraced one another as two bare embers, there was a moment of lull, a single moment where they stared into one another's eyes, sharing a type of intimacy that eclipsed their flesh and bone.

"God, I've missed you," Nate whispered against her jaw before his nose skimmed up against the peak of hers and their eyes met once more.

"Nate...I..." Ava swallowed the bundle of flames in her throat, trying to suppress the fire into the pits of her heart that could no longer contain the magnitude of it. "I love you."

He stared into her eyes, failing to hide the surprise on his face as those three words that he had longed to hear finally reached into his heart and made it whole.

"I love you so damn much," he rushed his words, choosing to show rather than tell as his lips crashed down against hers and his hands fisted her hair to bring her closer.

Ava wrapped her arms tightly around his neck, feeling like he was pushing her towards supernova as their kiss grew hotter. Their bodies naturally found one another as her lips spread against his, swallowing each other's moans as his manhood filled her silky walls in one effortless tilt of their hips.

Nate growled into her mouth, his body and soul aching for her as he rolled slowly in and out of her. She felt incredible, sheathing his length, and connecting him to the deepest parts of her.

With the backs of his fingers trailing across her cheek, they found their way down and around her neck, squeezing the sides as he brought her attention back to him. He loved it when her eyes scrunched with pleasure like that, loved the way her jaw descended as he angled himself right at that spot that made her putty in his hands, and loved the way her wild eyes watched him as if awaiting instruction.

"Say it again," he demanded breathlessly despite only having just begun.

"I love you," she moaned, back arched as she brushed her lips against his. "Makes me yours, Nate."

A deep animalistic growl left his lips as his self-control faded and he felt his primal urges resurfaced, desiring nothing more than to grant her wish. With his hands in her hair again, and without any warning, his hips suddenly jolted into her with sharp movements that made her yelp and mewl for more as her nails scored down his back.

"*Fuck*," he ground out against the delightful pain as he tilted his head back before peering down and summoning her attention once more. "I need to feel you *now*."

Ava didn't know what he had meant until his hand appeared between her legs, fingers twirling around her bundle of nerves and making her see stars as she begged for more.

"Mmhh!" she whined as everything pulsed and ached for him, her body trembling with pleasure and struggling to hold back the flood of euphoria. Her back arched high until her stomach pressed against his, her neck craning back as she closed her eyes and felt herself become weightless, like a balloon filling with helium, ready to burst at any moment.

Nate felt her on the brink of an orgasm, the way she clamped him and made his dick beg for release. No woman held the level of power over him like Ava did. He couldn't hold back any longer, dangling over the edge with his body feeling overloaded with emotion, sensation, and love for her.

"Open your eyes," he all but begged her and the moment her beautiful sapphires opened, creased with pleasure and full to the brim with adoration, his body finally betrayed him as he groaned loudly and yelled her name. It was like her body was in sync with his, her orgasm wrecking him as she spasmed around his manhood and brought on his warm silken spurts to bathe her insides.

For such a short-lasting moment of physical intimacy, the high they both felt was endless.

Ava had foolishly always lived her life under the presumption that *duration* qualified for good sex, but nothing could ever come close to what she just experienced moments ago with Nate.

Their bodies glistened in the morning sun with sensual sweat, Nate lying atop Ava as his hips undulated lazily with his face nestled into her shoulder. He wanted to freeze time and hit replay, specifically to the moment she confessed her love for him. Reaching up, he stared down at her with a love-sick grin, palming her cherub face.

"Mine," Nate affirmed, drowning in her oceans as she nodded her head.

"Yours."

FORTY-FOUR

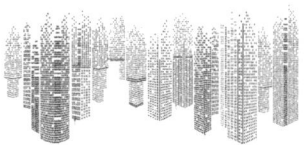

NATE STARED up at Ava in awe, their heavy breathing slowly returning to normal after several more sessions of lovemaking that morning. His mouth stroked against hers, a grin on his face as he tried to grab her lip between his teeth.

"Wait right there—I need to pee!" Ava beamed down at Nate, sprawled across his bare body as she awkwardly clambered to her feet, scolding any help he attempted to offer her. Walking was a struggle when half her leg was wrapped in white stone, but she was adamant that it wouldn't hinder her ability to walk without aid. If athletes could sprint on prosthetic limbs, then she could walk with hers in plaster.

"If you ain't gonna use your crutches at least use the walking aid," Nate sighed, running his hand through his messy dark locks, the roots saturated with sweat as he lazily turned onto his side to admire Ava's beauty—even if she was comically hobbling about the living room without any clothes on.

"*Don't need itttt!*" she said in singsong, clumsily staggering her way towards her bathroom.

"Whatever you say, hop-a-long!" Nate chirped, rolling

onto his back with his hands cradling his head as he grinned from ear-to-ear up at the ceiling. He couldn't remember a time where he'd felt such peace, as though the sun pouring through the window was filling his soul and bringing him a euphoric high. Ava changed his perspective on things and sweetened everything bitter in life. The rain was no longer depressing, it was cleansing, and the wind was no longer cold, it was refreshing. She made him feel overflowing with bright and warm sunshine.

Eyes closed, he listened to the birdsong outside before a shrill buzzing interrupted his moment of bliss as his cell darted across the coffee table causing him to squint at the caller ID that pulled a dark cloud over his soul.

"So, I was thinking we could maybe try going for a walk to—" Ava cut short as she wandered back into an empty living room and frowned, fastening her dressing gown around her. "Nate?" She heard chatter coming from the balcony extending from her kitchen as she padded as quietly as she could towards the white curtains blowing gently in the wintery breeze.

"Whoa, look just slow down, your *padre*? You mean your dad?" Nate spoke in hushed tones on the phone, stood shirtless upon the balcony as a pair of loose jogger bottoms hung from his defined hips. "Oh, Nat, I'm so sorry..."

Ava's stomach sunk upon realising who he was talking to. For the past few weeks, she had been drowning so much in her mourning that she had completely forgotten about the other woman. This morning, without a second thought, she greedily grabbed on to the first chance of happiness as a way of respite from that dark place inside of her, but now she realised she was simply swinging from one high to the next low.

There was a point in her life, not so long ago, that she

felt like she had everything, that she held all the puzzle pieces to a complete jigsaw. She had her best friend, a blooming career, wealth, and good health, and in her blinded state, she had a passion that consumed her with love.

Now she had *nothing*.

Her friend was gone, her father had dismissed her as his assistant, her health was in tatters, and the love she experienced was all just a dream, rendering her puzzle in pieces on the ground.

How foolish of me, she thought. *How foolish to think that things were that simple and that the one good thing left in my life was mine to keep.*

"Of course, Nat! I'll get the next flight out—shit, wait, no, I...I can't. I've got this...this work thing I—" Nate clamped his mouth shut as his wife screeched down the phone at him, the cell phone held away from his ears as she did. "I'll figure something out..."

Ava didn't know what bothered her more: the fact he was lying to his wife calling her a "work thing" or the fact that he was leaving her to go back to his wife. However, then it loomed on her that this whole time she had thought of his wife as "the other woman" when in fact *she* was the other woman.

She was the homewrecker, the adulterer, the *slut*... not Natalia *Brooks*.

Ava retreated towards the living room with her stomach lodged in her throat. The room with high ceilings was shrouded in shadows as the sun hid its head in the dark snow clouds. She felt entirely alone in that moment, like a little boat straying far out into the big black ocean. As her eyes glanced at a picture frame upon the cold fireplace, she released the breath she didn't remember holding. The picture was taken by Suzy many years ago, a young Ava dressed professionally after her first big day stepping into the working world. Sam was with her in the photo, showering Ava in champagne as they both screamed and laughed. That was the first time in Ava's life that she felt a sense of completeness, that all the boxes in her life were ticked and yet she had so much still to achieve and look forward to. Now she felt completely lost and had a desperate need to get her life back on track.

Glancing up at the mirror suspended above the mantel, she didn't recognise her own reflection. Her complexion was washed out, her hair wasn't quite golden, and dark crescents hung beneath her eyes. Whatever light was inside her was gone.

Closing her eyes, she materialised Sam in that room with her, imagining her friend stood behind with a hand on her shoulder. In her mind was the only place Sam now existed and these little delusions had been Ava's only saviour this last month.

Ava's eyes opened as she heard Nate's slippers slop against the floor as he stepped in from the snowy balcony and joined her in the living room.

"You need to go back to America."

"You heard?" he asked, cautiously moving towards her and stopping when she turned around and he saw the grave expression on her face. "Her father passed away suddenly last night, but it's fine, I can find a way out of atten—"

"No."

"Excuse me?" Nate's thick brows pulled into the bridge of his creased nose as he watched her cold eyes slice into him in the dully lit room.

"You need to go home and be with your wife."

"Not this *again*... Ava, I told you, Natalia is just my—"

"She is your *wife*, Nate. It is as simple as that." She lifted her shoulders with her lips turned inwards at the corners. "Whether you try and make it as black and white as the contract you signed on your wedding day or not, she is still your spouse and I'm...I'm just your mistress. I am anything but yours and you are anything but mine which is why we cannot be together right now. You cannot keep lying to Natalia."

"*What?*" Nate said, winded as his hand swept across his face in bewilderment. "Did we *not* just make love moments ago on that couch?"

"We did but—"

"Then where the hell is all of this coming from, Ava?!" Silence befell the room as he watched her avoid his glare. It was ludicrous to backtrack to square one when they had come this far. He began pacing up and down the living as he ranted, "I have told you before and I will tell you this again and again until I am blue in the face. She means *nothing* to me, and I mean *nothing* to her. That heartless *bitch* wouldn't give two craps if I walked up to her today and confessed where I've *really* been this past month or even that I have spent the last couple of months being madly in love with you because I am nothing but financial gain to that woman!"

"And so, what if she doesn't care, Nate? Does that make it the right thing to do?" Ava hissed as she angrily limped towards him. "You know what you're doing to her isn't fair and I know that you are a better man than that, which is precisely why you need to go home and sort your bloody life out!"

"And I will, Ava! The second I'm back in Manhattan it is over with her and we can start a life together!"

"No."

"Fucking give me strength!" Nate roared as he threw his hands into the air and sunk down onto the edge of the couch. "You are an impossible woman!" His hands covered his face as his neck began to ache, unsure if it was from lying on the couch or the emotional whiplash that this Brit was giving him.

"You need to go home and fix your life. Stop letting people dictate how you live your life. You work to live, not live to work so stop living by other people's rules and put yourself first, Nate—not your title, not your reputation or even your career."

"That's goddamn hypocrisy at its finest when you stand there and dictate what I should do with my life when I am perfectly happy with what is right in front of me right here!"

"I am not saying that we can't be together. I am saying we can't be together *right now!*" This brought on a lull of silence in their debate as Nate's frown softened ever so slightly and a small flicker of hope glimmered in his honey gems that peered up at her. Ava hobbled over to the sofa and stood in front of him. "Nathaniel, my *best friend* just died... I don't have a job to distract myself with, I need to make amends with my father, and I am like *this*," she croaked as her hand slapped at her broken leg. "My life is a mess right now and I don't have any more space for unbalance. I need to *be* better and *do* better. It's what Sam would have wanted me to do."

Nate dropped to his knees before her, his eyes pleading for mercy as he gazed up. "Ava, *please*. I...I just got you back...you said you loved me, I thought we'd—"

"I *do* love you, of course I love you!" she whimpered, hating to see him so vulnerable and wishing she could drop to her knees to join him. "Your heart is the perfect storm.

When I am with you, it's chaos. The most amazing, mind-blowing chaos that sets my soul on fire and makes me feel alive. But right now, I don't need chaos in my life. I need structure and I need to get back on track, starting with me, Nate. Can you please just try to understand?"

"I can't lose you again." His voice broke as tears blinked past the barrier of his eyes and trickled down his face. "It nearly killed me, Ava. That night...that video...not knowing if you were okay or not... I...I can't—"

"You will *never* lose me," she vowed, wiping away each of his tears as her own began dripping from her chin. "I am not saying we can never be together, but right now is not our time. Everything isn't in place. We need time apart and need to sort out our own train wrecks before we are ready for each other."

"Ava... I don't think I have it in me to wait anymore to start living my life..."

"Then don't wait for me...start living it on your terms," she soothed despite the tears thickening her voice. "But I think a part of me will always be waiting for this. Have you ever heard the saying about love and lust?" When he shook his head, she gave him a small smile and said, "Lust blinds you but love lets you see. You opened my eyes, Nathaniel Brooks."

It took him a moment to rationalise the bomb she dropped on him after such a blissful morning. Part of him wanted to grab on to her legs like a petulant child and scream her name until his lungs burnt out. However, he knew he couldn't be selfish and had to face the fact that she wasn't in the same headspace as he was right now. She had her own demons to contend with and had to heal herself from the inside out first.

His legs trembled as she pulled him up onto his feet and

wrapped her little arms around his neck. "We're really doing this then? We're going our separate ways after everything we've been through these past couple of months?" he asked with a tired sigh, feeling the last thread of hope snap as Ava weakly nodded up at him. All the words crumbled into a heap inside his heart and all he could do was pull her close and bury his face into her hair. He filled his lungs with all of her, committing her to memory like the picture of them that would forever remain inside his wallet.

Pulling back from her embrace, he watched the silver lines of heartbreak slip down her cheeks and wiped them away with his lips, tasting the salt of her sorrow on his tongue.

"Fate has shitty timing," Ava said, pouting up at him before nuzzling her face into his throat.

Nate chuffed sadly through his nose as he rested his chin on top of her head and squeezed his arms around her petite frame. In that moment, he made himself a vow: one day he was going to defy fate and marry this woman.

"Yeah, it really does, sweetheart."

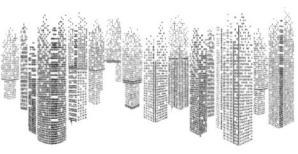

EPILOGUE
TWO YEARS LATER...

INSECURITIES AND FEARS are a lot like waves. If you let one overcome you, it will pull you under and drag you out to sea. However, if you decide to dive right in and surf your inner torment, you may find a new ability to breathe underwater.

That was what Ava had spent the last two years learning: how to breathe underwater.

She swam through her loneliness and focused on her needs rather than her wants. No more were there unfulfilling one-night stands. No more did she cry with a gin glass full of wine, and no more did she lie to the people she held dearest. She was bettering herself from the inside out and slowing finding her way back to her cornerstone in life.

It was no easy feat. Hard conversations were conquered, all her tears had been drained, both mental and physical therapy was undergone, and it wasn't until she was broken down into fragments that she was finally able to start rebuilding herself.

"Sometimes ye gotta break a few eggs to make some scrambeed eggos!" Sam used to tell her and by golly was her bestie right. Now here she was, thirty years old and finally at the top of her game.

In her chair, Ava sat with her back to the grand mahogany desk and marvelled at her daily view of London's skyline. For an entire decade, she had watched her father admire this view and now it was her turn. It was something she would never tire of and something she would never again take for granted.

"Coming to lunch then, bossy pants?"

"Suzy," Ava chuckled, her new shoulder-length waves swishing as she swivelled around in her chair to see her baby sister stand in the middle of her office. "Can you at least *attempt* to maintain a semi-professional rapport with me while we're at work?"

"Uhm...make me?" Suzy poked her tongue out before perching her bottom on the edge of Ava's desk.

"Well...I mean, I could always find *another* intern to hire as my assistant..." Ava teased, hiding a smirk behind her coffee mug and watching Suzy begin to fret. "I'm kidding! Anyway, have you finished organising the case file for the Kensington tr—?" She stopped short and frowned at the odd look her sister was giving her. "What?"

"Sorry, it's just a bit hard to take you seriously when you're drinking out of a llama-shaped mug with a wonky ear..."

"Hey, don't talk ill of Barry!"

"Point and case: managing partner of this firm and you call your coffee mug Barry."

"Shh...don't listen to the mean intern," Ava huffed, covering Barry's one good ear.

"Ava...?" Suzy sighed, waiting until Ava had finished coddling her mug and snapped out of her daydream before pointing to the door. "Lunch?"

"SO, have you heard from Dad yet?"

"Nope, he's too busy sunbathing and drinking Bahama Mamas on that cruise," Ava chuckled and took a sip of strong coffee as she and Suzy sat at the nostalgic spot next to the window inside the quaint cafe. "But I did see the picture he posted on Instagram with Steph and he looks like he's having a rare old time!"

Stephanie was a blessing that came into her father's life just in the nick of time. She was ages with him and they both retired at the same time. The pair had met each other at a garden centre after Steph dropped a plant pot and her father came to her aid. It was perhaps the sweetest meet-cute that Ava had ever heard.

"You're on Instagram now?! Bloody hell, first Face-book and now Instagram...someone's going up in the world!" Suzy guffawed but was interrupted by Ava's work phone loudly ringing inside an otherwise silent and tran-quil cafe.

"*Bugger*," Ava hissed and quickly silenced her call despite several notifications popping up on her screen at once.

Suzy sat smiling in admiration at her as Ava quickly replied to several emails on her phone. "I still can't believe my big sister is running the show now."

"I know," Ava sighed, turning her phone screen down as she smiled up at her little sister. "I still can't believe it either. It feels like I'm waiting on majorly fucking something up."

"Don't be silly, you won't." Suzy's brows lowered as Ava shot her a dubious look. "*You won't*! You're doing amazing, you've already completely changed the reputation of the firm as one that serves on the side of justice and innocence rather than serving those high rollers... Sammy would be proud of you."

Ava's breath hitched in her throat upon her friend's name filling the air. Hearing Sam's name still managed to pinch at her heart and pry apart the void she had spent two years trying to close. She was starting to realise that no amount of time could take away the pain of losing a friend; it could only numb it ever so slightly.

Ava looked down at her watch before peering back up at her sister with a small smile. "Time to get back to work. I'll go get the bill." She didn't give Suzy enough time to protest as she hurried over to the cashier, her walking aid tapping against the floor as she tried to avoid any more flattery or shovelling up of the past.

It wasn't that she hadn't made her peace with Sam's death, it was more to avoid the feelings associated with that turbulent time in her life. A lot of it still haunted her... certain *men* still haunted her every waking thought.

Rushing towards the barista stand in such a hurry, she didn't realise the person in front of her as her shoulder abruptly collided with theirs. A gasp left her lips as she knocked their wallet from their hands and sent copper coins scattering across the floor.

"*Fuck me!*" she rudely blurted, forgetting her company and surroundings as she dropped to her knees and began picking up coins. "That was so ignorant of me for not looking!" However, as her hand picked up the brown leather wallet that was opened on the floor, she noticed the folded photograph inside the clear plastic pouch. The blood rushed from her head as all of her ghosts began materialising in person as she gawked down at a picture of her and an old flame pulling funny faces inside a photo booth. That flame had left a fever inside her, and when he left, her soul had turned to winter.

Sat upon her knees, she gingerly tilted her head up and felt the air rush from her lungs as her ghost stared at her also in disbelief. He was exactly as she remembered: chiselled jawline, full lips, and whisky irises. The only difference to him now was that his dark hair had the subtlest hint of salt and pepper peeking through and his stubble had bloomed into a full thick beard.

"Nate..." She swallowed his name alongside the rising panic she felt.

"Ava..." he replied, sounding a little winded as his lashes blinked in disbelief at her knelt there before him and all his pathetic brain could conjure up in that moment was, "You've cut your hair." His random statement caused her to touch the ends of her blonde tips resting upon her shoulders before he shook his head from its daze. "Sorry, here," he finally said, extending his hand to her and trying in vain to hide the flutter inside his heart as her fingers laced through his and he helped her to her feet. His stomach was in a tight knot as she stared at him, remaining eerily silent with a pale expression on her face as though she had seen a ghost. Of all the coffee shops, she was here, in this one.

"Is this who I think it is?" Suzy cut in, passing Ava her walking stick and grinning up at the man she was with. "Mr. Brooks, right?"

"*Nate*, please," he admonished with a smile and blinked in shock with his hands raised defensively as Little Archer suddenly hugged him.

"You're a sight for sore eyes, Nate!" Suzy beamed and reluctantly released him as Ava tugged at the hem of her sister's shirt.

"Were you both just starting lunch or finishing?" he asked with hopefulness clear in his voice.

"We're just—" Ava began.

"Starting lunch!" Suzy interrupted Ava and ignored her sister's jaw-dropped expression. "But I need to go now because I forgot I left my computer unlocked but *you* should stay and keep Ava company!"

A clear lie that Nate saw right through, his amusement noticeable as he licked his lips and smirked, shyly unable to meet Ava's eye. He was glad by her flustered and useless attempts of trying to make her sister stay, musing to himself that she was like a schoolgirl avoiding speaking to their crush. "I'd love to catch up if you'd like to join me...?"

Ava felt the fever reach her cheeks, cursing her biology that was betraying her with a cherry blossom that spread from her cheeks, down her neck, and back to the apex of her ears. With her heart pounding in her chest, she peered up at Nate and gave a meek nod of her head.

"I'll go get you an Earl Grey to go," he quipped cheerfully, making his way towards the kiosk before Ava suddenly tugged on his arm.

"Can I have a cinnamon latte instead, please?"

"You drink coffee now?" His brows rose before creasing in confusion.

"Well...yeah...it kind of became part and parcel with the new job title," she mused with a flare of confidence before it blinked away in a heartbeat and her eyes fell upon her feet again as she tucked a golden curl behind her ear.

Her sudden submissive manner drew Nate in like a bee to honey and he had to restrain himself from tilting up her chin and kissing her there and then.

"I heard, congratulations!" Nate grinned, adoring the smitten smile she gave him. "I always knew you'd be a perfect fit for that role ever since that day you barged into my office barking about that damn coffee machine," he chuckled.

"I think you mean my office," she teased as she peeked out of her shell and caused Nate to release a small chuff from his nose.

"How is the new job going, then? That'll be coming up to a year, right?"

"Yes, almost a year." Ava nodded as she sat down at a table with her hot beverage and swept her tongue across the top of the frothy cinnamon-coated cream. "It's different. Good different. It's odd though..."

"How so?"

"Well, I kind of feel like I've always done the job and now I just have more control over everything...but with that comes the dreaded accountability when things go wrong," She grimaced and watched Nate laugh in agreement. "But what about you? How is the new job going? I think you'll also be coming up a year, yeah?"

"Yup! It's going great actually, although, my assistant could use a kick up the ass." He smirked but his smile dropped slightly as the melancholy saturated his eyes, the longing there for his old assistant to be by his side. "It's actually why I'm here...they set up a new branch in London so wanted me here to run the show."

Ava nearly choked on her drink as she gawked up at him. "You mean you're here for the—"

"The foreseeable, yes," he interrupted, staring at her and trying to figure out her thoughts from her reaction, however, she was ever the glacial fortress that gave nothing away. "How's the leg? I see you're still rocking the nine-inch stilettos, at least you're finally using that damn stick!"

"Why, of course!" She lit up at the mention of her heels

but then pouted as she looked down at her stupid cane. "The leg is as good as it can be. The stick is only there for walking in these heels. It was either flat shoes and no stick or heels and stick so naturally I had to choose fashion otherwise my fashionista of an assistant would chastise me for such a crime!"

"Oh, but of course!" Nate laughed, a genuine hearty laugh that filled the air with warmth and filled Ava with a feeling of home as she giggled with him. "I've missed your laugh so damn much..." he blurted and then gulped as Ava stopped laughing and watched the way he marvelled at her like a long-lost treasure.

He saw her walls go back up again as she focussed her attention on her coffee, her palms cradling the paper cup. "Look, I gotta ask"—leaning forward he placed his hands over hers and met her gaze—"are you seeing anyone, Ava?"

The abruptness of his forwardness left her feeling breathless and her mind foggy. Her life had only just calmed like the dust from a sandstorm settling across the dunes, but Nate was like a hurricane that brought chaos back into her life.

"Well...it's a bit hard to pick anyone up when you rock up to a date like an eighty-year-old with a walking stick..." She meant it quite seriously but Nate began chuckling as his thumb brushed across the back of her knuckles and sent shivers down her spine with such a simple touch.

"So, would you be free tonight then...for dinner...with me?"

No way was he giving up this chance to be a part of her world again, not when the universe was practically screaming at him. Why else would she bump into him on this day inside this random coffee shop thirty minutes from her office when there are thousands of them in this city. It was now or never.

"I...I don't know if that is such a good ide—"

"I'm a free man," he blurted, quickly realising that the last she knew was that he was intending on getting a divorce but couldn't since he took pity on the difficult time Natalia was going through after losing her father. "Yeah...it was probably karma working its magic but I walked in on Nat and my best man at her mother's funeral, so it was kind of my get out jail free card, I suppose."

"Oh my gosh, that's awful!" Ava gasped, her heart fluttering from the way he refused to remove his hands from hers, like the simplest of touch was a burning craving for them both.

"Really, it's fine. It was perfect timing and she's better off with him on my yacht halfway across the world." He shrugged, uncaring of what his ex-wife was doing with a good chunk of his money and his favourite boat which she won through their divorce. "So, is that a yes to tonight?"

"Nate..." Ava pulled her hands back, retreating from his embrace as she looked out of the window and onto the street outside. "We haven't spoken for over a year and so much has changed... I'm not sure what place I'm in now but...us going back to where we were... I don't know if that's such a good idea."

"What? But you asked me to give you space. You told me to back off for a while since you were dealing with the first anniversary of Sam's de—"

"No, I know that...it's just... I finally got everything back on track and everything is settled...and I just know that if you were to come back into my life that it'd be—"

"Say no more," he interrupted, not intending for it to sound quite as clipped as it did.

"Nate, please I don't mean to—"

"Ava, honestly, it's fine. We all heal at difference paces and I accept you're still figuring everything out. Everyone on this earth has demons in their closet and is dragging their baggage up the mountain that is life, so honestly, I get it."

He did get it but just because he understood didn't mean he wasn't crushed by it. The hardest moment in his life was forcing himself onto that plane two years ago, fighting with himself the entire trip to not turn back around like a selfish bastard and tell her he didn't care about her feelings or needs, that he wanted her, *needed* her, and couldn't live without her. But he couldn't go through with it so every day for the last seven hundred days was spent thinking about her, wondering how she was getting on, dreading the idea of her with another man, constantly staring at his phone deliberating on calling her, deleting the text he should have just damn well sent instead of watching the black cursor erase the words forever to be left unsaid.

There was so much distance between them, a distance that manifested its way into their relationship and opened a void of silence between them. It got to a point where he couldn't bear it anymore and when her father retired and she assumed his position, there was no way in hell he could work with her so close and yet so far. He'd drink himself into a coma if that had happened.

Nate had vowed to himself that day two years ago, stood in her apartment, that he would wait for her and he had. But right then, as he had spoken to a wall that she refused to lower for him after all this time, he made a new promise—that this would be the last time he tried to win her heart.

"Nate, I—"

"I best get back, but it was nice to see you again," Nate said with a pearly white grin as he stood up and looked down at the hopeless expression on her face. "Maybe we'll bump into each other, right?"

"Right..." Ava exhaled as though someone had placed a weight inside her stomach that rooted her to her chair. She couldn't move or speak, helplessly staring at the love of her life walk out of the cafe.

It wasn't until the entrance door swung shut and the bell chimed that she finally snapped back into focus and stared down at the empty seat in front of her. A seat that was always full whether that was Sam or her sister, but now it was empty, left vacant moments ago by the last remaining person her heart sang for.

Suddenly, Ava felt more alone than she ever had and realised in that moment that she hadn't been swimming in her loneliness but was barely managing to tread it.

She was drowning and Nate was her life ring that was floating far out to sea.

With a shaky hand, she pulled out her phone from her coat pocket to check the time before a hand came in front of her vision.

"Excuse me, miss?" The barista leaned down to her and passed her a small white piece of paper. "This just fell out of your pocket."

"Oh...thanks..." Ava replied, frowning as she took the small rectangular piece of paper and wondered why a fortune cookie message found its way into her pocket.

"Lust rushes but love waits."

The message hit her in the heart and all she could think of was Sam standing there, whacking her over the head with her walking stick and screaming at her to get off her arse and run after him.

"Shit, what am I doing?" she gasped and abruptly stood

up, tipping her chair back and causing an old woman to jump slightly. "Sorry!"

"That's alright, my love," the elderly woman spoke with a familiar Welsh accent. "Go'an get him!" She grinned, pointing a sun-spotted hand towards the door.

For the first time in years, light flooded into Ava's heart as she bolted out of the cafe like Bambi on ice without her walking aid, but it didn't matter, she *was* going to catch him. She mustered all of her willpower into pumping her legs one in front of the other, her damn thigh feeling heavy as she pushed it hard.

"Oh, fuck it!" Ava squealed, skidding to a stop halfway up the street in the middle of a busy market square before she ripped off her designer heels and passed them to a fish-monger. "Hold these." She didn't wait for a response as she sprinted up through the heavy traffic of people, her eyes on her prize as she suddenly saw dark stylish hair. "Nate, wait!"

Ignoring the people that looked at her like the madwoman she was, she finally reached him, grabbing his shoulder and turning him around.

"Can I help you?" The stranger peered down at her with his nose scrunched in offence.

"Wrong person," Ava squeaked, the blood surfacing to her cheeks before her stomach sank and the light inside her drained to empty. She felt like a right tit watching the man walk away until a familiar accent spoke behind her.

"Ava? What are you doing? Is everything alright?"

"Nate!" she gasped as she turned around to see him frowning down at her in confusion. "I came to ask you..." She finally broke breath only to realise how much her lungs burned from the lack of oxygen and how her mind hadn't thought this far ahead as to what she'd say when she caught him. "Do you like Thai?"

"Do I like *Thai?*" His eyebrow rose.

Ava grimaced up at him, realising she was a failure when it came to romantically trying to quote what he had asked her those years ago in the office. How else were you meant to tell someone you loved them and that you were a complete bloody tit?

"Oh, bugger it!" Ava blurted, grabbing the lapels of his grey peacoat and yanking him forward until her lips smacked into his with the force of a freight train.

For a moment, Nate didn't close his eyes, shocked to his core as the Aphrodite suddenly kissed him and fed his soul with what it starved for. Soon, his eyes closed, and his arms snaked around her waist as his fingers interlocked behind her back. His lips kissed hers back with such ferocious passion that for a moment he forgot that they were stood in the middle of a bustling food market inside London where people were applauding and *awh*ing at their display of affection.

Breathless, he pulled back and couldn't help but laugh at the ballsy, ferocious, and helplessly unromantic Ava Archer for pulling the most cliched and wonderful trick in the book.

"What?" She laughed, peering up at the amusement on his face.

"I thought you said we weren't a love story?" he chuckled, cupping her cheek.

"We weren't...but we are now."

THE END

ABOUT THE AUTHOR

Holly Dixon has always been passionate about writing and story-telling. She describes herself as a curious author who loves exploring the darker side of Romance. As part of her writing process, she loves immersing herself in her projects —diving head-first into the research, production, and fine-tuning of the stories she feels are the most worthy of telling.

A Scottish lass at heart, Dixon enjoys the fact she could bring a part of her heritage to this story through the character of Samantha Eastley. She sees pieces of herself in every character she writes, but relates most to the spirited and wacky best friend in ILLICIT AFFAIRS.

She first started writing on Wattpad at the age of twenty-five in late 2019, but it wasn't until the COVID pandemic hit in early 2020 that Holly began to get serious about publishing her work for real. Towards the end of 2020, she began writing ILLICIT AFFAIRS and completed her first draft in four months with a view of releasing her debut novel in September 2021.

"Writing this book has been the most wonderful pastime in lockdown for me, but I'd be lying if I said that publishing it hasn't been the most exciting yet nerve-racking process ever! I went into indie-publishing blind and fairly naive as most new authors do. A lot of research went into this and a

lot of people online through writing communities have given me so much priceless support in launching this book that I am forever grateful for. My advice for any new aspiring authors would be: to take advantage of the wisdom you receive from writing communities, do a tonne of research before hand, save your hard-earned money and pay for a good and creditable editor, don't skimp on the marketing of your book, and give yourself at least six months to promote it. Anyone, and I mean ANYONE, can write a book but polishing that beauty up and promoting it in a highly competitive market is where the climb really begins!"

GLOSSARY

- "A complete tit." — A complete idiot
- "Bloody Nora!" — Expression of surprise
- "Don't act the goat." — To behave in a silly way
- "For a game of soldiers." — Used by somebody who does not want to do something because it is annoying or involves too much effort
- "Help ma boab!" — Term of surprise
- "Jesus, Mary & Joseph!" — Term of surprise
- "My heid's mince!" — My head is scrambled. Term of confusion.
- "Spaniel ears for tits." — Saggy breasts
- Ae — Of
- Aye — Yes
- Bellend — Vulgar term. An annoying or contemptible man.
- Bloody — Term used to add emphasis to something
- Braw — Good
- Chip — A French fry
- Couldnae — Couldn't

- Cuppa — Cup of tea
- Da — Short for Dad
- Didnae — Didn't
- Doesnae — Doesn't
- Eejits — Vulgar term for a couple of idiots.
- Fanny — Vulgar term. Can be either a silly person or used to described a woman's genitals
- Fud — Vulgar term. A foolish person
- Gob — Mouth
- Hen — A girl or young woman.
- Ken — Know
- Knobbed — Can be used to describe sex or the action of being hit over the head
- Knobbing — To have sex with someone
- Lass — A girl or young woman.
- Ma — My. However, can also be short for Mum.
- Mare — More
- Maw — Short for Mum
- Nae clue — No clue
- Naw — No
- NHS — National Health Service
- Old Geezer — British term for an old man.
- Oot — Out
- Pish — Vulgar term for the word piss.
- Ruddy — Term used instead of bloody. Used to add emphasis to something.
- scrambeed eggos — Scrambled Eggs
- Soz — Sorry
- Tinky — Dirty
- Top Shagger — Vulgar term. A person who "has sex, especially one who has numerous casual sexual encounters.

- Twat — Vulgar term to describe a silly person or a woman's genitals
- Wee — Little
- Wise-arse — Used similarly to smart-ass
- Ye — You
- Yer or Ya — Your/ You're
- Yin — One

Printed in Great Britain
by Amazon